THE LIGHT THIEVES

There was a folded note on the bedside locker, and Grian opened it.

Gone to the Tipping Point! I can't stay here and do nothing when the world needs me. I want to help, even if none of you do. Don't come looking for me until I've saved the planet.

This series is for Jo and Bobbie – I love you both
all the muches.

First published in the UK in 2022 by Usborne Publishing Ltd., Usborne House,
83-85 Saffron Hill, London EC1N 8RT, England, usborne.com

Usborne Verlag, Usborne Publishing Ltd., Prüfeninger Str. 20,
93049 Regensburg, Deutschland, VK Nr. 17560

A CIP catalogue record for this book is available from the British Library.

ISBN 9781474991094   7144/1   JFMAMJ ASOND/22

Printed and bound using 100% renewable electricity at CPI Group (UK) Ltd CR0 4YY.

MIX
Paper from
responsible sources
FSC® C171272

THE LIGHT THIEVES

HELENA DUGGAN

USBORNE

CONTENTS

MAP OF
BABBAGE

QUANTUM

QUANTUM DISTRICT

THE TIPPING
POINT

TURING

TALLYSTICK

TURING DISTRICT

HOPPER DISTRICT

PROLOGUE

Grian Woods stared out the classroom window at the rapidly swaying treetops in the distant forest that surrounded his home town of Tallystick. Because it was a sweltering summer's morning, the sun high in the bright blue sky, the window beside him was open, but there wasn't even the slightest of breezes passing inside. The morning had been eerily still, so still he'd pointed it out to his sister as they got on the school bus only an hour ago.

So, if it wasn't windy outside, what was making the trees dance?

It was the last day of school and his teacher was busy handing out small tasks to set up for their end-of-year party. Everyone was in great form, and giddy laughter swept the classroom. Grian wasn't giddy though – he didn't like parties, especially school ones. Parties meant he'd have to make up random stuff to say to the people in his class, almost none of whom he'd really call friends.

"Bob," he whispered to his Hansom watch, "are there any weather warnings for this morning?"

Bob, his watch avatar, opened its eyes and smiled out at him from the watch face – Hansom's latest update meant the avatars were almost lifelike. Some people in his class had designed their avatars to look like famous singers or film stars or football players, while others had modelled them on what they wanted to be when they grew up.

One girl had even made hers look like her dog, because she said it was her favourite thing in the world. Grian had left Bob's avatar at the default setting, which looked a little like Howard Hansom, the owner of the Hansom company, because he didn't know what he wanted to be when he grew up.

"That's a negative, Grian," the watch replied. "The weather will be hot with prolonged sunny spells. Although some summer showers are expected in south-western Babbage, where there is also a risk of thunderstorms..."

Grian gasped, as a small hairline crack spontaneously darted down the centre of the windowpane beside him.

He muted his hEarPods so he couldn't hear his watch and was leaning in for a closer look when the benches and bins in the yard outside rocked, then fell over.

He stood up in shock, knocking his chair back, as the crack suddenly dispersed across the glass like a spider's web. There was a faint splintering sound before Grian roared "DUCK!" and jumped under his desk, just as the window burst inwards. Terrified screams filled the air as glass smithereens flew through the classroom.

Grian covered his ears, pushing his palms into the side of his head. Everything in the room rattled as if a giant had suddenly grabbed hold of the school and was shaking it like a money box. Books, pencils and hTablets flew through the air like missiles as the rest of the class now cowered, terrified, under their desks too.

Everything happened so fast and so slow all at once. Grian's thoughts scrambled as he tried to figure out what to do. He closed his eyes for a moment and breathed deeply through his nose until the chaos dulled to background noise, leaving only the sound of his heart thumping wildly in his ears.

He swiped at his Hansom, but the screen was blank. Bob wasn't working. Grian's chest tightened.

His teacher, was shouting something and beckoning everyone to follow her. Her usually perfectly pinned hair had fallen loose from its bun and she only wore one shoe, her other sandal lost somewhere in the mess of stationery, desks and broken glass.

Grian followed the rest of his class as they all climbed out over the jumble of stuff that blocked the door his teacher had shouldered open.

The school corridor looked like it had been looted by an angry mob – fallen lockers, broken hTablets and books were strewn across the floor. He scrambled through the wreckage, joining the masses of petrified children who screamed and jostled each other to escape out the main door.

Once in the yard, Grian followed instructions and raced into the middle of the playground where teachers roared at their students, herding them away from falling debris. He looked around for Solas but couldn't see his sister anywhere. He swiped Bob again, hoping it would locate her, but his watch was still dead.

Grian shivered uncontrollably, as though he'd been dipped in a bath of ice-cold water. What had happened? How would he contact his parents? Were they okay? Where was Solas?

A girl nearby screamed, pointing skywards. The day suddenly darkened like storm clouds had just rolled in.

Grian looked up, but there wasn't a single cloud in the clear blue sky.

"The sun...the sun," his teacher stuttered, her voice a whimper.

Grian couldn't understand what his eyes were showing him. He rubbed them, afraid the dust and dirt might have caused damage, but it didn't make a difference.

A black shadow had formed on the bottom right-hand quarter of the sun. Almost as if that same giant he'd imagined rattling the school earlier had taken a juicy bite from the orange circle in the sky.

He wheezed in air as the thumping in his chest beat harder. Stunned silence wrapped the school yard.

"It's the end of the world!" someone cried.

THREE YEARS LATER

CHAPTER 1

SCHOOL'S OUT

The vibrations raced up his arm and into his shoulder, shaking Grian awake. He wished Hansom hadn't added their latest software update.

"I said not to use that alarm, Bob!" he groaned, pulling the duvet back over his head.

"Last night you directed that I was to wake you by any means possible, Grian!" Bob chirped.

"I didn't mean that way! Vibrate mode is too far."

"I'm a watch, Grian, I interpret literally. It's hard to decipher what you do or don't mean if you are not clear," Bob stated, before continuing. "You've your last test this morning then school is out for summer. Your grandfather will not be home for a few hours today, so you're scheduled to accompany Solas to the *PEOPLEPOWER* rally this afternoon."

Grian didn't respond as he dressed, pulling on navy tracksuit bottoms and a grey hoody. Then he dragged his feet out of his room and across the carpeted landing towards the toilet.

"Hold it! Me first!" Solas cried, rushing into the bathroom just ahead of him. "I've to get ready, Grian!"

His older sister slammed the door and left him standing in the chilly landing. Ever since the earthquake three years ago, the mornings were colder and the days a little darker. It was July now, but it felt like autumn.

Grian waited patiently for Solas to finish – she always took for ever. He didn't understand why girls spent so long getting ready. Most of the time he wished he had an older brother and not a sister.

"Would you like to revise for this morning's big summer hTest?" Bob piped up. "We could go over your long division again, as you were a little weak on that last night."

"Just give me a break, Bob," Grian moaned, sliding down the wall onto the carpet to wait.

He was glad that the normal end-of-school party didn't go ahead any more, so at least he didn't have to make awkward conversation. The principal said it wasn't right to celebrate on the anniversary of the earthquake – the day the world tilted – so the party had been replaced by the end-of-year hTest instead, which seemed a little unfair.

The summer test took the morning and then they were getting a half day off so everyone could attend the *PEOPLEPOWER* rally.

"Breaks never a master makes!" the watch replied.

Grian stabbed the off button and his watch's avatar closed its eyes before the screen darkened to a sleek metal grey. A moment later the double H of the Hansom logo lit up and Bob smiled as the watch turned back on.

"What?" Grian fumed, glaring down at his wrist.

"The new parental controls update. You can't turn me off when my advice is for your own good, Grian! Now, I think we should do some revision."

Bob began asking long division questions.

Grian took off the watch and shoved it into his pocket. He'd done his study and was pretty confident the test would go well. He liked learning, though he'd never tell that to anyone in school in case he was teased.

"Any advice on how to get out of my pocket, Bob?" Grian mocked.

His watch didn't reply and was mumbling mock exam question number four by the time the bathroom door flung open. Solas walked dramatically out, her hair now a silvery pink. Mam would fume, which was probably why

Solas had done it while she and Dad were away. Grian could swear his sister was wearing some kind of make-up too. He never understood why people, especially girls, put stuff all over their face. He'd worn some once for Halloween when he dressed up as the Barber from his favourite computer game, "Beat the Barber"; it was a pretty cool costume, but he'd wiped the sticky make-up straight off the minute he got home.

"He's not even going to see you, you know!"

"Who's not?" Solas replied as she swished past.

"Howard Hansom. All of Tallystick will be there, there's no way he'd even look at you!"

"Oh, shut up, brother!" She glared, then slammed her bedroom door.

Grian stomped into the bathroom and slammed the door too. If Solas could do it, so could he.

"Will you two ever stop banging doors!" his grandad called from his cupboard office downstairs.

He'd probably been up all night talking on his ancient radio set again. There were way easier ways to speak to people all over the world. He could never understand why his grandad didn't just get a Hansom, like everybody else.

Grian brushed his teeth and tried to pat down some of his more unruly curls so they didn't stand out too much. A little happier with his reflection, he trudged back onto the landing and was just pulling Bob from his pocket when Solas opened her door and pranced down the stairs ahead of him. She was dressed in some sort of ridiculous sparkly skirt and the same neon multicoloured *PEOPLEPOWER* T-shirt everyone was wearing lately.

"Morning, Solas." Bob smiled as Grian strapped the watch back onto his wrist.

Grian cringed, popping in his hEarPods and bluetoothing them to his Hansom so Bob couldn't speak out loud any more.

"Why do you have to be nice to her when she's always so mean to me," he sniped as he searched for his shoes.

"Your runners are under the bed," Bob replied, "and it's nice to be niccccc…"

The watch face flickered and Bob's avatar froze for a minute mid-sentence, before coming back to life.

"What was that?" Grian gasped, his heart skipping.

"Just a signal disruption. Those trees blocking the signals again," the watch replied, its human replica voice suddenly sounding robotic.

Bob had been flickering quite a bit lately, which made Grian nervous. It's true, he did take the watch off sometimes, when it was annoying him, but he definitely didn't want it to ever stop working again. The first and only time Bob broke was awful – it had happened exactly three years ago, the day of the earthquake.

Ever since, that day became known as "the Tilt" because it was later discovered that the earthquake had been so strong it knocked the world off its axis, just before a mysterious black mark appeared on the sun.

"Your school bag is in the kitchen. I'm hoping your grandfather has remembered to make lunch, but because he refuses to wear a Hansom I can't tell." Bob sounded frustrated as it pulled Grian's thoughts back from his most scary memories. "The school bus is exactly four minutes and twenty-three seconds away. Get a move on!"

Grian raced down the stairs past his grandfather's room. The door was ajar as always, so the squeaks and squeals of his radio system whizzed and whirred out into the hall. Sometimes the sounds were broken by the chopped and usually fuzzy voice of someone from somewhere far away.

Grian had to turn the kitchen light on even though it was already twenty past eight. His lunch box was sitting on the wooden worktop. The plastic lid was half off, revealing an apple and a sandwich oozing disgusting purple jam.

"Jam!" Grian huffed, leaving his home-made lunch on the table. "Where does Grandad even get this stuff?"

He opened the press and pulled out a packet of crisps and a chocolate bar, then grabbed his bag and stuffed them inside, before pushing past Solas in the hall. She was poking her head in Grandad's door, probably sucking up to him for money. Since their dad's job had been under threat, Grandad handed it out more easily than his parents did.

Grian's dad, Cam Woods, was a postmaster, which meant he was the head postman in the Turing district. Grian didn't tell anybody about his father's job, purely because he wasn't proud. It was embarrassing really and total fuel for teasing. Nobody sent letters any more – it was last-century old.

That's where his dad was now, away at a work conference. His mam had taken time off to go and surprise him. They were to spend a few days together. "We'll be back Sunday evening," his mam had said with a smile as she kissed Grian on the head early that morning, before slipping downstairs and out the front door.

His mam, Saoirse Woods, was a solicitor in Turing – the city a few bus stops from their small town. She said she "represented the underdog" – Grian wasn't sure what that meant, except that her clients hardly ever had money. She was stubborn, his dad often joked, and only worked for people she liked. His mam said that was because she couldn't do her job if she didn't believe in the person – which kind of made sense.

"T minus one minute!" Bob cried as Grian threw open the front door.

"Good luck in your test," his grandfather called.

"Thanks, Grandad!" Grian shouted, dashing down the garden path and out the gate.

The bus was just pulling into the stop as he arrived. Solas was a little way behind. His sister never minded if anyone had to wait for her, whereas Grian got embarrassed even thinking that he might cause a delay. He wished he was a little more like Solas – she didn't care what anyone thought.

Grian was already settled in his seat when his sister mounted the steps and swung into hers. She was just in front of him, sitting beside her best friend Amz. Everyone thought Amy Alton was one of the coolest girls in school, but Grian knew she really wasn't. She was mean, just like Solas.

Grian sat in the middle of the bus. It was the safest place to be. He was alone, which was what he preferred. He'd tried making friends once when he was younger and it hadn't worked out well. His mam said he'd just met the wrong ones and that not all kids were mean. But Grian wasn't so sure and, besides, nobody ever got his jokes.

"Jeffrey is here," Bob suddenly said as a blond-haired boy, with light blue eyes, a thin upturned nose and bright-red cheeks, puffed and panted up the steps. "Why don't you ever make friends with him? I keep telling you, you two have such similar interests. Jeffrey likes history and excels at maths. He also likes gaming and is an ace at "Beat the Barber". He's on level sixteen and is the number-one player in the Turing district. Maybe he could give you some…"

Grian was turning purple. His stupid watch was always trying to force him into making friends, especially with Jeffrey Slight. Someone giggled behind Grian and, paranoid, he turned the volume down on his hEarPods, in case anyone could hear.

Grian knew Jeffrey a little, as they were practically neighbours and went to the same school. But those weren't reasons to hang out and he made sure they didn't, even when his mam encouraged him to.

Jeffrey seemed nice enough, if a little weird and annoying. People teased him though, and Grian didn't want to be friends with someone who got teased. It drew too much attention and he had worked hard at avoiding the eyes of bullies ever since his first experience of them. Sometimes he even got the answers wrong in his tests on purpose. It made life easier. People didn't like know-it-alls, and Jeffrey Slight was definitely a know-it-all.

Jeffrey always came out with one hundred per cent in his tests, and he tried to talk to everyone about all the stupid stuff he liked. Sometimes his clothes didn't fully fit him either – his trousers stopped at the ankles or his shirts were a little too tight – but he didn't seem to notice when others sniggered.

"If you'd like to go to the toilet before the hTest, then it'd be quicker to enter school via the back door. There is a queue up in corridor five, as a fight has broken out between two sixth-class pupils," Bob said as the bus pulled up at the school gates.

Quickly Grian raced round the school and in the rear entrance. He always needed to go before a test. Pre-exam nerves, his watch called it. He banged the toilet door shut, dropping his bag to the floor.

"Hurry, you've six minutes and forty-two seconds to get to the classroom. Most people are at their desks, but Mrs Norman is not there yet," Bob said, as Grian hurriedly washed his hands.

He sprinted down the corridor and was just settled at his desk as the teacher began to hand out their papers.

"Watches to exam mode," Mrs Norman said, turning to face the class before setting her timer.

Grian swiped across Bob's interface, switching his Hansom to exam mode so it couldn't help him, before logging into his school hTablet.

The exam was easy. Even taking into account the questions he got wrong on purpose, Grian was sure he'd done well. His summer report would be good, and though his parents never really cared about exams, he knew they'd be happy.

"Your results will be hMailed home early next week."

Mrs Norman smiled as she collected up the papers. "Now enjoy your lunch, and then you're on holidays! I'm sure I'll see most of you at the *PEOPLEPOWER* rally later today – what an exciting way to start the summer!"

His classmates whooped and shouted before hugging each other as if they'd never meet again. Grian bid a few quick goodbyes before turning Bob back on and leaving the classroom.

There wasn't a cloud in the sky when he stepped outside, though the black mark on the sun meant the days weren't as warm as they would once have been. This didn't really bother Grian – he'd never been a huge fan of too much heat.

The black mark, or what it meant for the planet, really bothered everybody else though, which was why the whole world was excited about *PEOPLEPOWER* – Howard Hansom's plan to save them all.

PEOPLEPOWER was everywhere. The ads flashed across Bob's screen every few minutes, it was even all over the school hTablets, the hTV, the hNet, hNews, and all anybody ever talked about on the radio or wrote about in the papers. Even the fridge and the bus stop regularly showed the adverts – so much so that Grian was kind of sick of it.

"You've to meet Solas by the school gates in thirty minutes," Bob piped up with a reminder. "I've contacted

Petra and it's let your mother know you'll be here for a while longer before going with your sister to the rally. Now, time for a quick lunch."

Grian hated it when Bob talked to Petra. Petra was his mam's Hansom and it was set on really strict mode, meaning it basically told Bob that Grian wasn't allowed do anything. Grian had ignored its instructions once and Bob had to report back – he was grounded for a week.

When Solas turned thirteen, some of Petra's permissions were cancelled and it didn't have to know everything about where his sister went any more. Grian couldn't wait until he was thirteen so he could stop Petra spying on him too.

He sat on the bench just inside the school gates and pulled out his lunch of crisps and chocolate.

Hundreds of kids were now piling out the entrance doors, wearing the same multicoloured neon *PEOPLEPOWER* T-shirts. They all seemed just as excited as his sister.

Would anybody really be as excited about saving the planet if Howard Hansom wasn't involved?

Grian loved Hansom's technology – his company made the best products. He couldn't live without Bob or the hNet, and definitely wanted Hansom to keep releasing updates and building all the latest gadgets. But none of that meant he had to swoon over Howard Hansom, even if he was trying to save the world. Mr Hansom would be better off sticking to his day job, instead of trying to be some sort of superhero – at least, that's what Grian's grandfather said.

Grian munched his way through his food before settling back into "Beat the Barber". He was finding it hard to get past level fourteen. Maybe Bob was right, maybe he should go talk to Jeffrey.

He was still trying to chop a crew cut into a knife-wielding customer without getting butchered, when his Hansom spoke again.

"Solas is late!" the watch stated. "I normally give her a ten-minute window; factoring in lunch, I gave her a half-hour today and she's still not here!"

Grian looked up.

Almost everyone in the school yard had gone, and the caretaker was closing up. A chill crept over his shoulders. Without anyone about, the place felt eerily quiet. The street was empty too; only a single car waited at the traffic lights on the road outside the gate.

Suddenly he startled, as a distant roar filled the sky.

CHAPTER 2

PEOPLEPOWER

The sound was coming from the direction of Tallystick stadium.

"It seems your sister is already there," Bob stated in its angry tone, as it checked Solas's GPS signal. "I'll let Petra know Solas hasn't collected you again – your mother won't be pleased. Now let's get going before we miss the show!"

Bob navigated Grian towards Tallystick football stadium, while he continued to concentrate on his computer game. The closer he got to the grounds, the more people filled the streets, and he had to keep looking up to avoid collisions.

Grian didn't think this many people lived in his small town, and wondered if some had taken the bus in from the city just to see Howard Hansom. Tallystick was a suburb of Turing, which was the second largest city and acting capital of Babbage now that Quantum, the capital, was a no-go area because of the damage caused by the earthquake.

Bob honed in on Suzi, his sister's watch, and navigated Grian through the crowds until he saw Solas's sparkling skirt and silvery pink hair in the distance. She didn't stand out half as much here as she did at home – everybody was dressed just as colourfully.

Solas was with Amz, and they both threw their eyes to heaven as he fell into step beside them.

"I thought you were with Grandad for another half hour!" Solas sighed, her shoulders falling so far from her ears he was sure they'd touch the ground.

"I wasn't with Grandad at all! Don't pretend you didn't know you were meant to meet me. You left me alone outside the school…again!" he snapped.

"So? You're not a baby," Solas snapped back. "Anyway, don't come near me – pretend we don't know each other!"

"As if I'd want people to know we're related," Grian said, falling in behind her now.

Solas's sparkly skirt almost blinded him as it reflected light with every step.

"How was your test, Grian?" Amz asked, turning around.

"Why are you even talking to him?" Solas said.

"Good, Amz." Grian smiled. "I think I did well!"

"Nerd!" Amy smirked as she pulled on Solas's arm and the pair almost fell over laughing.

Grian blushed. He should have known Amy wasn't being nice. Why did he always fall for it? He had to remind himself a lot why he didn't want or need friends. Being on his own was easy – at least he'd never poke fun at himself.

The crowd tightened as the gates to the stadium appeared in the distance. Solas didn't look round when Grian was pushed by the masses and stumbled sideways. He grabbed hold of a man's arm to stop himself from tripping over.

"Thank you," he stuttered, looking up.

The man, who held a placard high in the air, smiled back down at him. Grian had accidentally fallen into a group of protestors congregated outside the entrance gate. They held signs with messages like *THE TILT IS A LIE* and *HOWARD HANSOM HOLDS YOU TO RANSOM*. Right in the middle of the group, Grian spotted his grandad loudly chanting an anti-Tilt slogan.

People laughed openly at the protestors and some even shouted nasty comments as they walked by into the stadium. Grian ducked his head, afraid he'd be seen, and quietly slipped away, his cheeks flaming hot with embarrassment.

Quickly Bob navigated him back to his sister, who was standing in the middle of the pitch, screaming and shouting excitedly at the empty stage.

"Your brother is back," Amy stated as he arrived.

"Thank god, I've been so worried," Solas mocked.

Grian ignored his sister as he turned his game back on. He didn't tell Solas that Grandad was with the protestors at the gate, though he was tempted to in front of Amy – his sister would be even more mortified than he was.

Grian had just beaten the Barber on level fourteen by slicing his hand and stealing his golden scissors, when music pumped from huge speakers on both sides of the stage, and beams of neon light moved through the air and washed over the crowd.

The place suddenly erupted in a frenzy and Grian watched Solas and Amy jump around, screaming at the top of their lungs.

"Welcome to *PEOPLEPOWER*, a movement powered by people, to save our planet!" a deep and dramatic voiceover announced.

Everyone screamed again, though Grian was pretty sure Solas screamed the loudest. Even the noise-cancelling on his hEarPods couldn't dull down her high pitch.

All around him tall people blocked his view of the stage. He looked down at Bob, who was broadcasting the whole event on its screen.

"Tallystick, give your best and warmest welcome to Howaaaard Hansoooom!"

The crowd went wild once more. This time Grian was sure Solas and Amy were about to fall over from heart failure. He was on the verge of ordering Bob to call an ambulance when a man with sun-streaked brown wavy hair walked onto the stage.

Howard Hansom seemed tall, though it was hard to tell on Bob's screen. He also had a deep tan and looked a little like one of those surfers who was practically born on a beach.

Grian looked towards the stage again but he still couldn't see, as the taller people had now put shorter ones on their shoulders. He thought about asking Solas for a lift just so he could fart on her. She probably wouldn't find it funny, though, and she definitely wouldn't be able to hold him up for more than a second.

He looked back at Bob's screen instead. Howard Hansom was now bending down to shake hands with people in the pit at the front of the stage. A woman had even managed to climb up and threw herself round him before being shepherded off by a security guard.

"Wow, what a welcome!" Hansom smiled, throwing his arms out wide as if embracing the whole audience. "It's great to see so many of you here. I've been told the whole of Tallystick has come out! What a super little town. You clearly care about each other and this precious world of ours!"

Everyone screamed again.

"Now, are you ready to use your powers to heal this beautiful planet?" Hansom shouted.

The whole stadium responded with a deafening "Yes!" – except for Grian, who stayed quiet. Because of Grandad, he wasn't fully sure how he felt about Howard Hansom and his plan.

"Do you remember where you were exactly three years ago today – the day the world rocked, the day of the Tilt?" Hansom asked, his voice falling sombre.

Everyone started shouting random answers, though surely Hansom didn't really want to know. Grian did remember where he'd been, even though most of the time he didn't want to. He'd been in school that morning; his dreams were still haunted by the sound of breaking glass and piercing cries.

They had been lucky in Tallystick, the damage was mainly broken windows – the place hit hardest by the earthquake was the capital, Quantum. People said lots of buildings there had been toppled, the roads were broken and bent like a toy racetrack, and the huge industrial centre was almost completely destroyed. At the time, emergency crews had to act fast to stop deadly chemicals leaking out into the rest of Babbage. The whole city was evacuated and newsreels gave minute by minute updates as the rest of the country held its breath. People everywhere were petrified to leave their homes in case they choked on the poisonous gases.

Grian would never forget watching the news a few months later, the day they put in place the huge dome, which still sat over the capital city, to keep all the toxic air inside. His family celebrated that night – it was the first time since the quake that he'd seen his parents not looking so worried, and daring to walk outside without a mask on. After that a large exclusion zone was set up around the dome and nobody, except those involved in the clean-up, had been allowed near Quantum since.

Eventually the day of the earthquake became known as the Tilt, because it was discovered the quake had been so strong it had knocked the earth further over on its axis. All the experts said the earth's new angle caused the sun to appear as if it had a black mark on its surface.

At the time it was very confusing for Grian as he'd only just learned in geography class that the earth revolved around the sun at a tilt of 23.5 degrees. He had to unlearn all his schoolwork, as the world's most famous physicists and geologists fought on the airwaves about what exactly had happened and what angle the earth's new axis was at. Before the Tilt, Grian didn't know what a physicist was, but now physicists and geologists were celebrities.

It took scientists a while to come to a consensus about the Tilt, but when they did the news was everywhere. It was all anyone could talk about and his parents started to look worried again.

Studies began to emerge about how the earth's new axis made the planet unstable and experts on every news programme warned about the dangers of this instability and how at any moment the world could spin off into outer space.

Airline travel stopped, freight ships were docked, all mining and drilling was brought to a halt, even wind turbines were taken down, as people were petrified that anything could tip the fine balance the earth was now in.

Grian would also never forget the goosebumps he got the day Solas put on her expert hat and tried to explain it simply to him.

"Watch this," she said, taking an apple from their fruit bowl and placing it on the table, its stem pointing upwards.

She tapped the apple gently.

"See how it doesn't move. That was the earth," she said in the voice his sister used whenever she thought she was being very intelligent. "Now watch this – here comes the earthquake!"

Solas hit the apple hard, knocking it over on its side.

"Now the stem's pointing away and look how unstable

the apple is," she said as the fruit rocked gently back and forth before eventually rolling off the table.

"That will be us," she whispered as the apple smashed against the floor.

Grian was petrified, until it was explained to him that "at any moment" meant over a hundred years, which was ages away. But still it seemed as if everyone was terrified until Howard Hansom, the world's most famous tech entrepreneur, came up with a plan.

"*PEOPLEPOWER* can fix our problem," Hansom shouted from the stage, pulling Grian back from his wandering thoughts, "but we need you!"

Hansom explained how an enormously heavy weight in a specific location on earth could shift the earth back to its correct position, saving the planet from bouncing off into outer space. He pointed out how it was not physically possible to manufacture such a weight, but if enough people gathered together that would do it.

He had pinpointed the spot. Since Quantum had been the epicentre of the quake that had thrown the world off balance, then south of Quantum, in remote West Babbage, was calculated as the place that if enough force were applied, the earth could be shifted back to its correct axis.

And Howard Hansom was putting all his money on it.

"I am paying families to move to the Tipping Point, a smart city I've created in the exact geographical location needed to tilt the world back. If we get enough people there, we will have critical mass to shift the earth to its original axis, saving the planet! As you already know, all those who lost their homes in Quantum are living in the Tipping Point now, but we need much more weight. That's why we need you.

"We at Hansom will ensure that your houses and jobs here in Tallystick are maintained for the duration of your move. When you have helped us save the world, you can return home to your old life. This is a risk-free opportunity in a city beyond your wildest dreams. So, join me and become real-life superheroes!"

The crowd lost it this time. Grian huddled in closer to Solas. It was probably the first time in his life he'd ever turned to his sister for comfort, though he convinced himself he was only using her as a human shield.

"We're going, Amz! We're soooo going!" Solas screamed as Hansom pointed behind him and the stage backdrop turned into a huge cinema screen.

A film played, showing the Tipping Point and all its amazing facilities. The smart city had hoverboards and holograms and the Hyperloop – a super-fast underground train. It even had a "Beat the Barber" theme park with an augmented-reality gaming experience. Grian had seen videos of the city a million times and he had to admit, Hansom was right, the Tipping Point seemed pretty cool.

"I swear I'll convince Mam and Dad to move!" Amz roared.

"I will too!" Solas screamed back.

"Agh...no you won't!" Grian shook his head as he pulled on her sleeve. "I don't want to move to the Tipping Point!"

Grian wasn't a fan of change, and the Tipping Point might be cool, but it was sure to be a bit cramped. He'd seen all the *PEOPLEPOWER* moving vans on the roads around Tallystick – it definitely looked like they already had lots of volunteers. And anyway, he liked his home and had no desire to save the world when so many others were lining up to do it already.

"They won't want you there anyway," his sister laughed. "I read they don't want scrawny twig people that don't weigh enough... I'll go on my own!"

"Oh, they just want whales, is it? Then you'll fit right in, Solas – enjoy yourself!" He smirked.

"There are information points around the pitch," Hansom's voice cut through. He was pointing to the large multicoloured neon stands erected at all corners of the stadium. "You can find out more details or even sign up there. But this is a big decision, so think about it carefully – and sign up online or come on a Tipping Point day tour to check out the city for yourself. We understand that not everyone will be comfortable with this idea, so don't feel under any pressure. This is a global movement and I assure you we will get enough *PEOPLEPOWER* to save us all!"

"See – they'll have enough people. We don't need to go!" Grian felt relieved as he looked round for his sister.

Solas and Amy had already disappeared. He spotted his sister's shimmery skirt a little way away in the information desk line-up – the pair were busy talking and smiling weirdly to some boy in a multicoloured neon *PEOPLEPOWER* T-shirt.

Grian sighed. The centre of the pitch had cleared a little, so he sat down and resumed his game.

Solas was fourteen, so surely she wasn't old enough to go on her own. She could waste her time trying to convince their parents to move, but he knew they wouldn't leave Tallystick, as long as his dad kept his job. And even if his parents did want to leave, Grian knew his grandad definitely wouldn't go.

He looked around for the placard holders and was relieved when he couldn't spot Grandad anywhere among the few remaining protestors.

Adler Rothe wasn't like most other people – he didn't believe in the Tilt. He talked to his radio friends all over the world about it almost every night. Grian's grandad was a "Tilt denier", which meant he didn't think that the earthquake three years ago had knocked the world sideways at all – he said the whole thing was a lie.

Everybody else said Tilt deniers were stupid, but that confused Grian because Grandad was one of the cleverest people he knew. When they played puzzles or riddles Grandad never lost; he even got a Rubik's Cube for Christmas one year and had it finished by dinnertime.

"Solas is leaving," Bob piped up. "I've spoken to Suzi and it's going to get your sister to wait for you in the left-hand corner of the car park near the forest. Solas said she'll only wait ten minutes and you know what your sister is like, so get a move on."

Grian sighed as he picked up his bag and threw it on his back.

The late afternoon was almost fully dark now and the reflective patches on the *PEOPLEPOWER* T-shirts that everyone wore illuminated in the passing car lights as they pulled out of their parking spaces.

Solas wasn't where she said she'd be and there was no sign of her anywhere else in the car park.

"She's gone and it's not even been ten minutes," Bob stated. "Suzi's signal is moving down Main Street towards home. If you cut along Forest Drive you'll catch up with her."

"But…" Grian hesitated, looking down the quiet road ahead.

On one side of the road was a long line of houses, each

with a small square patch of garden and a paved driveway to the front. Across from the homes was a wooden fence that spanned the edge of Tallystick Forest. Grian knew he could walk through the housing estate as a shortcut home – Bob had brought him that way before, but only in daylight. Going that way in the dark didn't seem such a good idea – people called the Wilde lived in the forest and there were lots of scary stories about the Wilde.

Lately one of the girls at school said the Wilde had locked her granny in her house for days until she didn't have any food left, and she was so hungry she ate her own toes. Other stories told of stolen dogs or bikes or clothes robbed from washing lines. His grandad defended the Wilde whenever Grian said anything negative about them; he told him not to believe everything he heard. But whether the stories were true or not, Grian knew the Wilde were weird – after all, who'd choose to live in a forest?

"I can see your heart rate has spiked, Grian, but I've told you before, the Wilde are simply a social group who have chosen to stay separate from the outside world and live sustainably in the forests," Bob stated. "The Wilde are nothing to be afraid of – regardless of the stories."

Grian shivered as he headed along the estate road. He knew Grandad would be annoyed with him if he wasn't back at the same time as Solas – even though she was the one who left him behind again.

He was on edge the whole way home and jumped as a cat raced out from under a car, almost tripping him up. He reached his house just in time to see Solas walking up the path to their front door.

"Huh, what's up with you?" his sister moaned as he pushed past her into the hallway.

"You were meant to wait for me," he snapped, heading upstairs to his room.

"Stop being such a baby, Grian," Solas called after him. "You know – most people grow up sometime!"

"Yeah – and they normally leave home when they do," Grian shouted back at her. "I hear the Tipping Point is great!"

He slammed the door and bounded onto his bed, fuming in silence at his sister. Frustratingly he failed to make it on to another level of "Beat the Barber" before his eyelids felt heavy and eventually closed.

What felt like only minutes later, Grian almost fell off the bed as darts of electricity raced through his arm. He jumped up in a daze.

"What…agh…Bob, stop!" he cried, trying to swipe at his watch. "Turn off vibrate mode. Now! Bob! What are you doing!"

He was trying to pull his Hansom from his wrist when suddenly it stopped buzzing. Grian looked around, wide awake now but totally confused. He was still in his room and in the same clothes as earlier, but his tummy was rumbling, and he could see through the open curtains that it was dark outside.

He must have fallen asleep on the bed.

"I'm sorry, Grian..." Bob stated. "I know it's late and I don't mean to cause alarm, but you wouldn't wake up when I tried gentler means. Can you get Adler for me? I'd like to speak to him... I'm worried about your sister!"

CHAPTER 3
RUNAWAY

"What? Solas...? What do you mean?" Grian asked as he rubbed his sleepy eyes. "Speak to me, Bob!"

"Well, I heard some strange noises coming from her room, but when I tried to track Suzi's GPS it wouldn't give me a reading," Bob responded. "Though it's slightly outside the remit of my regulations, I logged into Suzi's operation system – just to check if everything was okay. Your sister's pupil dilation, skin conductance, brain activity and heart rate all indicated a major stress response. Then Suzi's system went dead. I haven't been able to access the device since."

Grian raced to his sister's door, bursting inside. She was lying in the bed under the covers.

"Solas, Solas!" he cried, reaching to shake her shoulders.

His hands disappeared into the soft blankets. He pulled back the duvet to reveal pillows carefully placed to suggest her shape.

There was a folded note on the bedside locker, and Grian opened it.

Gone to the Tipping Point! I can't stay here and do nothing when the world needs me. I want to help, even if none of you do. Don't come looking for me until I've saved the planet.

She'd left lots of love hearts and Xs at the end of the note too, like what she was doing was normal and not something totally stupid. *Saved the planet*, as if she was doing it all by herself, Grian fumed. His sister was always so dramatic.

He grabbed the page in his fist and raced downstairs, barging into his grandad's office.

"The white rose? No, I, ahem…I never heard of them, Vermilion… Oh, Grian!" Grandad said, looking up in shock. He grabbed a piece of paper from the desk, trying to hide it. "I've got to go, grandson here. Over and out."

Grian knew his grandfather was talking to one of his radio friends, though it was a little unusual that they were

45

talking about flowers. Normally Grandad said sentences with lots of letters and numbers, or words that didn't make sense, as if whatever he talked about on his radio was top secret and very important.

The room was small, pokey and smelled a bit, squashed under the stairs like a forgotten apple at the bottom of a school bag.

Grandad's large figure was hunched over a small desk, and huge black earphones cupped his neck as he looked over his shoulder at Grian. His shovel-like hands grasped a microphone just centimetres from his mouth and he seemed flustered.

"Is everything okay? I thought you'd gone to bed. It's very late!" he spluttered.

"I know but...Solas is missing! Bob noticed her heart rate spike. It thought she was in trouble, so it woke me. When I went into her room she was gone. She left this note!"

He read out loud and watched with a mix of emotion, wavering between guilt and satisfaction, as his grandfather's face dropped.

"She's gone to the Tipping Point!" Grian added as he finished. "She told me she was going to earlier, but I didn't believe her."

"No, Solas wouldn't do that." His grandfather shook his head. "Your sister would never run away..."

Grandad looked up at the old-fashioned clock on his

wall, the ancient one with two hands that Grian could never understand.

"Tell your watch to get me the phone number for *PEOPLEPOWER*…quickly!" he ordered.

On Grian's instructions Bob dialled the movement's hotline. The ringing tone punctured the silence as they waited for someone to pick up.

"*Thank you for contacting PEOPLEPOWER. I'm afraid all our lines are closed at the moment…*"

"I'm sure they wouldn't allow a minor to volunteer without their family!" The old man sounded flustered. "Hansom must be staying somewhere in Tallystick – perhaps we can find her that way…"

"I've checked all social channels," Bob stated. "Howard Hansom has posted recent pictures of himself in the Tallystick Palace Hotel, and an image of his dinner taken in their restaurant has just popped up online. You should catch him there if you hurry."

"Good…great! I'll go now. Solas is in a lot of trouble when I find her," his grandad snapped, before grabbing his coat from the hanger by his desk. "Go to bed, Grian. I won't be long. And don't get any funny ideas of your own, please. You children will send me to an early grave!"

Then the door banged, after a moment the gate screeched, and Grian's grandfather disappeared into the dark night.

CHAPTER 4
THE INTRUDERS

Solas was in a whole heap of trouble. Grian was sure she wouldn't be able to smile her way out of this one. He rubbed his eyes, fighting off the tiredness. He wanted to see his sister's face when Grandad brought her home.

Grian had never been in his grandfather's room alone before – in fact he hardly ever came in here at all. He normally just poked his head in if he needed something whenever his grandad was there. Now he slipped into Grandad's warm leather seat and looked at the shelves of black radios across the pokey desk in front of him, the dials all set at different angles. Bending forward, he began to fiddle with one of them.

"Don't touch your grandfather's possessions!" Bob corrected.

Annoyed, Grian stood up to leave, when he noticed – taped to the back wall behind the door – a map of the world with lots of bits and pieces stuck around it. Some were notes on how the radios worked and others were what looked like strips torn from magazines with stuff about the Tilt. There were postcards too, from people Grian had never heard of, in countries he'd never been to.

He laughed. If his grandad would only jump into this century, he wouldn't have to stick paper all over the walls – he'd have all the information he needed on his Hansom.

His tummy rumbling, Grian walked into the kitchen to get some food.

"Bob, has Suzi turned back on yet?" Grian mumbled, finishing his toast.

It was after midnight now, and his grandad still hadn't come home.

"No. It's still offline. I believe the best course of action is bed. Adler will not be happy if you're here waiting up when he gets back."

"But I want to see Solas! She's really in trouble this time."

"It's not polite to gloat, Grian!" his watch replied.

Suddenly Grian's wrist began to tingle and a strange groggy sensation slipped up his arm before wrapping his body.

"What are you doing?"

"Hansom's latest update has a sleep-cycle generator – people are severely sleep-deprived these days and it's one of the pillars of good health, Grian. Now get to bed, you will see Solas in the morning."

Reluctantly, but also now sleepily, Grian climbed the stairs to his room. He was just getting into bed when he heard the garden gate squeak outside. A rush of excitement broke his sleepy mood, and he ran to the hall window to see his sister returned.

Strangely the street lights were off and it took a few seconds for his eyes to adjust to the darkness outside.

Grian tensed. It wasn't Grandad or Solas on the path. Instead, three figures crept slowly towards his house.

Their faces and bodies were completely engulfed by large, dark, hooded capes that swept to the ground, making it impossible to see who these strangers were. Their movements too were oddly smooth, as if they glided instead of taking steps, the bottom of their capes slipping silently over the paving.

His heart thumped and he swallowed hard.

"Bob...Bob!" Grian stuttered, hoping his watch could tell him what to do.

His Hansom was blank. He swiped frantically at the screen, but it was completely off – totally dead.

The figures were at the door now.

Grian snuck down the stairs, trying not to panic; then raced to the kitchen and hid behind the large island worktop as the front door creaked open.

Petrified, he watched the intruders slip straight up the stairs without making a sound, even on the step that always creaked.

He had to get out of the house.

Grian held his breath as he slid open the large glass patio door at the back of the kitchen, wincing as it closed, and crept across the tidy terrace, down into the garden. His grandfather had insisted on making the place a home for bees and for the first time Grian saw a bonus to this – the overgrown weeds were a perfect place to hide.

He ducked into the long grasses, trying to catch his breath as he watched dark shadows move around inside his home. Who were these people? And why were they in his house?

Soon the figures were back downstairs and at the patio door.

He ducked down further into the tall grasses as one of them slid open the large glass door and floated outside. Grian shivered as the cloaked figure stood dead still, watching.

Without a second thought, Grian eased backwards and slipped through the rickety wooden fence that separated his garden from a small lane that ran behind the houses.

He moved at pace along the lane, swiping at his watch again, willing Bob to turn on. But his Hansom still wasn't working. He needed to get help. Scrambling through the bush at the back of one of his neighbour's gardens, he then snuck up towards the house.

There was a light on in an upstairs window. Jeffrey Slight was sitting at his desk, his head millimetres from a huge screen, playing "Beat the Barber". For the first time in his life, Grian was happy to see Jeffrey.

He scoured the manicured lawn, looking for something suitable to throw at the window, like he'd seen someone do in an old film his parents watched once. His fingers brushed over a few loose pebbles, and he fisted them up.

Grian hated PE – he didn't see any use in running or jumping or throwing or any of that stuff. Nobody else liked it either, except the teacher. But now he wished he'd paid a little more attention, as his first attempt failed to hit Jeffrey's window.

He glanced behind him towards the laneway, as the pebble ricocheted off the red brick wall. Then he closed his eyes and took a deep breath before trying again. This time the stone tapped gently off the glass.

Jeffrey looked down, smiled and waved, as if not at all

surprised to see Grian out in his back garden at this time of night. Somehow the other boy's reaction was irritating. Jeffrey Slight never seemed fazed by much.

A minute later his neighbour appeared downstairs to let him in.

"How nice…" Jeffrey smiled, opening the patio door. Grian darted inside.

"I need your help!" he panted, breathless. "There's robbers in my house!"

"You mean intruders?" Jeffrey asked, his eyes saucer-wide. "Unfortunately, it's bad timing – my parents aren't here right now! We're alone, and that may not be a good thing when there are intruders lurking about."

"What about your Hansom, is it working? Mine's dead!" Grian stammered. "Call the police!"

"Betty," Jeffrey ordered his watch, "contact the police, please!"

Betty sounded like a name Grian's grandad would choose for a Hansom – if he ever wore one.

"Mine's dead too!" Jeffrey sounded surprised as he swiped at his watch screen.

"The Wi-Fi must be down or something?" Grian shuddered, looking over his shoulder.

The Wi-Fi signals dropped out a lot after the Tilt, which had caused all sorts of trouble. People and cars were constantly getting lost, fridges ran out of milk and businesses were disrupted for days. But they'd mostly stabilized now – there hadn't been a drop in a long time. And usually when the signals went down, Grian could still see Bob's avatar, he just couldn't talk to it. But he could take pictures or do other stuff like that if he wanted to. This time was different – Bob was blank, almost as if its battery had died. But that was impossible with a Hansom; they had endless battery life. Something similar had happened only once before – the day of the earthquake.

Something clanged outside. Jeffrey startled.

CHAPTER 5
THE WILDE

Grian peered through the window and gasped. A dark hooded figure moved across the grass towards the house. They must have seen him go into Jeffrey's! But why did these strangers seem to be coming for him?

"I...I have to get out of here!" Grian choked, the words catching in his throat.

He snuck down the hall towards the front door, looking back only as Jeffrey grabbed his arm. The other boy pointed at the patio door, which was sliding open. One of the dark figures swept inside without a sound.

A chill snaked up Grian's spine as his mind raced.

"I'm not staying here alone!" Jeffrey whispered.

The pair crept outside, closing the front door behind

them as quietly as possible. The street lights were still off as they snuck along the path towards town.

When they reached the crossroads, Grian looked over his shoulder. The hooded figures were behind them.

"They're following us!" Grian panicked, darting left through Forest Drive, the housing estate, and retracing his steps from earlier that evening.

He began to sprint, as terror took hold. He could see the forest ahead. He ducked under the fence and broke through the first thicket of trees, Jeffrey panting loudly a few paces behind.

"What...what about the Wilde?" the other boy heaved as branches scraped Grian's face, tearing at his skin as he raced forwards.

"We've no choice..." Grian wheezed, when suddenly, mid stride, he stumbled over a fallen tree trunk.

A branch punched him in the stomach as he fell. He stayed down, winded, struggling to grab some air. Jeffrey scrambled down beside him.

"Are you okay?" the other boy rasped. "They've... they've gone... I think we've lost them, Grian!"

Grian dragged himself up to sitting, still heaving for breath. What had happened? Who were those people? Why were they chasing them?

Suddenly a pair of yellow eyes fixed on him from the deep.

He yelped and scrambled backwards, trapping himself against the fallen tree trunk as the dark outline of a four-legged creature stood in the middle of the forest, snarling.

"Run!" Jeffrey called, darting right.

Grian turned and scurried over the fallen tree just as the animal pounced and a huge force landed on his back, knocking him face forward onto the forest floor.

His whole body trembled as damp, warm breath seeped over the back of his neck and something wet dripped onto his skin. The creature's low growl vibrated in his ears. He could just see the edge of a large paw, the thick claws digging into his shoulders.

"What are yous doing in MY forest?" a voice boomed from the surrounding darkness.

Grian couldn't speak.

"We're…ahem…we're…" Jeffrey stuttered.

"You're what?" It was a girl's voice, and she was angry.

"We're…we're hiding," Grian spluttered, the words stumbling out onto the dirt as he tried to breathe against the weight on his back. "I was chased by hooded people. They broke into my home. I'm sorry, we didn't mean to come here, we just needed somewhere to hide."

There was a long silence. All the while, Grian's heart thumped in his ears, as if about to explode.

"Nach! Stand down," the girl ordered.

The weight lifted as the creature sprang off and landed

with a soft thud on the ground beside him.

Grian pushed himself up from the dirt as the small patch of forest around him illuminated in a gentle light.

"You said hooded people came to your house?" the girl probed. She was holding a glowing rectangular piece of rock that pulsed slowly.

"Yes." Grian nodded. "They wore long black capes with huge hoods. They didn't seem to walk either…they moved like…like…"

"Like ghosts…" Jeffrey interrupted. "Though of course ghosts aren't scientifically recognized, at least not in the conventional way we portray them."

The girl grimaced. "Who are you, poshy?"

"I'm Jeffrey, his neighbour. And I'm not posh, thank you!"

She snorted and looked back at Grian.

The girl was pale, with flaming red hair tied in a long, frizzy plait. Her large amber eyes sat either side of a wide nose in a strong, square, freckled face. Her gaze and grimace were fierce, as if she could slice the boys in two if she wanted. She wore an oversized jacket that looked to be woven with twigs and clumps of dried moss, making her small frame almost dissolve into the thicket around her.

"Follow me!" she ordered, before disappearing into the trees.

Grian looked back, trying to catch sight of the forest edge. He wasn't sure what to do, but it was either this girl or the hoods.

The strange dog growled just metres from him and all thoughts of making a run for it vanished.

"This way!" The girl's voice reached back from somewhere as Grian stumbled forwards, Jeffrey just in front of him.

The dog nipped at Grian's ankles whenever he hesitated while scrambling over roots and fallen branches. He could just make out the other boy's figure ahead, but the pair moved in terrified silence for what seemed like an age. They were following a distant pool of light that danced like a firefly through the darkness, marking the weird girl's position.

Suddenly the light disappeared. Jeffrey stopped dead, and Grian knocked into his back. Filtering through the quiet all around were human whisperings, like tired ghosts on the wind. A shiver crossed his shoulders.

Then the light reappeared above them.

"Yous two – up here!" the girl hissed from the treetops.

She cast her light on some shallow steps cut into the bark of a tree beside them. Grian looked at Jeffrey – for the second time ever, glad to be with him – before putting his foot on the bottom step.

He struggled with the climb, his hands and feet often

slipping from their hold. Jeffrey groaned behind him as the girl huffed impatiently above.

Grian's arms and legs were shaking as he heaved himself onto a wooden platform suspended above the forest floor.

"Wait in there," the girl ordered, pointing to the open door of a round hut built high in the trees.

A railing of twisted branches ran around the perimeter of the platform and Grian grasped it, wobbling up. He steadied himself before edging across the floor and in through the door, Jeffrey just behind him. Petrified, he tried to forget all the bad stories he'd ever heard about the Wilde.

The interior was lit by candlelight that flickered shadows up and down the curved wooden wall. The building swayed, a little like a boat at sea, and Grian flopped down on a purple beanbag by his feet, his stomach churning.

"Curious, isn't it?" Jeffrey said, walking sure-footed around the space.

The hut was decorated with a huge wool tapestry of trees, birds, insects and animals that hugged the curved wall like a wallpaper, while a large, woven straw rug covered the wooden floor.

Jeffrey sneezed. "I imagine this straw may bring on my allergies," he sniffled, rubbing his nose.

A noise startled him and Grian turned towards the door.

An old woman had stepped inside the hut. In one of her hands she held a long branch that she tapped gently across the floor, as if using it as a guide.

The woman was old, but it was hard to tell if she was older or younger than Grandad. Her hair was white and her skin was milk white too, making her ice-blue eyes jump from her face. Her startling gaze swept across Grian and Jeffrey almost as if she didn't see them.

"Welcome to de Wilde forest," she said, dimples dotting the end of her smile like full stops.

Though her colouring was cold, her presence warmed the room.

"My name is Mother and I'm keeper of this forest."

Grian's lip quivered. Something about the woman's presence reminded him of his own mam and how he really needed her right now.

"What is it, son?" The woman stepped towards him. "What has you scared?"

When Grian didn't answer, Jeffrey spoke. "Earlier we were pursued by men in rather large black hooded capes, before almost being attacked by a wild animal in your forest and then finding ourselves here," he stated. "It's a little overwhelming."

Grian snorted a laugh, his anxious mood broken by Jeffrey's directness.

"Hmm," the woman said. "Shelli did mention something like that."

"Shelli?" Jeffrey asked.

"The girl who brought you here," the woman answered. "Now take me back to the beginning of your ordeal and tell me everything."

Grian swallowed a lump in his throat and found his voice, spilling the whole story out for Mother.

"It's de Proctors. It's them, Mother!" the girl interrupted, just as he reached the bit about entering the forest.

Grian hadn't noticed that Shelli had been quietly sitting cross-legged by the door, listening.

"You know who those hooded people are?" he asked.

"No, not exactly – but we have come across them before," Mother replied before changing the subject. "Now, your grandfather must be worried, he'll have come home to an empty house. Your parents too…" She nodded at Jeffrey.

"Oh, don't worry about my parents," Jeffrey replied, shaking his head. "I expect they may not even arrive home tonight. Father says I'm old enough to take care of myself – though not by state regulatory standards, I might add."

The old woman frowned.

"Well, give me your names and addresses and I'll send someone to fetch them anyway…or to leave a message if they're not there," she added. "I don't want you two going back home alone until we're sure there's no one lurking about!"

"I'm Grian Woods."

"Grian? That sounds like a Wilde name..."

"Oh," he answered, surprised. "Mam said Grandad told her it meant 'sun' and she liked the idea of calling me something happy like that."

"And who is your grandad? How does he know our old tongue?"

"I don't know." Grian shook his head, confused. "His name is Adler Rothe..."

"Adler Rothe!" Mother gasped.

She stopped speaking for a moment, feeling her way along the tapestry wall until her hand brushed over a weaving of three white-blonde children huddled together in a forest clearing.

"You're Adler's grandson?" she asked after a minute.

"Yes, why? Do you know my grandad?"

"I'm afraid I did..." she snapped.

Grian blushed at the sting of her reply.

"I'm sorry," the woman said, "I've forgotten myself – memories do that to me sometimes."

She looked towards the door, where the Wilde girl sat in stern silence.

"Shelli, go wake whoever is on call tonight, tell them

to bring Adler and Grian's sister here. They must be back home by now. Tell them to check in on Jeffrey's parents too and if they are not there leave a note," she ordered.

"Yes, Mother." The girl nodded before disappearing outside.

"Now," the woman said, tapping the stick across the floor towards the door, "you two relax here and we'll have you back with your families soon. If you'll excuse me, I need to go consult with the Aunties, my council. It's been an eventful night."

Without another word she disappeared outside.

"Contrary to popular opinion I find the Wilde quite hospitable, don't you?" Jeffrey whispered.

"What does 'hospitable' mean?" Grian asked, still a little wary, though he was finding himself increasingly sleepy in the warmth of the room. The beanbag fitted cosily round his shape and as the hut rocked back and forth on the wind his eyes were slowly closing.

"Courteous," Jeffrey answered as if it were obvious.

"That doesn't…make…it…any clearer," Grian slurred as the candlelight haloed round the edges of his eyes until he couldn't hold them open any longer.

CHAPTER 6

MOTHER AND THE AUNTIES

Grian opened his eyes as morning light warmed his face. He'd been dreaming he was on a ship rolling across a huge ocean. He jumped up suddenly as a snore rattled the air. Was someone else in his room?

He tripped on the edge of a straw rug he didn't recognize, before spotting Jeffrey snoring on another beanbag, his mouth open wide as if catching flies.

Suddenly, Grian remembered he wasn't at home. He was in the forest! Had he spent the whole night in a Wilde hut? That woman, Mother, had said she'd get Grandad to take him home. So why was he still here?

He swiped at Bob, but his Hansom still wasn't working,

so he stepped out onto the platform to see if he could pick up a signal.

The early morning was greyed by a cold mist gathering low over the forest floor. He shivered, holding firm to the railing that wrapped the edges of the platform.

Birdsong rang from the canopy above like an invisible orchestra, louder than he'd ever heard before. Birds rarely sang in town, but then there weren't any trees outside this forest.

Stunned, he sat with his back to the hut wall, listening. As he listened shadows emerged from the thinning mist. All around were other wooden huts, linked by a series of rope bridges. Now the phantom sounds he'd heard the night before made sense – the trees were home to the Wilde.

The other huts were circular too. Most had pitched roofs of straw or grass, though some roofs were made of wood and painted in stripes of red and white. Hanging from branches between the bridges were numerous wooden rings tied at the ends of long chunky ropes. The rings were just like the ones he'd seen gymnasts use, making the whole place appear like an old-fashioned circus.

A large group of birds were dancing around a mound of earth by the base of a neighbouring tree. One of them had a beak full of what looked like red fuzzy hair. Grian startled, as a hand shot up from the mound to shoo the creatures away.

Shelli, the weird Wilde girl, was asleep in the undergrowth – like some sort of animal!

He shuddered and crept back inside to his beanbag, wanting to go home. Where were his grandad and Solas? Why weren't they here yet? Grian sat down, lost in thought.

The morning ticked on and he was just wondering if he should run away, when soft footsteps padded across the platform and Shelli poked her head inside their door.

"Yous are wanted in de council meeting hut," she said, her voice a little croaky with sleep.

"Where's my grandad?" Grian stood up.

"De council will tell ya. Wake him!" Shelli pointed at Jeffrey before stepping back outside.

Nervous and frustrated, Grian woke Jeffrey and they both joined Shelli on the platform.

The mist had cleared now, and the Wilde world was alive around them.

A toddler giggled in the middle of a rope bridge a little away. Her chubby legs were dangling between the wooden boards, as the bridge swayed on a breeze, high above the forest floor. In another tree nearby, a man weaved straw into the roof of a home, while a woman swung from ring to ring like an acrobat as she cut through the camp at lightning speed.

"Yous take de bridges and…" Shelli took a short run and launched herself onto a nearby set of gymnastic rings before somersaulting forwards to catch another set. "… Follow me!"

"Oh my!" Jeffrey rubbed his eyes. "She's impressively fearless."

Grian wavered. He could see the ground far below, between the gaps in the planks.

"Come on." Jeffrey pushed past him onto the bridge, skirting across the thin wooden steps. "We'll lose her if we hesitate. She's quite nippy."

Grian's stomach did a flip.

"All the greatest minds say fear is a construct," Jeffrey called as he raced across another bridge, trying to follow Shelli's path through the forest.

Grian wished he understood what Jeffrey said half the time, because bits of it sounded like it might be useful.

He closed his eyes and took the first step.

The planks beneath him swayed and he gripped the rope sides until his knuckles turned pinkish white. He was sure he didn't breathe for the whole journey.

"Took your time!" Shelli smirked when he finally arrived. She was dangling her feet over the platform edge of a very large hut. "Your posh friend's already gone in…"

Grian gulped as he opened the door and stepped inside.

The stillness hit him first, followed by the waft of heat.

Ten women of about his grandad's age sat cross-legged on colourful mats arranged in a circle around the room. Their eyes were shut and everyone was humming, deep in concentration.

"Good morning, Grian. Sit down beside Jeffrey," Mother instructed, looking up at him.

In the morning light he noticed how her eyebrows were as white as her hair. Her lashes were white too, making the red rims of her eyes pop almost as much as her pale blue irises. She stared straight at him but just like the night before, Grian wasn't sure she could see him at all.

She gestured towards two mats in the middle of the circle. Jeffrey was already sitting cross-legged on one, humming. Grian stepped round another grey-haired woman, who appeared to be in a trance, and sat down on his mat.

Everyone opened their eyes and looked at him.

"Grian and Jeffrey, let me first welcome you to our council gathering – as you know, I'm Mother and these are the Aunties. Together we make up the Wilde council..." The woman stared at the two boys. "And we have a few questions we would like to ask you—"

"Where's my grandad and my sister?" Grian

interrupted, swallowing his nerves. "You said you were sending someone to my house to get them! I thought I was going home. Why are we still here?"

"I know, Grian, and you will go home," Mother soothed. "Please just help us here, and then we will try to answer all your questions. I assure you we don't mean any harm."

Grian looked at his watch. Usually, Bob had a plan if he ever got into a difficult situation, but his Hansom still wasn't working. He nodded at Mother, unsure what else he could do.

"Can you describe the hooded people for me, Grian?" she asked.

He closed his eyes and tried to remember them in detail. He shivered, describing their capes, how the dark pits of the large hoods hid their faces, and the eerie way they moved.

"Was your grandfather at home when the hoods arrived?" one of the Aunties queried.

Grian shook his head.

The Aunties didn't seem interested in Jeffrey at all as the questions continued; most of them were about Grian's grandad and his radio friends, and not about the night before.

"And Adler is a Tilt denier, isn't he?" another Aunty probed.

"Yes," he replied frustrated, "but I don't see what that has to do with last night!"

"That's enough!" Mother finally told the Aunties as she stood up. "Grian, I'm sorry. We've caused you stress. You've had enough of an ordeal already. You mentioned your parents are away – if you give me their details I will contact them. Your father is on the way, Jeffrey. We managed to speak to him this morning. You will both stay with us until they come to collect you."

"But Grandad? Why isn't he coming? My parents are on holiday – Grandad wouldn't want you to call them. Where is he…and my sister? You sent someone to get them last night. What's going on?" Grian stammered.

"Your grandfather wasn't at home last night, Grian, but we will find him. I promise it's nothing to worry about," Mother said, as Shelli stepped inside. "Ah, Shelli, my love, take our guests back to their hut and make sure they are given a full Wilde breakfast. I'll be talking to your parents straight away, Grian, and I'll come get you myself when I know more."

Despite Mother's reassurance, Grian's worry grew legs as the Aunties filed in silence from the room, and he barely noticed the rope bridges as he followed Jeffrey back to their hut.

"I for one am over the moon we get to stay here longer." Jeffrey smiled, falling back onto his beanbag.

"And I'm ravenous – this Wilde breakfast sounds good!"

"You don't even know what it is yet – probably fried rabbit or something! And your dad is on the way, Jeffrey," Grian sniped as he sat down. "You'll be gone soon anyway."

"No I won't. Father always says he's coming to get me when I'm staying in my cousin's house but sometimes he doesn't turn up for days. It's character-building, he says. A child is not a puppy, you know – we should be able to take care of ourselves!"

"I don't want to stay here!" Grian paced the room. "Why were they asking all those questions about Grandad? Why isn't he home yet? I don't trust the Wilde! I mean, the Aunties all call that woman Mother, but she can't be their mother, they're all the same age! The people in Tallystick are right about them. They're weird!"

"I understand your frustration, Grian," Jeffrey said, stroking his chin, "but maybe you should trust Mother. She seems like the good sort of adult."

"But she didn't tell me anything!"

"Yes, but that's just the way adults are, especially the good ones. I expect she thinks she's protecting you from whatever it is she's hiding." Jeffrey shrugged.

"So you *do* think she's hiding something?"

"Of course." Jeffrey smiled. "But all adults hide things – it's part of being grown up, I think!"

"Then all adults are liars and I don't want to grow up!" Grian said, whacking the beanbag so hard that a cloud of dust tickled his nose.

He was mid sneeze when Bob beeped and a familiar name flew across its screen.

Solas had sent him a message.

CHAPTER 7
THE TRACKER

Grian had just swiped to open Solas's message when Bob's screen went blank again. Then, just as quickly, it turned on once more before dying a third time.

"What is going on?" he snapped, desperate to know what Solas had said. "There's something weird happening to my watch."

Jeffrey was standing by a small round window in the hut, peering out. "Over here! Quick, look," he whispered, pointing.

Shelli was sitting on the platform outside playing with a small black box in her hand. A tiny red light blinked in the corner of the box.

"Watch! When that light turns green, our Hansoms

come back on!" Jeffrey breathed.

Grian watched the girl chuckle as she swiped across the screen of the small box. The light turned green and Bob was alive.

"She's cutting the power somehow," Jeffrey whispered. "It must be an electrical blocking device. Hansom have some in development – TechNow had a podcast on it last week. How the Wilde came upon one is quite perplexing. I had thought they were technophobes."

Grian was only half listening as Jeffrey rambled on. He swiped in frustration at Bob, trying to open Solas's message when the watch turned off again and he raced outside.

"What are ya doing?" Shelli jumped up as he swiped the black box from her hand.

"What am *I* doing?" Grian replied, running inside with it. "I could ask you the same thing!"

"That's mine, give it back!" She chased after him into the hut.

Bob's name, product ID and registered owner were listed across the screen of the box, beside the words ON/OFF. Grian swiped across the word ON and his Hansom lit up once more.

"I wouldn't if I were you." Jeffrey shook his head at Shelli as he stepped in front of the furious girl. "He's just received a message from his sister – the one who's run away. Where did you get technology like that anyway, I thought the Wilde didn't have any?"

"I found it on de edge of de forest last night. One of them Proctors dropped it when they were chasing yous, so I went back and got it... And just because we don't like technology doesn't mean we don't have any – we're not stupid!" Shelli snapped.

"Oh, those hoods had it! That might explain how all the power went out last night then," Jeffrey mumbled to himself.

"Solas knows she's in trouble." Grian looked back up from his watch. "Grandad must have found her!"

He read his sister's message aloud.

"grandad here help"

"Are you sure Solas sent that message? It could be interpreted a different way. Maybe your grandfather sent it and he needs our help?" Jeffrey quizzed.

"It's Solas's watch! Grandad doesn't know how to use a Hansom – he's never even turned one on before!" Grian shook his head.

"Maybe he's with your sister, maybe they both need our help?" Shelli whispered.

"What do you mean? Why would they both need our help? I know where Solas is, because she left a note –

she went to the Tipping Point! The only one who's kind of missing is Grandad and I'm sure he's bringing her back... Like her message says – Grandad is there with her, she's obviously in trouble with him for running away and she expects me to help. So he must have found her! They just got delayed, that's all. Why does it feel like you Wilde people aren't telling me something?" he said frustrated.

"I'm not hiding anything. I don't know more than you do, but de Proctors turning up at your house makes me worried," Shelli answered. "And I think Mother and de Aunties are worried too!"

"But why are they worried? And who exactly are the Proctors anyway?" Grian asked.

"I don't know really... All I know is de Proctors bring trouble."

"Trouble how?"

"Whenever they are spotted, people disappear. A few years ago there were lots of sightings of them in Wilde areas, then our people would vanish without a reason. Once even a whole tribe disappeared overnight – things like that happened to de Wilde all over Babbage. After de earthquake it stopped for a bit.

"But lately de Proctors have been spotted again, de disappearances are smaller this time – one or two people at a time and they're not Wilde – they're brainy people like scientists and doctors and all. Most are part of some colour council – at least that's what I heard Mother and de Aunties say. Mother's worried – she won't tell me anything, though, she thinks I'm too young."

"Oh, this fires a neuron," Jeffrey said. "Hansom was interviewed on Babbage One hNews about a Geology Professor in Turing University who vanished a few weeks ago. Some of the professor's students saw people in hooded capes on the campus that night. Hansom was irate. He said something about a gang called the Proctors who are trying to discredit him and the Tipping Point."

"So you think the Proctors have taken Grandad?" Grian asked, alarmed.

Shelli nodded, looking straight at him. Her amber eyes startling. "I listened in on de Aunties' meeting last night. They think so too."

"But why?" Grian asked. "All of Tallystick think Grandad's weird not brainy! And it doesn't make sense… why would the Proctors come looking in my house last night if they'd already taken Grandad?"

"Maybe they were looking for something of his?" Jeffrey replied.

"I don't have all de answers," Shelli continued, "but I know de others who went missing were never found and I don't want that happening to your granda. Any good tracker will tell ya that de sooner ya act de better. And

I'm de best tracker de Wilde has ever seen. Your granda's scent will still be strong – we could save him!"

"It sounds like a fine idea to me!" Jeffrey smiled.

"You're serious?" Grian asked.

"Never seriouser," the girl stated.

"But what about the police or Howard Hansom or something? Shouldn't we go to them first? We're just kids! Mother told us to stay here. She's calling my parents!"

"De police won't help us – like ya said, we're just kids, they'll say we're wasting their time and send us home. And how are we meant to get to Howard Hansom, de most famous man in de whole world!" Shelli replied, her eyes large. "And do ya really think your parents will be happy to let ya go off looking for your granda? Adults work slow and are too careful – they think too long about things and there's no time to think. We have to act, like, soon – really soon!"

"Most are valid points," Jeffrey nodded, "but I do dispute that we're 'just kids' – children are capable of quite a lot. Now where do I sign up?"

"You're not coming!" Grian blurted. "Ahem...I mean, this isn't your problem, Jeffrey – and anyway, your dad is on the way to get you!"

"Thank you for your concern, Grian," Jeffrey replied, "but my father, if he does turn up, won't mind – as I told you before, he'll say an adventure like this is character-building."

"So we've a plan!" Shelli announced. "We'll leave as soon as possible. We'll go to your house first, so I can get some of your granda's stuff – for his scent."

Grian hesitated as he rubbed the back of his head and walked away. Solas's message said Grandad was there with her. But what if he'd read it wrong? What if Shelli was right – what if he didn't go now and Grandad disappeared and Grian never saw him again?

"But how do I know I can trust you – why do you want to find my grandad anyway? I mean, why does it matter to you now that the Wilde aren't going missing any more?" He turned and stared straight at her.

"Because…my ma was one of de first disappeared. I was six. I haven't seen her since – no one has." Shelli looked away.

Grian looked away then too, his cheeks flushed. Silence slipped between them.

"Ahem. Okay – if you really think Grandad's in trouble," he replied unsure; he really hadn't thought through the idea.

He loved his grandad more than anything. He couldn't never see him again.

"I have listened with an open attitude and I admire your spirit, but I must now object, Grian," his Hansom piped up. "This is in breach of my guardian guidelines. If you persist, I will send an alert to your mother."

"Pass it over." Jeffrey nodded at the watch.

Grian hesitated before undoing the strap.

"Do you know your mother's hMail address?" Jeffrey asked fiddling with Grian's watch.

"SaoirseWoods@hMail.bab," Grian answered, a little curious now.

"And perhaps you know her password too? Most parents aren't tech aware so it may be something like a birthday or anniversary. If I had my hTablet of course I wouldn't need to ask for any of this information. I have a database of passwords."

"Ahem. I think it's her date of birth," Grian replied, remembering how he'd recently watched his mam buy a coat on her favourite website. "She uses the same password for everything."

"Parents really do make it easy," Jeffrey smiled as he concentrated on Bob.

"Security breach, security breach," Grian's Hansom repeated as Jeffrey expertly accessed its security system before handing back the device.

"I hacked your mother's account." Jeffrey smiled as Grian's face dropped. "Don't worry she won't know and I merely removed parental controls."

"Poshy might actually come in handy!" Shelli half smiled before turning to leave. "I'll be back. Be ready."

CHAPTER 8

GOING HOME

Grian grew more uneasy as the time passed waiting for Shelli's return. The hours were broken by the Wilde breakfast, which wasn't as bad as he'd thought it might be, bursts of sleep, a Wilde lunch which was equally as good as the breakfast, and a visit from Mother, who did seem like the "good sort" of adult. She said she'd been in touch with his parents; his mam was on her way and should be with them the following morning.

Sitting on the platform as the day wound on, he felt guilty and anxious and angry all at once. Guilty because his mam would turn up in the forest and he'd be gone. Anxious because his grandad could be held captive by some weird, hooded gang and because Shelli still hadn't turned up, and angry – well, angry because it was all Solas's fault. If she hadn't run away, he wouldn't be in this mess!

He'd sent his sister loads of messages since he'd received hers but she still hadn't replied, which only made everything worse.

As the night settled in he strode back and forth across the hut, itching to leave. Where was Shelli?

The animated sounds of the forest quietened to rustlings in the undergrowth, until only ghostly snores floated through the trees.

Then a single knock sounded on the door and Shelli slipped in, a small black rucksack strapped to her back.

"What took you so long?" Grian blurted angrily.

"One of the Aunties saw me with de Proctors' black box and I was made to hand it up. She locked it in our tech hut. I tried to get it back – I mean, it'd be so good to bring with us – but I couldn't, so I gave up cause we don't have much time. Are yous ready?" she asked.

"As we'll ever be!" Jeffrey replied.

Grian cringed, still unsure why Jeffrey was coming, as they slipped onto the platform and wobbled down the rope ladder, aided solely by moonlight.

"Shush," Shelli whispered as Grian landed with a soft thud on the forest floor.

He closed his eyes and forced himself not to be

irritated by his companions this early in their trip. Then something brushed past his leg and a low growl met his ears. He looked down as Shelli's animal crept past without a sound.

"Is the dog coming too?" he asked, a little surprised.

"Nach goes everywhere with me," Shelli answered, "and she's not a dog – she's a fox!"

"Foxes are smaller than dogs and have flatter skulls than their canine cousins," Jeffrey whispered. "They're not very like dogs at all actually."

Grian breathed deep again, unsure any of this was such a good idea.

As they travelled onwards through the thick trees, Grian concentrated hard on not falling over large roots or getting lost. The light from Shelli's strange glowing rock was a good guide but sometimes the snap of a branch was the only indicator of her whereabouts. He was relieved when his feet eventually met a worn path that wound into a clearing and under the fence back into Forest Drive, the sleepy estate.

When they reached his house, Shelli held her hand up, stopping Grian as he opened his gate. Then she closed her eyes and for a moment looked a little like she'd fallen asleep.

Suddenly Nach, her fox, stood to attention and began sniffing down the garden path to the grey painted door, before racing back to Shelli. She nodded at Grian, giving him the go-ahead.

Grian's hand shook as he typed the code into the front door lock. There was a faint click and carefully he pushed it open. Nach leaped across the threshold and sniffed around, before Shelli nodded again, and the threesome followed the fox inside.

"Show me to your granda's room," Shelli ordered. "Yous pack food and anything else ya need."

"What exactly are you looking for?" Grian asked, a little put out by her bossiness as he led her upstairs.

"Something that has your granda's scent and his… I don't know how to explain it…his energy, I suppose."

Grian cringed as he pushed open his grandad's door. Shelli was definitely weird.

Straight away she started searching the room, the girl's features set in a kind of concentrated scowl as her fox sniffed round the cream carpet.

Something inside Grian shook as everywhere he looked he was reminded of his grandad – from his worn red slippers under the bed to his glasses on the locker. He took a deep breath and stepped back into the hallway.

For some reason he found himself walking into Solas's room and sitting on his sister's bed.

Suddenly overwhelmed, he punched the pillows that were meant to outline her shape. Why did she have to run away to the Tipping Point? Even though he knew it didn't make sense, he blamed her for all of this. Maybe if Grandad hadn't gone looking for Solas, none of this would have happened.

Could the Proctors really have taken his grandad, like Shelli thought, or was Grandad just in the Tipping Point trying to persuade Solas to come home? She still hadn't responded to the messages he'd sent her, and Bob had just told him that his sister's Hansom had now gone offline.

Frustrated, he picked up Solas's diary from the bedside locker. Even though he'd joked with her about it, he never thought she'd actually run away. Maybe he didn't really know his sister at all. He took the small book out of its pouch, feeling only a tinge of guilt.

"We're done," Shelli said, poking her head in the half-opened door. "You said your granda had another room?"

Grian nodded and took the diary with him as he led Shelli downstairs and into his grandfather's pokey study. Jeffrey followed behind, carrying a bag bursting with what looked like every bit of food that had been in Grian's kitchen cupboards.

"I was a two-way radio fanatic when I was younger – I even built one myself!" Jeffrey boasted as he pushed past and fiddled with some dials.

"Don't break Grandad's stuff!" Grian said anxiously.

Shelli stood with her arms folded, staring at the map on the back wall, while Nach ate something under the desk. Grian imagined it was a bit of mouldy cake. His grandad loved cake.

Shelli moved her fingers across the hand-drawn map as if circling the world. "Who does your granda work for?"

"Grandad?" Grian laughed. "He doesn't work for anyone. He retired; he's ancient! He used to be a postmaster like Dad – that's how Mam and Dad met – but that was ages ago!"

"But you said he doesn't use technology at all, so he must, like, travel to other countries or something to record this stuff? I thought it was only de important people or people with work passes who are allowed to visit other countries now?" Shelli asked, looking confused.

"He doesn't travel." Grian shook his head. "I don't think I've seen Grandad outside this room much. He does use technology though, it's just really old tech. He's got radio friends all over the world, so he probably gets that information from them."

They were all staring at the map of the world now. Grian had never paid much attention to it before.

Along the edges of the map were a series of hand-drawn boxes, each relating to a different country in the world. At the top of each box were what Grian presumed to be names, because he recognized one of them – Vermilion. He'd asked his grandad once what the word meant, when he'd seen it written down on a Post-it note, and Grandad had said Vermilion was a radio friend of his. He remembered now that his grandad had even been talking to Vermilion on his radio when Grian interrupted him with Solas's note the night before.

At the bottom of each box was a series of numbers, letters and angles.

"The information is not accurate – your grandfather should get better friends," Jeffrey stated from his seat at the desk.

"What do you mean?" Grian asked, a little annoyed.

"According to your grandfather's map, the earth hasn't tilted at all! Look – by his calculations the daylight hours, the sunrise and sunset times and the seasons haven't changed for any country in the world, which is simply incorrect! It's the stuff of a Tilt denier. I fail to understand why some people don't listen to science."

"Grandad loves science," Grian answered defensively. "If you think his map is wrong then maybe you should check your science!"

"So you believe Howard Hansom and the whole world is wrong, and your grandfather is right?" Jeffrey frowned.

Grian opened his sister's diary, to distract himself from hitting his neighbour with it.

I HATE GRIAN! Solas had written in huge letters across the middle of the opened page.

He flung the diary on the desk and walked outside.

CHAPTER 9

THE HIDDEN ROOM

Grian was pacing up and down the garden path when Shelli appeared back outside, shoving his grandad's favourite socks and an old shirt into her bag. He hoped she really was a tracker and not some sort of weird thief.

He pulled his own bag onto his back. He'd packed a small load of necessities – some food he'd taken from Jeffrey's haul and a change of clothes. Jeffrey snuck into his own home and came out with a small purple backpack crammed with more food, an hTablet, a tiny folded mechanical tripod thing, a strange metal box with no sides and an array of other odd bits of technology Grian had never seen before. He also had a pencil case filled with screwdrivers, glue, computer chips, memory cards, chalk, wire and anything else you might find in a random drawer.

"This pencil case of oddities always comes in handy, and I imagine more so now we're on an adventure!" Jeffrey explained as he shoved it into his bag.

"Won't you need clothes?" Grian asked, amused.

"I have limited room – a change of socks and underpants will do. After all, you can't eat a shirt and it certainly won't help you decode a lock." Jeffrey shrugged. "I have Mum's hPay," he tapped his watch, "so should we need anything else, I'll have the funds."

Grian blushed. His parents gave him a tiny monthly allowance on his Hansom, mainly for bus journeys and things like that. They would never allow him to have their hPay details. Jeffrey's parents were obviously much cooler than his.

"Great, let's go!" Shelli smiled as she bent down and held Adler's clothes to her fox's nose.

She leaned forward so she was eye to eye with the animal. Grian squirmed as the silence grew awkward. What was she doing? Could he really trust this girl to find his grandfather?

Then, in a flash, the fox turned and disappeared into the shadows of the street. Shelli raced after her, leaving the two boys behind like a pair of bobbing bottles on the open sea.

"Are yous coming?" she shouted back.

"You mean, run after you?" Jeffrey called. "I'm not sure I've run much since I was a very small child!"

"You'll figure it out!" Shelli laughed before disappearing round the corner ahead.

As Grian panted along the Tallystick streets, he wished he'd listened to his grandad more and exercised – even a little. Shelli was way ahead, only stopping now and again to make sure the pair hadn't collapsed. At least he wasn't as bad as Jeffrey, he thought, as he stopped to catch some air while the other boy struggled a distance behind.

Grian shivered as a cold blast of wind whipped round the street. He'd never been in Tallystick this late at night – the dark shadows and the silence seemed huge, as if they'd swallow him. He glanced over his shoulder, trying to shake the feeling that someone was watching.

He'd just looked down at his Hansom when the bright bus stop billboard beside him flickered and went out, along with all the street lights. He gasped as Bob stopped working too.

Looking up, Grian spotted a black shape hovering in silence on the footpath opposite, almost hidden in the shadows of a bookshop doorway. A chill slithered down his spine – he tried to run, but his feet were welded to the path.

The caped figure appeared to be looking straight at him, though he couldn't see a face in the dark pit of its hood.

Jeffrey stopped beside him. He seemed not to have noticed the figure as he bent at the waist, sucking in air.

Grian stared straight at the huge black shape, its cape billowing on the breeze, until suddenly the Proctor swept out from the doorway and moved towards the pair.

"Je-Jef...Jeffrey..." Grian stuttered, grabbing at his jumper.

"What...what...are...you doing? That's...quite enough ...I just...need...a...breather," the other boy panted.

"Across the road...b-by the bookshop," Grian said, just as three other figures moved out of the shadows and glided towards the pair like a hunting pack.

"The P-proctors!" Jeffrey inhaled.

Grian shot forward, pulling the other boy with him. His mind raced as his feet moved faster than they ever had in his life.

"Where are we going? Where's Shelli?" Jeffrey wheezed, sprinting round the corner of a bus depot and down the deserted main street of Tallystick.

As they raced ahead, the street lights, bus stops and billboards flickered before turning back on.

"The post office!" Grian blurted. "We could hide in there."

He'd practically grown up in the building, playing in all its hidden corners after school while waiting for his dad to finish work. His Hansom was on the access network and so had a key code for the door.

Grian glanced down at his watch – it was working again.

"Bob," he whispered, "find the post office."

"Calculating," his Hansom replied as Grian desperately searched the street for the shiny golden P – he wished he'd paid more attention to directions instead of always depending on Bob.

The Proctors rounded the corner behind them, their pace slow but definite as they moved without seeming to touch the ground.

"In thirty metres, turn right down Letters Lane," Bob stated.

Grian ploughed forward, his lungs heaving as the rucksack banged up and down on his shoulders.

He darted into the lane, not looking back as he caught a glimpse of the golden post office *P* shining like a beacon from the darkness ahead. They were nearly there.

Then Jeffrey cried out, the sound cutting the night.

Grian swung round.

He could just see the outline of the boy on the ground – he must have tripped and fallen. Grian dashed back and grabbed Jeffrey's arm, pulling him up as the Proctors entered the lane.

Jeffrey scrambled forward in a panic just as another terrifying wail, like a bawling baby, echoed off the narrow walls, and something sped past them, launching itself at their hunters.

A frenzy of growls and yelps filled the air behind them as the pair sprinted towards the end of the lane and broke out onto the open street, almost colliding with Shelli.

"Nach, did she find yas?" the girl cried.

"She's...she's in the lane with the...the Proctors. She saved us," Jeffrey wheezed.

"You've reached your destination," Bob stated, while Grian's hand shook as he swiped his Hansom across the entrance panel of the post office doors.

The doors slid open and they rushed inside, disappearing behind a large orange couch usually reserved for waiting customers.

Even Shelli gasped for air as all three crouched on the floor.

"Nach sensed something was up," she panted. "I was following her when she turned and sprinted back to yous..."

"Will she be okay?" Grian gulped.

"She'll be fine." Shelli nodded, peering around the side of the couch. "It's us I'm worried about..."

Grian followed her gaze through the large window. The Proctors were crossing the street, heading straight for the post office.

"The vault!" he hissed, crawling away. "Dad showed it to me a few weeks ago. No one knows about it. Even if the Proctors do get in here, they'll never find it."

Keeping low, Grian and the others crept along the cold, marble floor, passing numerous white plastic desks inlaid with self-help screens, before slipping behind a wall of glass into a green carpeted hallway lined either side with staff offices.

Grian stiffened as the gentle swoosh of the front doors broke their silence.

"They're in," Jeffrey whispered.

Grian increased the pace until they reached the postmaster's office at the very back of the building.

"This is Dad's," he whispered, hurrying inside.

The keys to the vault were hidden in a box in the middle drawer of his dad's large desk. The desk was old, with thick carved wooden legs and a dinted tabletop. His dad never felt comfortable with anything new – he'd once told Grian that was why he loved the postal service.

Grian jolted as a crash rang through the building from the front foyer.

Quickly he opened the stiff middle drawer and removed an ornate wooden box. It was a puzzle box Grandad had given Grian's father as a present. Grandad had a weird obsession with puzzles, which he'd tried to pass on to his family.

Grian steadied his breathing and tried to block out all thoughts of the Proctors just metres away. He needed precision to unlock the puzzle. Concentrating, he moved the delicate wooden pieces from memory, until he heard a faint click and the middle compartment slid open.

Reaching in, he grabbed the tiny key fob and crawled two paces across the office to a plain white wall before tapping the key off a sensor hidden in the side of an electrical socket.

Jeffrey's mouth dropped open as the office wall zipped across, revealing a hidden room beyond.

CHAPTER 10

THE POSTAL TUNNEL

"Quick!" Grian whispered, racing inside.

Once they were all in, Grian swiped another sensor and the wall closed. Then he turned on Bob's flashlight.

The room was small and dark. Every surface from floor to ceiling was covered in grey sheet metal that was lined in a strange mesh of thin interlacing metal strips, like a weird geometric wallpaper.

"Wow," Jeffrey said, the torchlight casting deep shadows across his face. "Is this a real Faraday cage? I tried to build one once, but I didn't have enough metal…"

"Yeah, I think that's what Dad called it," Grian replied, relief seeping in a little. "The Proctors won't find us here, hardly anyone even knows it exists!"

"Can someone please tell me what this place is?" Shelli whispered, looking more terrified in the tight space than she had facing the Proctors.

"A Faraday cage – it blocks electromagnetic signals," Jeffrey said, pointing at his Hansom.

Betty, his watch, was on, but apart from basic functions it wasn't working.

"Oh," Shelli replied, her expression confused. "But why would de post office need a place like this?"

"Dad said this place was part of the old sorting room for the underground postal trains before they stopped running. When they did up the building it became storage and wasn't used any more, so—"

"So they turned it into a Faraday cage?" Jeffrey interrupted. "Why would the post office need a room that blocks electromagnetic signals? I've heard of government agencies having them, and I see the logic in that. But the postal service – I mean, it's practically obsolete."

"I didn't ask, but I doubt the reason is anything exciting." Grian shivered. The small space was freezing – it was almost like standing in a fridge. "Dad's job is pretty boring. I don't really listen when he talks about it!"

"Maybe his job is not *that* boring." Jeffrey raised his eyebrows. "Maybe that's why the Proctors are after you and your family…"

"They're not after my family!" Grian stiffened.

"Forgive me if I'm wrong, but the Proctors did break into your house, they possibly have your grandfather and they are chasing us tonight. It would seem plausible to me that they are after your family. They could actually be tracking your Hansom! It'd be one way to explain how they found us tonight. I'm confident they won't be able to locate us in here though, now the Faraday cage is blocking signals," Jeffrey stated.

"But why would they be tracking me?" Grian said, shivering again, though this time not from the cold.

Jeffrey pointed at his watch. "Give me Bob and I'll change it to incognito mode – it will hide your device ID and IP. I'll do Betty too, to be safe. No one, not even Hansom himself, will be able to track us then! As to why anyone wants to track you – well, I presume we'll find answers to that question when we locate your grandfather. Isn't that right, Shelli?"

"Shush!" Shelli glared as she paced the walls like a tiger in a zoo. "De Proctors are still out there. They're looking for us and we're trapped in a tiny metal box like… like caged animals! I can't track your granda from here. I have to get out!"

Grian handed over his watch and Jeffrey fiddled with it as Shelli slipped down one of the walls and disappeared inside her oversized coat of moss and leaves. A few moments later she re-emerged, holding a long stick of rock crystal. Its warm glow filled the corner of the metal box and Shelli seemed to relax a little, her fiery red hair almost golden in the soft light.

"What is that? How does it work? Is it battery powered?" Jeffrey asked, handing Grian back his Hansom.

"It's called a Glimmer. I just think about someone I love and it turns on," Shelli replied, her voice a little lighter. "Mother Wilde gave it to me. She said her sister made it years ago by trapping sunlight – she was kind of clever, I think."

"How curious – of course, you know love can't power anything. There must be a mechanism in it somewhere," Jeffrey said, moving closer to inspect the jagged rock crystal.

Shelli growled, instantly pulling her rock away so the Glimmer's light drifted across the back wall for a brief second illuminating something etched into the grey metal. Intrigued, Grian directed Bob's torch towards the etching. What looked like a rectangular framed map was highlighted under the glare of his Hansom's stark LED.

On the top left-hand corner of the map was a small, raised plaque with *The Turing District Postal Railway* etched in tiny letters. The map appeared to show a trainline running from their suburb of Tallystick into the city of Turing and beyond, listing ten numbered stations along the way. The last station was labelled *Babbage*

Central Sorting Warehouse. Hand-scratched into the metal by station number nine were the letters T.P.

"It looks like a map of the underground postal railway," Grian whispered. "Dad told me they closed the railway lines years ago."

He snapped a photo with his Hansom before noticing a discreet silver button on the bottom corner of the map and pressed it on impulse.

Grian gasped and jumped back as the map lit up and the wall it was on came alive. The outer layer of mesh raced downwards and disappeared into the floor before the rectangular map moved aside, revealing a large entrance hole in the wall behind it. A swift breeze whipped round the tight room.

"Well, I never…" Jeffrey said, stunned. "You seem to have unearthed some sort of passage!"

"Maybe it leads to the postal railway?" Grian replied.

"Come on." Shelli jumped and pulled herself straight up into the cylindrical passage. "I'm not waiting around here for de walls to close in on me or those Proctors to find us!"

Grian was speechless as she crawled forwards on her hands and knees along the passageway, the Glimmer in her grasp emphasizing the curve of the metal walls.

"The passage dips down – it's steep …" her voice echoed back.

"That must be the chute where they'd drop the post—" Grian was mid reply when Shelli gave a tiny squeal and vanished into the darkness.

He swallowed a lump in his throat and turned around to Jeffrey.

"I suspect she went down the chute." Jeffrey smiled.

"Shouldn't we at least have made a plan?" asked Grian, feeling nervous.

"She does appear to be quite impulsive. But we can either choose the Proctors out there or the unknown down that metal pipe." The other boy shrugged.

Grian pictured the Proctors and shuddered, before climbing quickly into the passage. His arms shook as he crawled along, stopping just before the metal sloped away from him. He shone Bob's torch down.

"It's a bit of a sheer drop," he stuttered.

"On a risk versus benefit analysis, I'd go with the drop." Jeffrey's voice echoed round him.

Grian closed his eyes and tried to slow the thumping in his chest. Then he shuffled round in the tight space so he was feet first, and edged forward.

"One, two, three…" he whispered before pushing off.

Suddenly the air rushed round him as he catapulted downwards. His heart was in his throat as he flew free of the pipe and somersaulted into a heap of rough brown sacks, releasing a cloud of dust.

He spluttered and dived forwards to avoid a sideswipe from Jeffrey, who shot out of the tunnel directly behind him.

Almost choking on the new wave of dust, Grian stumbled off the sacks and steadied himself against the side of what looked like a large rusty wagon on wheels, that must have been used for carrying post. It was resting on similarly rusty railway tracks.

The cement ceiling above was low and curved. A row of cobwebbed industrial strip lights ran along its centre like a spine. Some were broken but others flickered a faint light into the space.

Grian gazed about full of wonder.

"Dad told me about the postal railway lines, but he talked about them like they were gone! The underground lines run all over Babbage... He said they'd closed them years ago..."

"Strange how the lights are on then..." Jeffrey commented.

Grian was about to reply when he noticed a faint murmur playing on the air. He tugged at his ears, the sound so low that at first he wondered if it was inside his own head.

He spotted Shelli sitting cross-legged in the middle of the tracks, just like Mother and the Aunties had sat in the Wilde meeting hut. Her eyes were closed and she had

104

his grandad's shirt and sock on her lap.

The low murmur grew until an intense buzz filled the tunnel.

Grian's right leg started to itch. He scratched it but the itch grew until he was swatting at his legs but he couldn't shake off the irritation. It felt as if his skin was crawling, until all of a sudden his calves were on fire.

"Agh!" he cried, jumping about as he looked down.

Millions of tiny ants streamed over the bottom of his tracksuit.

Jeffrey cried out too and the pair hopped around as though they were sizzling sausages on a hot pan. But the ants kept coming until Grian's legs were blackened to the knees and rising.

"Stop moving!" Shelli roared, her fierce voice bouncing around the tunnel. "Don't harm them or I'll batter yas!"

Grian stumbled backwards, almost falling into the black moving mass of ants that now carpeted the ground beneath him, before steadying himself against the small, rusted train.

"What...is happening?" Jeffrey stuttered, standing so stiff only his eyes moved.

More of the tiny creatures streamed in thick waves across the curved ceiling, moving down the walls to join the advancing army on the floor. Grian looked away in horror as the insects blanketed Shelli until she was only a dark blob in the middle of the tunnel, before continuing onwards behind her.

The buzz fizzled to a hum and slowly died out as the mass of ants passed through the space and disappeared into the distance, revealing Shelli sitting dead still on the tracks.

She opened her intense amber eyes and fixed the pair with a stare.

"Let's go!" she said, springing up and dashing after the ants.

CHAPTER 11
THE NOTE

"I asked de ants to track your granda's scent. They've great noses. When they pick up something they'll head above ground and follow it. If them watches are any good, I think yous should be able to pinpoint where exactly de ants have broken out above ground. Then we just need to find a way up, find de ant trail and follow them," Shelli shouted back from somewhere ahead.

"So ants are now looking for Grandad – is that better or worse than a fox?" Grian whispered to himself, not totally convinced he wasn't dreaming.

"I can hear ya! Do ya want to find your granda or what?" Shelli's voice bounced off the walls, startling him.

He pulled a face, sure she couldn't see that at least.

Shelli was pretty bossy, sometimes making her nearly as annoying as Jeffrey. Still, Grian raced faster up the track after her, his lungs heaving, as she disappeared further and further into the distance.

Soon tiny bits of dirt and dust started to fall onto his hair and eyebrows. As he stopped and brushed off the debris it felt like the walls were beginning to rattle.

"Beep, beep!" Jeffrey's voice rang out from behind. "Jump onboard!"

Grian swivelled just in time to see the large rusting wagon careening down the track straight for him. Jeffrey, who was tucked inside, held out his skinny arm as he flew past. Astounded, Grian grabbed his opened hand and jumped clumsily onto the side of the moving metal vessel, before shimmying over the edge inside.

"We'll catch Shelli in no time now!" Jeffrey laughed above the clatter of the rattling wagon.

Grian held on for his life, his white knuckles gripping the rusted metal sides. His heart pounded, the sound almost louder than the speeding wagon itself. He was terrified and electrified all at once.

Jeffrey's eyes were large and the wind whipped through the top of his hair, making him look a little like the crazed Barber in Grian's computer game, as he squatted by a small operation panel screwed to the front of the wagon. Each time Jeffrey pressed the dirty red button on the dashboard their vessel picked up speed, until they were rocketing down the track and closing in fast on Shelli.

Suddenly the wagon jolted and Grian walloped into Jeffrey as they swooped off course, diverting downhill on a different track.

"Stop the train!" Grian roared.

The brakes screeched their protest as Jeffrey pulled on a long lever attached to the side of wagon, then he flew backwards as it broke in his grasp. They were now hurtling at lightning speed down the track.

"Duck!" Grian cried, shoving Jeffrey down as they sped headlong for a red and white striped barrier spanning the tracks ahead.

A huge crack split the air as they hit the barrier, and the pair jerked forward, ramming into the front of the wagon. Time slowed. Chunks and splinters from the barrier spun over Grian's head as the wagon spiralled off the tracks, before crashing into a wall and stopping dead.

Warm blood trickled down Grian's chin and he tasted metal as he wiped it away. The tunnel spun around him and he was groggy as he climbed out of the battered wagon. He sat on the dirt and pushed his head between his knees. Jeffrey dragged himself across the ground to sit beside Grian and they both stared in numbed shock at the crash scene.

"My ankle's a bit worse for wear," Jeffrey croaked, pulling up the bottom of his grey trousers.

It was hard to see in the dim light, but it looked okay. At least there weren't any bones jutting out where they shouldn't be.

"Can you walk?" Grian coughed, pulling himself off the ground to test his own limbs.

"I think so." Jeffrey winced as he stood up. "Just a war wound!"

Grian snorted – they weren't exactly at war, though the place did look a little like the trenches in "The Troops" – a new Hansom game.

"Looks like an abandoned station," Jeffrey said, dusting himself off.

"Bob, where are we?" Grian asked.

"According to online records, Grian, and using GPS, we appear to be on a maintenance line for the old Turing District Postal Railway."

Standing on the tracks, Grian could see up to what seemed to be some sort of platform.

Still a little dazed, he stood on a piece of metal jutting out from the wall and hoisted himself up onto the platform to look around. Everything here was covered in dirty white tiles, from the floor to the back wall and even the columns that held up the low ceiling above him. Bits of electrical cables draped down the walls like curtains, while a fallen bin was picking up dirt in the middle of the floor.

A bench was broken and lonely, left on its side to rot. Maybe people had sat on it once, but nobody had been down here in a while.

Curious, Grian walked towards a dark doorway in the back wall. A large spider's web hung across it and he had to pull a host of soft grey threads from his face as he inched into what looked like an old office.

Jeffrey coughed, startling him.

"Shush," Grian whispered as his friend stepped inside behind him, "there could be someone about!"

"There clearly isn't!" the other boy replied.

"Flashlight, Bob," Grian ordered.

The room lit up under his Hansom's glare.

A battered table was shoved up against the back wall, covered in odd bits and pieces of mechanical parts. Screwed to the wall above the table was a cabinet of small wooden drawers. Tiny metal label holders were screwed to the front of each drawer, holding worn pictures of various screw types, nails and tools. Grian opened up a few drawers to be greeted in turn by an old coin, a petrified mouse, a chewed pencil and a cloud of dust.

"As I said, clearly there hasn't been a soul down here in years," Jeffrey stated.

Grian noticed something poking out from a half-open

drawer in the cabinet. He opened it fully to see a small yellow envelope resting inside. The envelope looked fresh and clean, which seemed odd.

"How strange," Jeffrey said, peering over his shoulder. "No name or address either. Open it!"

"I'm not sure," Grian said. "It's not ours, Jeffrey, and it looks new. Maybe it's here for someone else to collect?"

"Who? Look around, nobody's been down here in millennia. No, it's just been protected by the drawer."

Wary, Grian turned over the envelope.

There was a wax seal on the back, just like the ones he'd seen in movies about Ancient Rome or old places like that. The seal was stamped with what looked like the outline of a strange flower, the circular petals interlacing over each other.

Feeling a little guilty, but curious, Grian cracked open the wax. Inside the envelope was a piece of paper, which he shimmied out.

Suddenly he felt sick, like he'd just poured sour milk on his breakfast.

V – Find out exactly what Adler knows about the White Rose. The postmen found a letter. Urgency needed. Y.

"Adler?" Jeffrey said in a deadly whisper. "They

couldn't be referring to your grandfather, could they? It's not an entirely common name."

Grian's hands shook, and he was about to reply when a bell dinged on the other side of the office, followed by the sound of footsteps heading in their direction.

CHAPTER 12
THE STRANGER

Grian shoved the letter in his pocket, and with nowhere to hide in the office he raced back out onto the platform with Jeffrey. Ducking down behind the broken bench, both held their breath. Light flashed around inside the office and there was a rustling, as if someone was looking for something.

Then footsteps emerged out onto the platform.

Grian tensed, afraid whoever it was had seen them.

He peered up and caught a glimpse of a tall thin man standing in the middle of the platform. Light pooled by his pointed black polished shoes from the torch held in his grasp.

The stranger sighed and looked round as if frustrated.

He wore a wide-shouldered, long, black jacket, the bottom of which almost reached his ankles. His black hair was slicked back and parted stiffly to one side, giving him the air of someone strict and scary.

The stranger began to pace the platform. Grian ducked down every time he turned in their direction.

Eventually the man stopped. He seemed angry as he pulled a deep orange envelope, some paper and a pen from his inside jacket pocket before leaning against the wall to write. When he finished, he folded the note inside the envelope, removed something else from his pocket and lit a match. The flame highlighted the man's large, crooked nose and stubbled face as the smell of burning wax wafted across the platform. Once finished, he disappeared back into the office, rustled around once more, then the torchlight disappeared and there was silence.

The boys waited in hiding a few minutes longer.

"I think he's gone," Grian whispered.

"What are the odds he left that note he wrote in one of the drawers?" Jeffrey said, echoing what Grian was thinking.

Together the pair crept back across the platform.

"Voila!" Jeffrey smiled as Grian held up the orange envelope he'd just pulled from the same drawer he'd found the yellow one in.

More curious this time, Grian didn't wait to peel back the still warm orange wax, which was stamped in the same interlacing circular pattern as the other envelope that remained in his pocket.

His hand shook as he pulled out the piece of paper. What if this note mentioned his grandad too?

"What are yous two doing?"

Both boys jumped in fright.

"Shelli!" Jeffrey gasped. "It's not polite to sneak up on people!"

"Well, poshy, it's not polite to leave me in an underground tunnel on me own either! I've been waiting ages for yas!"

Grian ignored the pair as he unfolded the short message.

As no orders received, I'm heading back in. I will make contact again soon. V

"What's that about? Where'd ya find that note?" Shelli asked.

"A man left it a few minutes ago. He's just gone. We found an earlier note too," Grian replied, taking the yellow one from his pocket and handing it over. "We think it might be about—"

"Grian's grandad," Jeffrey interrupted. "This is turning into quite the mystery!"

"It's not a game, Jeffrey – it's real life!" Grian said, still feeling queasy.

"Yous think de Adler in this is your Adler?" Shelli asked.

"I don't know," Grian replied, suddenly remembering the last time he'd seen his grandad. "But…I heard grandad say something about a 'white rose' the other night on his radio, when I walked in to tell him about Solas. I thought it was strange because I didn't think he liked gardening."

"You heard your grandfather speak about the White Rose, then he goes missing and we get chased by Proctors. Now we find this note mentioning Adler and a White Rose – I suspect there are too many coincidences here to actually be coincidences," Jeffrey stated.

Even though he didn't want to believe it, Grian thought Jeffrey might be right – but then what did it all mean? Where was his grandfather, why were people looking for him and what was the White Rose?

Just yesterday he was a normal boy with a normal family doing normal things – he wished he could rewind time.

"We can't worry about all that right now. We'll find your granda and figure it out. I promise," Shelli said, as if reading his mind. "Just stick to de plan. De ants went above ground a while ago but I don't know where cause yous weren't with me. It's not far from here though, so when we get outside we should see them. And if your mystery man got down to this station then there has to be a way up to de outside from here!"

"Yes okay, you're right… Let's go." Grian nodded, putting both notes in his pocket.

He needed to focus his racing mind.

A door on the far side of the office led out into a pokey, dark and dingy hall covered in more dirty white tiles. Cobwebs decorated this space too, particularly favouring a solitary dust-caked bulb in the middle of the ceiling.

Recessed into graffitied walls was an elevator shaft. The silver metal doors were battered and smeared with patches of dried liquid. Jeffrey pushed a rusted button set in the middle of a silver plaque on the wall. A bell tinged and the doors cranked open.

The three looked nervously at each other and Grian was the first to step inside, eager to get out of this creepy place and find his grandad as soon as possible. He pressed G on the lift panel and waited. The doors shuffled shut and a light flickered behind a dirty plastic panel above their heads as the lift rattled upwards. Moments later, there was another faint ding and the elevator opened to a dingy landing which led out onto an early morning street.

"What? How did she know?!" Grian stuttered as he spotted Nach standing to attention outside the lift.

"Animals are smart!" Shelli smiled.

"But not...I mean...they're not intelligent – not like humans?"

"You think humans are intelligent?" Shelli laughed. "Have ya ever listened to birds singing or stared right into de eyes of a fox? That's real intelligence. We think that humans own de world. De problem is we think too much – and think that makes us clever! If humans really were intelligent, we'd know we're just a tiny part of everything and we'd stop trying to wreck de place! We need nature and nature works best when we leave her alone!"

"A natural event caused the Tilt," Jeffrey stated. "I expect that hasn't done much good for our planet, now, has it? And as usual us humans have to clean up the mess!"

"Us humans usually cause de mess!" Shelli's face reddened and she buried it deep in Nach's coat.

"Ahem, so...where are we exactly?" Grian piped up, keen to break the tension.

He walked across the landing out onto the street and looked around.

The entrance to the lift they'd just stepped from was in the side of an old brick building battered by time and dwarfed by its shiny sky-scraping neighbours. He recognized the place from visiting it once or twice with his dad.

"This is Turing Central Post Office," Grian said, amazed, as the others joined him on the path.

Shelli shifted uneasily as well-dressed people scurried past, coffee cups in one hand, satchels over their shoulders. They all talked at speed to their Hansoms, organizing their day ahead. It was morning rush hour. They must have travelled all night.

"There's soooo many people," she said, her eyes large.

"You've led us to the city," Grian explained feeling a little tired. "Turing's a lot busier than Tallystick!"

For the second time since he'd met her, Shelli didn't look so fierce. Grian realized how small she was, her tiny bird-like frame dominated by her large scruffy coat, which was even more out of place in the bustling city.

"De ants!" she croaked, dropping to all fours. "They're around here somewhere. If we're going to find your granda, we have to find de ants!"

CHAPTER 13

TRUST NOBODY

Grian felt very silly and his neck ached as he walked around the street, studying the paving stones for ants.

"How do you know your ants are actually near here? They could be anywhere by now," he argued.

Shelli was crawling on her hands and knees nearby, almost knocking over a few angry pedestrians in her determination.

"Just trust me," she answered, her nose almost touching the concrete. "They're streaming out somewhere round here. I can feel them – so can Nach."

"I presume you mean *smell* them… Pheromones," Jeffrey muttered, snooping low around a manhole. "I expect that's how ants track too."

"There...look!" Shelli sprang up and raced across to a dustbin a little away.

A line of ants was streaming out from a crack in the paving stones, down onto the busy road and up over the curb to the pavement on the other side. Shelli almost collided with a car as she skipped across the road, her eyes set on the line of tiny creatures. Nach barked and danced from paw to paw beside her, drawing attention from wide-eyed bystanders. Clearly, just like Grian, these people had never seen a fox in real life before.

Embarrassed, Grian kept his head down and hurried after Shelli, hoping nobody would recognize him – Turing wasn't that far from Tallystick.

The tiny insects now seemed to pour out of every crack and cranny, and the single ant line grew to double, then triple its width, until it spanned the whole pavement.

A woman in the ants' way screamed and dropped her bag when the insects marched over her shoes and up her tights as they continued on their journey. Another caught in the tiny creatures' parade danced from foot to foot before jumping off the path onto the road, almost knocking over an unsuspecting cyclist. Soon pedestrians were screaming all over the pavement.

A little way up the street, a man was shouting and waving his arms frantically outside his shop.

"I'm being invaded! I'm being invaded!" he cried.

T E C H were the last four letters Grian could make out of the sign above the shopfront before the blue plastic letters were engulfed by the sea of insects. Horrified, he watched the ants black out the shop window like something from a scary movie, before streaming inside.

Shelli raced in the door, past the hyperventilating shop owner, with Nach bounding round by her heels. Grian and Jeffrey followed just behind them.

Along the walls of the now darkened shop were white shelving units lit up in blue neon. The shelves were filled with secondhand digital devices and the insects seemed to be attracted to one particular item. Shelli lifted up the small object covered in masses of ants and gently shooed the tiny creatures away.

"A Hansom?" Jeffrey said, bewildered. "Why would the ants track Adler's scent to that? I thought your grandad didn't have a Hansom?"

It was a Hansom, a bright pink H22 watch – the latest model.

"Grandad doesn't have one, and even if he did it wouldn't be bright pink!" Grian replied.

"Maybe it's your sister's watch?" Shelli answered, unwavering. "De ants brought us here for a reason. Your granda's scent's on this watch – so he has to be connected to it somehow!"

"No. Solas went to the Tipping Point, remember? She

123

even left a note!" Grian argued. "And I've never seen her without her watch, so there's no way that's hers!"

"But what about de message she sent? What if Jeffrey was right and it wasn't your sister but your granda who sent it – maybe he got hold of her watch somehow and that's why his scent's on it? Or maybe your sister and your granda were together somewhere?"

Grian shook his head, frustrated, as he asked Bob to pull up his sister's message.

"Look, it says '*grandad here help*'. I know my sister – she's probably in big trouble with Grandad, and she wants me to smooth it over for her somehow – that's all. Grandad doesn't have a clue how to use a Hansom. He'd never be able to send a message – he can barely even turn on the TV!

"Besides, like I said, Solas would never go anywhere without Suzi, so that can't be her watch. If you hadn't grown up in a stupid forest, you'd know people's Hansoms are their life! And if your ants worked properly then why wouldn't they find Grandad himself instead of a random watch? I thought you said animals are intelligent! Just admit the ants are wrong and this whole thing has been a waste of time!"

Grian's anger spilled out. How had he agreed to this plan in the first place? He'd followed a Wilde girl and Jeffrey Slight the whole way to Turing, without question, even when the trip involved talking to foxes and chasing after ants! And he still hadn't found his grandad.

"De ants aren't wrong! Adler's scent is on this Hansom," Shelli whispered fiercely, before turning to face the terrified shopkeeper, who was hovering from foot to foot behind them. "When did this arrive?" she asked.

"Ahem…ahem, I don't know…maybe… Yesterday! Our regular supply of Hansoms got delivered just before closing. I only put them on the shelf this morning."

Grian huffed and walked outside – he wasn't listening any longer. Shelli was grasping at straws now, instead of admitting she made a mistake. He plonked down on a street bench and toyed with Bob.

The note in the tunnel had made him believe something strange was going on with Grandad, but what was it? Even though her ants were clearly wrong about the watch, was Shelli still right about the Proctors?

He hadn't contacted his parents because they'd have told him not to leave the Wilde forest with Shelli, and now he knew he'd made a mistake by leaving. Even though he'd be in massive trouble, maybe it was time to contact his mam and dad and tell them everything? He hadn't heard from his mam so she mustn't have arrived at the Wilde forest. She probably didn't even know he was missing – maybe nobody knew yet.

"*I love it here!*"

The words rang loudly round the street. Grian looked up, baffled. It was Solas's voice. He'd know her anywhere. Desperate, he searched the faces around him, trying to pick her out amongst the crowd.

"I love it here!" she said again.

Her voice sounded huge, as if she were everywhere. Grian scanned the glass windows in the office blocks and department stores above street level until his eyes fell on a massive billboard covering the large skyscraper opposite.

The words *WHAT IS YOUR TIPPING POINT?* flashed across the enormous screen. Then videos of people carrying flags and posters, hugging and singing and crying at the *PEOPLEPOWER* rallies held all over Babbage played out. These cut to videos of the Tipping Point and interviews with volunteers who'd moved there, raving about what an amazing place it was to live in and how everyone should sign up.

It was one of the Tipping Point adverts. Grian had seen variations of them a million of times, everywhere, so much so that he even tried to block them on Bob – which was impossible.

But now Solas was on the reel. Stunned, he watched his sister jump around in front of a huge roller coaster, gushing about how much she loved the Tipping Point.

So she really had run away to live there – just like her note said!

Grian felt betrayed and angry and relieved all at once. Part of him had worried that maybe the Proctors had taken his sister too, like Shelli said. He'd gotten so wrapped up in the Proctors story and everything the Wilde girl had told him, that he hadn't stopped to think it through.

He felt stupid. He'd wasted all this time following Shelli, believing that she could help him find his grandad, when clearly she couldn't.

But Solas could!

Solas was the one who'd sent the message about Grandad – she obviously knew something. If he found her, he could sort everything out. If he contacted his parents now, he'd be in big trouble. But if he contacted them after he'd found Solas and figured out where Grandad was and what was going on, he wouldn't be in trouble at all – or at least Solas would be in more trouble than him.

Bob had tried to contact Solas a few times, but his sister hadn't responded – she'd turned her Hansom off and still hadn't turned it back on. His sister was either in serious trouble with Grandad or selfishly having too much fun to reply to anyone.

Well, she gave him no other choice. Grian knew Solas wouldn't like it, but he was going to the Tipping Point to find her.

CHAPTER 14

THE SPLIT

Grian hadn't taken his eyes off his sister since he'd first seen her on the screen. Her face flashed round on rotation about every three minutes. The more he saw her, the angrier her grew. Why had she run away – why did she always have to be so selfish?

"Isn't that Solas?" Jeffrey gasped, following Grian's gaze up to the large billboard. "Well, that solves one mystery – she did run away to the Tipping Point! It must be something very special if she's raving about it this quickly – she's only been there a day. Explains why she's not getting back to you, though – I've heard it's so good people forget about their old lives and are rarely heard from again!"

"Yeah, looks like she's having a great time," Grian grumbled.

"Are you annoyed that Shelli's animals appear to have failed?" Jeffrey sighed, sitting down beside him. "I had thought they'd lead us straight to Adler myself, but apparently things aren't that straightforward in the field of tracking!"

Grian didn't reply as Shelli walked over, the pink Hansom still in her grasp.

"De shopkeeper threw it at me when I tried to give it back – I don't think he liked de ants." She shrugged, handing the watch to Grian.

"I don't want it!" he scowled, shoving it at her. "You need it most. Might help you get back to the forest. You don't seem to be as good at tracking as you thought!"

The words were out before he could stop them. Shelli growled and her large eyes narrowed to amber slits.

"I'll take it, thank you," Jeffrey interrupted, breaking the tension. "One can never have too much technology." He smiled as he shoved the Hansom in his pocket.

"I told you, de ants and Nach are not wrong!" Shelli glared at Grian. "Your granda's scent is on that watch. It could be your sister's Hansom – maybe your granda borrowed it from her to send you that message! Like I said, maybe de Proctors have them both."

Jeffrey shook his head rapidly. "I think you are partially

wrong in that deduction. His sister is on that billboard! She's in the Tipping Point."

"Oh right... Well, ahem, that's strange." Shelli frowned, turning around just in time to catch Solas professing her love for her new home again. "That explains why he's so upset then!"

"I am sitting right here." Grian stared at her.

"Tell him I might talk to him if he wasn't so cross," Shelli addressed Jeffrey.

"Well tell her I wouldn't be so cross if she hadn't led us all over the place for nothing!" Grian stood up. "I'm going."

"And what about your granda? We've only just started looking and you're giving up already?" Shelli scowled.

"I'll do a better job on my own!" He began walking away.

"But what if the Proctors come for you again?" Jeffrey asked, running after him.

Grian didn't reply. He didn't want to think about the Proctors too much or he might lose his nerve.

"Well, I know whatever's going on, that watch is linked to it – whether you believe me or not!" Shelli hurled after him.

Nach started barking, the fox's shrill baby-like cry terrifying shoppers. Jeffrey stopped too and looked back at Shelli as if torn.

130

Grian didn't care if Jeffrey went back to her. He'd been right about friends all along – he didn't want them, and he didn't need them. All of this had been a big mistake. He was better off on his own.

He looked down at Bob. Now he was alone again he realized how much he missed the device's company. He turned up his hEarPods.

"Good morning, Bob," he said. "I want to take the Tipping Point Tour. Can you get a ticket for me?"

Hansom had created the Tipping Point Tour as a day trip so people could experience what the smart city was like before signing up. Solas had begged the family to go on one but they never did.

"My pleasure," Bob chirped. "Calculating…"

A small dial spun on the watch face.

"The next Tipping Point Tour leaves from Turing Central Station via Hansom's Hyperloop in twenty-nine minutes," Bob stated. "I'll navigate you to the station while I check for tickets…"

Grian followed his watch's directions through Turing, glad nobody was staring at him any more. Shelli attracted a lot of strange looks in the city.

He distracted himself from worry with thoughts of a trip on the Hyperloop. He'd seen the ads and it looked unreal. The Hyperloop was Hansom's superspeed underground transport system to the Tipping Point. A track had been laid from Turing to the smart city, and it was the only way volunteers could get in or out of the place. It also ran in a loop under the Tipping Point, as the city's main transport system.

Grian turned a corner and was greeted by the large glass facade of Turing Central Station. People wheeling bags and carrying rucksacks rushed past him into the bright atrium, which was decorated with a cascading chandelier of falling golden stars.

"There's an empty seating area 3.4 metres ahead," Bob informed him. "Sit and play a game while you wait. I'm having a little difficulty securing a ticket but I'm trying all available channels and should have more information soon."

Grian sat down and opened "Beat the Barber", slowly relaxing into the familiar comforts of his old ways. Depending on Bob felt great – his Hansom would organize everything.

"Give her a slick bob, then swipe the chair from under her before she swings round – that customer is an employee of the Butcher," someone said over his shoulder.

"Oh, Jeffrey... Right – yeah, thanks," Grian coughed out in surprise.

Jeffrey had come back? Grian smiled despite himself. The other boy sat down, and neither talked for a while, both busy with their games.

"Why did you follow me?" Grian asked, looking over after a while. "I thought you'd stay with Shelli."

"I quite like Shelli." Jeffrey nodded. "I think she'll make a great pal too and I told her I will pursue our friendship, but you're my best friend, Grian."

"Oh right." He coughed again at Jeffrey's bluntness.

The pair slipped into comfortable silence. Jeffrey began to fiddle with the pink watch Shelli's ants had found in the shop, while Grian continued with "Beat the Barber". He was about to smash level fifteen when his Hansom interrupted the game.

"Suzi is back online," Bob announced. "Will I send your sister a message?"

"Finally!" Grian said, sitting upright. "Tell Solas I'm on my way to the Tipping Point, and she's in big trouble for running away. Ask her if Grandad's okay too!"

A moment later a familiar message tone pinged very close by. Grian looked at Jeffrey, his friend's face whitewashed.

"I rebooted the system...it...it just needed a soft reset," the boy mumbled, holding the pink watch aloft.

"It is Solas's Hansom?" Grian gasped. "But...but...it can't be hers – she never takes it off!"

CHAPTER 15

THE TIPPING POINT TOUR

Grian felt sick – he'd never seen his sister without her watch. She loved her Hansom more than he did his!

He blushed – Shelli had been right. She had tracked down Solas's watch. But how? After all, it was his grandad's scent they were looking for. No matter how hard Grian tried, he couldn't think of any reason why Grandad's scent would be on Solas's watch, except if maybe he'd brushed off her wrist once or something. But surely that wouldn't leave a smell strong enough to track?

"A lot of Suzi's database has been wiped, so I can't find out the device's recent location history. There might be cloud backup…" Jeffrey muttered to himself.

"Maybe they give them new watches at the Tipping Point?" Grian reasoned out loud. "It's a smart city. The ads say they give the volunteers all the latest tech – the stuff nobody else has. Maybe she sold her old watch or something, once she got the new one – Solas is always looking for ways to make money!"

"Plausible," Jeffrey replied. "It still doesn't explain how your grandad's scent is on it though."

"Well her message said Grandad is there with her – he did go looking for her after all! If she did get a new watch in the Tipping Point, maybe Grandad tried on her old one for a minute or something and that's how his scent is on it? Solas will explain it all, anyway – she'll have lots of explaining to do when I see her," Grian answered, realizing he sounded a little too like his parents.

Another advert for the Tipping Point flashed across the large screen hanging above their heads. This one showed a classroom full of kids being taught by a hologram. They were learning about dinosaurs when suddenly the holographic teacher turned into a huge T. rex and stomped around the room. If every school was this cool in Hansom's smart city, maybe Solas had the right idea.

"The next Hyperloop leaves in eleven minutes, Grian," Bob piped up, "but I'm afraid I can't locate any tickets for the Tour. You can't board unless you've a valid day ticket or are a fully signed-up volunteer. The Tour seems to book up months in advance.

"Perhaps you'll have more luck at the ticket desk – they may have some last-minute cancellations."

Grian followed as his watch navigated him to a ticket desk, above which hung a huge sign advertising the Tipping Point day tours. Jeffrey was just behind him, still fiddling with Solas's watch.

The area was cordoned off by neon blue ropes shepherding the queue towards a black-haired girl in a blue *PEOPLEPOWER* fitted blazer and multicoloured T-shirt. The girl sat behind a large glass window, looking self-important as she adjusted her hEarPods. She held up a finger, topped with blue neon nail polish, to stop the pair as they approached the counter, while she babbled about Hyperloop times to a caller.

Eventually she pressed a button on her hEarPods and smiled, blinding Grian with her white teeth.

"Welcome to the Tipping Point ticket office! How may I help you today?"

"We would like two tickets for the Tour, please," Grian replied.

"I'm afraid the Tipping Point Tour is all booked up for today!" The lady tutted as she swiped across the screen in front of her. "There aren't any tickets available for weeks. You really need to book well in advance."

"But my sister's living there and I need to see her!" Grian pleaded.

"I'm afraid you can't just visit the Tipping Point. It's an exclusive resort. There are only two ways to gain access – the first is to become a citizen volunteer and help save our planet, and the second..." the woman recited, "is to book a tour on the day trip of your dreams!"

She looked over Grian's shoulder and nodded at the people in the queue behind him, just as her computer pinged.

"Well, you're a lucky pair!" She smiled, surprised. "This never happens, but I've just had two last-minute cancellations pop up on my screen! Would you still like those tickets?"

Grian jumped in excitement.

"Excellent! I'm always lucky." Jeffrey smiled, swiping his Hansom over the payment point. "We'll take them!"

"The Tipping Point platform is under the main train station – just head down the escalator." The woman sounded as if she was back to reading from a script. "Your tickets should be on your Hansom now. Please use the navigation link provided and board at least five minutes before departure. There is also a link to exclusive content on our Tipping Point website – this content will only be available for the duration of your visit."

Jeffrey swiped one of the tickets across to Grian,

which popped up instantly on Bob's screen. Grian pored over the exclusive online content as he followed Jeffrey down the escalator, looking for anything that might help him find Solas.

When they arrived on the platform, a man wearing another multicoloured *PEOPLEPOWER* T-shirt and carrying a *Tipping Point Tour* flag was talking to a group of very excited people.

"Here for the Tour?" He smiled at the pair when they approached.

Jeffrey nodded and waved at everyone in the group individually.

"Please just act normal," Grian cringed.

A girl squealed and hopped in excitement beside them. Jeffrey copied her and Grian shoved him in the ribs.

"That's not normal," he hissed through gritted teeth. "Can't you just fit in, or even better, fade back? It's not good to stand out!"

"What's wrong with standing out?" Jeffrey asked.

Grian didn't know how to reply. Things were just easier if you didn't stand out, but he wasn't sure Jeffrey would understand that. Jeffrey was a bit like Solas – he didn't seem to notice or even care what others thought of him.

"Just do what I do," Grian huffed, not sure that was good advice either. "And don't use big words!"

"Welcome, one and all," the man in the T-shirt said. "I'm your guide and I hope you're excited for your day trip to *the Tipping Point*!"

Everyone cheered and clapped loudly.

"Maybe some of you will even sign up to become Tipping Point residents by the end of the day and be part of the movement to save our planet. Out of interest, who here is considering the move?"

A family nearby shot their arms straight into the air, reminding Grian of Jeffrey in school. A lady towards the front of the group waved her hand while gripping tight to the arm of the grumpy-looking man beside her.

"Thank you sincerely, from all of us and from the world." The tour guide applauded. "What you are thinking of doing is selfless! The weight of your actions cannot be overestimated. Together with all the other volunteers, you will tilt our planet back and save humanity – you are real-life superheroes!"

The group clapped louder this time. Some nodded appreciation at the family and couple, while others patted them on the back. Jeffrey walloped the grumpy-looking man on the shoulder and smiled before walking away. Grian stifled his laughter – the man looked like he wanted to throttle his friend.

"You don't have to act that normal," he sniggered when Jeffrey returned.

"What was wrong with that?" Jeffrey asked, bemused.

"Now, has everyone got their tickets?" The tour guide clapped his hands to gather attention.

"Yes," the group replied, waving their Hansoms about.

"Great, then let's get going. This will be the day trip of your dreams!" he beamed, echoing the exact words of the ticket seller.

Everyone whooped and cheered again.

"I'll be hoarse soon if this jovial chanting goes on much longer," Jeffrey whispered.

Grian laughed as the wind picked up around the platform. Even though he wouldn't admit it, he was kind of enjoying Jeffrey being there.

Within moments, headlights pierced the dark tubelike tunnel to Grian's right and Jeffrey gasped as the Hyperloop shot out of the darkness and stopped smoothly in front of them, appearing to almost float above the tracks. The *PEOPLEPOWER*-decorated doors slid open without a sound.

"It works via magnetic levitation," Jeffrey said as he stepped inside. "Hansom truly is one of the greatest minds in the world."

The cylindrical interior of the Loop was crisp white, the neon-blue *PEOPLEPOWER* seats and multicoloured seat belts adding the only colour. It was pretty cool, Grian thought as he sat down, and the seat belt moved automatically into place around him.

Oohs and *Aahs* floated on the air as the group took their places. The excitement grew until it was palpable – Grian's stomach did flips as he got sucked up in the excitement, forgetting his worries for a moment.

"T minus twenty minutes to the Tipping Point." A tall, blonde woman smiled as she suddenly appeared in the middle of the aisle. "Your adventure starts here!"

The lady was transparent – Grian could see right through her to the smartly dressed couple behind.

"It's a hologram," Jeffrey squealed as she passed them. "I've seen them on the adverts, of course, but I thought it was camera work – I didn't think they really existed!"

"Onward to the Tipping Point," the holographic woman announced theatrically.

Suddenly the Hyperloop took off and the carriage lit up with screams of wonder and joy.

CHAPTER 16
THE REUNION

The hologram named April filled everyone in on what to expect from their trip. When they arrived at the Tipping Point exhibition centre they'd be taken straight on their two-hour guided tour of the smart city. They would then return to the centre, where they could enjoy the exhibits and souvenir shop before heading back to Turing on the Loop.

"Now all that is left for me to do," April announced as the Hyperloop stopped, "is to welcome you to the Tipping Point!"

Then April jumped into the air and dissolved into a virtual fireworks display, right in the middle of the carriage. Everyone, Grian and Jeffrey included, was swept up in the excitement, as if it was Christmas morning.

Grian was speechless as he stepped out into the Tipping Point exhibition centre Hyperloop station, the walls, floor and ceiling of which were tiled in tiny screens. On every screen was a silent video of a person talking, just their head and shoulders visible. He stepped closer to inspect the wall and touched his finger to one of the screens showing a boy of about his age. Bob vibrated and his hEarPods filled with the voice of the boy. He said his name was David and he excitedly told Grian all about his life in the Tipping Point and why his family had moved there.

"This is quite spectacular," Jeffrey whispered in awe.

All around them, like an interactive wallpaper, thousands and thousands of people poured out their reasons for signing up to the smart city. All of these people had moved here to save the planet. The effect was overwhelming. Grian felt guilty as he began to understand the frenzied crowds at the *PEOPLEPOWER* rallies and why Solas might have been drawn to the Tipping Point.

Their whole tour party were stunned into silence as they watched the moving walls. Then all of a sudden, music filled the platform and a holographic choir wearing multicoloured neon robes began singing the *PEOPLEPOWER* theme tune at the top of the escalator.

Everyone headed for the moving stairs.

"Impressive." Jeffrey smiled as they stepped off the

escalator and walked right through the virtual choir, who were all still clapping and dancing.

The pair were now in a narrow, mirrored tunnel which changed through a series of colours as they walked along. Inspirational quotes from famous people about *PEOPLEPOWER* and saving the planet floated across the reflective walls.

"I'm looking rather splendid." Jeffrey smiled at himself as he smoothed down a tuft of hair.

Grian stood on his tippy toes and peered over the shoulders of the couple just in front, who were snapping their Hansoms rapidly, recording everything in sight. He thought he recognized the woman, who was now pouting as she took a selfie – she looked like an influencer Solas followed.

A large man dressed in an electric-blue fitted suit and a multicoloured T-shirt stood at the top of the tunnel, scanning Hansoms before letting people pass into the huge auditorium behind him.

"Tickets, please?" he said as Jeffrey and Grian put out their Hansoms to be scanned.

Both boys were stunned as they walked past the security guard into the exhibition centre.

The place was huge – as if it could hold a million people. It was domed, and sunlight filtered down from what looked to be a curved glass ceiling, as though they stood inside one of those snow globes that only came out at Christmas. Above their heads, suspended from the middle of the ceiling, was an enormous 3D model of the world, the word *PEOPLEPOWER* arching above it in giant letters. And beneath their feet the floor was covered in an electric-blue carpet patterned in the *PEOPLEPOWER* logo.

Scattered throughout the auditorium were exhibition stands where growing crowds *Oohed* and *Aahed* as they interacted with the displays. In the far left of the huge space was a roped-off area leading to a door – a sign above it read *Tipping Point Tours*. A queue of people had formed inside the ropes, waiting for their time-slotted trip out into the smart city. Taking up the rest of the huge space were a cafe and a souvenir shop stacked with *PEOPLEPOWER* and Tipping Point merchandise.

Suddenly Grian jumped as screams echoed round him, and people began to point up at the domed glass ceiling. Flocks of birds swept in from opened windows to fly in formation across the cavernous space. For what felt like ages the birds mesmerized the stunned crowd as they danced themselves into one strange shape after another. Grian thought it was part of the exhibition until he noticed staff rushing around in alarm as they tried to get rid of the creatures.

"Your Tipping Point Tour leaves in five minutes," Bob interrupted.

Grian silenced his hEarPods, engrossed in the scene above him.

"People call it a murmuration," someone said behind him, "but de birds don't need to name it. They just feel it, not in any way most humans understand. We think we can explain everything but we can't explain that. Remind me – who was it said animals aren't brainy?"

Grian swung around. Shelli stood with her hands on her hips, smirking at him.

Then the Wilde girl closed her eyes and hummed something under her breath. When she opened them again the birds swept out of the auditorium, back to the world outside.

"Shelli!" Jeffrey gasped.

"How…did…you…?" Grian stuttered.

"Let's just say I smelled ya, Grian!" Shelli joked.

"But how did you get here?" Jeffrey asked.

"Hyperloop, same as yous. I snuck on…with some help. Then I asked de birds to do something big enough for me to get past de ticket man without him noticing. It worked!"

Jeffrey nodded, impressed. Grian stayed silent.

"Where's your coat gone?" Jeffrey asked.

Shelli's small frame looked smaller still in the neat *PEOPLEPOWER* jumper she was now wearing.

"I couldn't walk round here looking like a pile a leaves."

She smiled. "Someone left this behind on de Loop so I took it."

The jumper sat awkwardly over a too-big pair of brown trousers that were tied at the waist with a piece of thick string. The trousers, which were torn and a bit mucky, must have been hidden under the ridiculous coat Shelli had worn up to now.

"What are you doing here anyway?" Grian asked. "I thought you were still looking for my grandad."

"I am!" Shelli replied, her tone a little sharp. "I was confused when Nach and de ants found that watch in de shop. I know it's your sister's, whether you believe me or not. Somehow your granda must have had it lately. So I got a stronger nose on de job to keep tracking his smell and..."

"The watch is Solas's!" Jeffrey blurted. "I was able to revive it – a simple soft reset was all it took – then Grian sent Solas a message and the watch pinged!"

"What!" Shelli replied, excited. "You serious?"

Grian nodded, not meeting her eyes. He could feel his cheeks redden.

"I knew it! Then your granda must have had Solas's watch...which is interesting..." Shelli stopped mid-sentence and squirmed, grabbing the top of her trousers.

"Interesting why?" Grian encouraged.

"Interesting cause Fred...tracked Adler to here...de Tipping Point," she replied as the top of her trouser wriggled.

"Fred?" Jeffrey quizzed.

Shelli bent forward at an awkward angle and giggled as if somebody had just tickled her.

"What are you doing?" Grian whispered, embarrassed.

Shelli reached down her trousers and pulled out a large furry creature with a long, pointed, twitching nose and tiny bead-like eyes. Its bald tail wrapped round her wrist.

"Meet Fred." She smiled, crouching a little over him to conceal the animal from view.

Grian and Jeffrey coiled back.

"It's a rat!" they both whispered, disgusted.

"Well done!" Shelli smirked. "Fred's got de best nose I know!"

"And *it* thinks Grandad's here?" Grian replied, staring at the creature in her hands. "Then I was right about Solas's message. Even the rats agree!"

"Well FRED tracked your granda's scent to de Hyperloop and up to here." Shelli smiled. "Now he just needs time to pick up de scent again and we'll be off. Nach will help too – she's hiding in the station below until it gets quiet. A fox can't sneak round as easily as a rat."

"But people will see that creature." Jeffrey screwed up his nose as Shelli pulled her jumper further over the ball of dirty grey fuzz.

"No they won't. Fred is used to keeping out of de way. Most normal people don't like rats, ya see, so rats are

148

really great at hiding – even though they're everywhere, specially in cities!" She smiled.

Grian shuddered.

Shelli put her hand on the animal's thick grey coat, closed her eyes and lowered her head, just as Grian had seen her do before with Nach, with the ants and recently with the birds. Then she looked round to make sure nobody was near and popped Fred onto the floor. The creature scurried off to the side of the auditorium, sneaking in behind a black curtain by one of the exhibition stands.

"He can take a while to pick up a scent, so what'll we do while we wait?" Shelli beamed, standing back up.

"The Tour!" Grian gasped, remembering. "I silenced Bob's reminders – if we miss the Tour of the Tipping Point we won't be able to find Solas!"

CHAPTER 17

A WAITING GAME

Grian and Jeffrey raced across the room to the Tour sign. The queue had disappeared and a lady, dressed in the same *PEOPLEPOWER* uniform, stood smiling by the closed door.

"We have tickets for the Tour!" Grian panted, waving his wrist around.

The woman scanned their Hansoms.

"I'm afraid your tour's just left," she sighed.

"But my sister lives in there – I need to see her. Can't we just race after them or go on the next one?" Grian pleaded.

"I'm sorry but all Tipping Point Tours are guided and kept to strict numbers to protect the privacy of the volunteers who live here in our city. You've missed your slot so I'm afraid unless you're a volunteer or have a weekend pass you can't leave the exhibition centre," the woman replied.

"It's okay, Grian," Jeffrey said, trying to be cheerful as they turned around. "We'll find a way to see Solas."

Shelli was sitting on the ground near the entrance down to the Hyperloop, squinting as if focusing on something across the room.

"Fred's having a great time," she said when the boys walked over. "He's finding all sorts of food round here – people are weird de amount they waste! Fred's had an apple, crisps and some jellies so far. Think he's forgetting what he's here for – rats are easily distracted by food!"

Grian didn't reply as he slid down the wall beside her.

"What's wrong with him?" Shelli asked Jeffrey.

"We missed the Tour – he can't get into the rest of the city to find Solas. Apparently, we can't leave the exhibition centre without a guide."

"Yous are seriously letting that put ya off?" Shelli laughed.

"Do you have any better ideas?" Grian grumbled.

"We could break in..." she suggested, raising her eyebrows. "That was my plan anyway. It'd be easier to sneak round de city when it's dark, so I was gonna wait until tonight."

"Sounds like a sensible idea!" Jeffrey nodded.

"But how would we break in?" Grian tensed. "There must be security cameras everywhere. We'd be caught! Alarms would probably ring all over the place!"

"Not if we infiltrate their security system." Jeffrey smiled this time.

"Really – infiltrate Howard Hansom's security system?" Grian answered, raising his eyebrows.

The boy nodded. "You may not know this about me, but I'm an excellent hacker – in fact, I'm one of the best in Babbage. We just need to find a networked computer – should be one around here somewhere. I'll grant myself privileged access and upload some extremely discreet malware to Hansom's network. Then, using Betty, I'll be able to open doors and get the IPs of every security camera in the city so I can redirect their field of vision as we pass. It's child's play really!"

"Don't understand any of that, but I think it means we have a plan?" Shelli smiled.

Grian took a minute before agreeing. He was a little wary about the whole breaking-in thing, but if it meant he'd be able to find Solas and Grandad, he'd give it a try.

Together they decided they'd first all look for a networked computer to hack. Then when it got dark and everyone went home, they'd begin project break-in.

Grian was mesmerized as he began searching the huge exhibition centre for a suitable computer. All around him were the latest in Hansom's technologies. Virtual guides and helper holograms walked about, asking people if they needed assistance.

There were lots of nerdy exhibition stands that Grian thought Jeffrey would love. Virtual equations and diagrams filled large screens and people played around with them, doing things like adjusting the earth's axis more or less to see what effect it would have on the planet. Grian liked these stands the least – they reminded him of school.

The most popular exhibition was the virtual sun. The huge holographic fireball hovered high in the air towards the back of the auditorium, highlighted against an enormous curved black screen emulating outer space. Spits of red-hot flames leaped from the sun's surface, the effect so real that people underneath jumped and screamed in morbid excitement as if afraid they were about to be set alight. A virtual earth spun slowly as it moved around the sun. The blues of the sea and the greens and browns of the land were so vibrant and real Grian wanted to touch them.

He stared, awestruck, at the display, imagining he was an astronaut. Suddenly he jolted as the crowd cried out and the virtual earth shook violently before disappearing into the black abyss of outer space.

"That's what the experts predict will happen to us if we don't fix the Tilt," Jeffrey whispered over his shoulder.

"An excellent reproduction, isn't it?"

Grian shivered, feeling very small and unsettled. He didn't want to think about the Tilt and up until recently he was able to ignore it – a hundred years was ages away. But now, with the cold reality of that demonstration, one hundred years didn't seem all that much.

He moved on to the next installation trying to forget what he'd seen.

A gigantic screen covered the floor of this stand, attached to hydraulics beneath. On the screen was a huge 3D visual of the earth floating in space. The view was from above, as if the camera was on the moon looking down. The Tipping Point was highlighted on the virtual earth. Grian joined a crowd as they walked across the screen and stopped at the Tipping Point's location. All of a sudden, the screen began to rock backwards and forwards, mimicking the movements of the virtual world beneath Grian's feet. People laughed and cried and wobbled as they clung to each other, until finally the earth shifted on its axis and a huge virtual banner sprang across the space above their heads.

Congratulations, you've saved the planet.
Now that's what we call PEOPLEPOWER!

Grian was elated, swept up in the emotion of saving

the world. Straight away he felt like he wanted to do something to help. Maybe he should be trying to save the planet too? When all of this was over and they'd found Grandad, he'd talk to Solas about it. Maybe together they could persuade their parents to move here.

"You hungry?" Jeffrey asked, sneaking up on him again. "I'm famished. Sustenance is on my parents!"

Grian hadn't realized he was hungry, but now his tummy rumbled at the thought of food. He lined up with the other two, loading his tray full of all the things his mam probably would say no to. The three discussed their plans as he munched away on Tipping Point ice-cream tacos and *PEOPLEPOWER* peppermint piepops.

"I spotted an office earlier – it's accessed through a door in the souvenir shop. I suspect that would be our best hope to find networked computers," Jeffrey mumbled while eating a sprinkle-covered ice-cream taco.

"We should hide in the toilets," Grian whispered as a large hologram of Howard Hansom walked past, greeting all the diners by name, "then we'll be able to sneak into the office once everyone's gone home."

Shelli closed her eyes and sighed. She obviously didn't like his plan.

"Or, if you've a better idea…"

The girl opened her large amber eyes and shook her head. "No, I think it's great. I was just telling Nach – she's still hiding down in de station and she's a little nervous. She's not used to all de noise and people."

Could Shelli really talk to animals? And when they're not even near her?

"I don't talk to animals." Shelli fixed him with a stare.

Grian sat up, startled. He was sure he hadn't said that out loud.

"I feel their thinking," the girl continued. "Anyone could do it if they just tuned in. But people are too busy to listen to animals. They barely listen to each other."

"Grandad tunes into radios," Grian joked.

"I don't imagine that's the same thing," Jeffrey replied, deadly serious. "Anyway, however did you learn to communicate with animals, Shelli?"

"I didn't learn anything, Poshy. I've always been able to do it. One of de Aunties told me once that Mother Wilde can do it too, but she doesn't any more."

"Is that because Mother grew up in the forest?" Grian asked, curious.

"She didn't grow up in de forest, she ran away and hid in it with her sisters when she was little. Then they just ended up staying. She doesn't like talking about her past – least not to me. They ran away from de circus, that's what I heard. They were an act called 'de belle sisters'."

"A circus act, that must have been so cool," Grian said, imagining Mother on a trapeze.

"It wasn't cool. People just lined up to look at them like they were in a zoo!"

"As I suspected – she has albinism, doesn't she? I believe she may be blind too? Albinism is often associated with vision problems. It's diabolical that they used to put people on display like that," Jeffrey replied.

"But not awful that WE still do it to animals?" Shelli huffed. "People are de cruellest of all creatures!"

"How did Mother know Grandad?" Grian asked, changing the subject.

"I don't know." Shelli shrugged. "But I don't think she likes him."

Grian snorted – his grandad seemed to have that effect on some people.

"It's quite odd that everyone calls her 'Mother' when a number of the Aunties are at least the same age as her," Jeffrey stated.

"She acts like everyone's mother, I think that's how she got de name. She's my granny – though she's really been my ma since…since Ma was taken," Shelli looked down at her hands.

Grian choked on his piepop. He'd never met a kid who'd lost their mother, before Shelli. Guilt wrapped his throat and he couldn't speak.

"That must be rather lonely," Jeffrey replied. "I can empathize a little; sometimes mine goes missing too. I'm not sure she's good mother material though – or at least, that's what my father says."

Grian choked again. He thought of his parents and Solas and Grandad, and what he would do if anything bad ever happened to any of them. Then he thought of the two strangers opposite him and all he didn't know about their lives, and how despite his best efforts they were becoming his friends.

"I'm sorry for not believing you earlier," he stuttered, looking at Shelli.

His friend smiled, her eyes a little glassy.

"The crowds are beginning to disperse," Jeffrey whispered, waking Grian from a short snooze.

The auditorium was much emptier now. Robotic cleaners hoovered and dusted quiet corners as people bought the last of their souvenirs and headed for the Hyperloop.

Once the toilets were cleaned, the three snuck in one by one to wait hidden in a cubicle.

As time wound on the sound of hoovers died down, doors banged and voices crying out for stragglers echoed in the empty space, until finally the lights went out and the place descended into total silence.

"Right, let's go," Grian said, feeling less confident than he sounded.

CHAPTER 18

AREA 13

The three snuck across the branded bathroom floor out into the empty auditorium. The silence felt eerie in the huge space.

All exhibits were switched off, there were no flashing lights, no laughing or excited squeals, no virtual guides or delicious pastry smells. There was no life and the place felt hollow.

Grian shivered as he turned on Bob's torch and passed beneath the massive *PEOPLEPOWER* globe suspended in the middle of the huge space.

What was he doing here? If he was caught breaking out of the exhibition centre into the rest of the city he'd be in more trouble than Solas had ever been in her whole life.

He jumped as a large grey rat dashed across the carpet from one side of the auditorium and a fox flashed from the mirrored tunnel on the other. Shelli bent down, greeting them both with more enthusiasm than Grian had ever seen her give a human.

Then she closed her eyes – within moments both creatures darted off again, sniffing the ground.

"Yous go to de office, I'll follow in a bit. Nach and Fred are telling me that your granda's scent stops right here, exactly on this spot. But his scent can't just vanish into thin air. So, I want them to check one more time when there's no one about. All de people smells might have confused them earlier," she sighed.

Grian looked around. They were standing right in the middle of the vast auditorium and there was nothing at all in the spot Shelli indicated except the carpet under her feet. He wasn't going to say anything about her animals being wrong this time though.

The two boys left Shelli alone and headed for the souvenir shop. They passed the *PEOPLEPOWER* T-shirts plastered in slogans such as *PEOPLEPOWERed Planet* and *Tilting Time*, then the multicoloured mugs and Hansom posters, before sneaking in behind the tills. Quickly they opened the office door and slipped inside. The room was large and dark except for the tiny red dots on numerous screens and tablets.

Jeffrey pulled out his hTablet before sitting down at a random desk and riffling through the notebooks and family photographs that decorated the small space.

"Ah ha – the young woman who sits at this desk is called Susan Spence." He nodded at a name scrawled into the top corner of a small black diary. "People never fail to surprise me with the information they willingly leave about the place."

"It's only her name." Grian smirked.

"You'd likely be surprised what I can do with a name," Jeffrey replied looking very serious before typing into his hTablet.

"I have the passwords, biometrics and even the typing cadence of everyone in Babbage at my fingertips," he boasted before powering up the computer in front of him.

Then he bent down and pulled out what looked like a small metal tripod with thin movable metal arms from his backpack before inputting something into a tiny control panel on the side of the unusual machine.

He sat the tripod on the desk beside the lady's keyboard and watched with pride as the tripod's spindly arms began pressing letters on the keypad.

"I invented this device myself. In fact I call it the sClerk," he stated. "It will match Susan Spence's speed and pressure as it types her password into her computer. Quite a few companies monitor all of these metrics now and we're better safe than sorry. I don't want to alert any of Hansom's systems to a breach…

"…And we're in!" Jeffrey nodded a few seconds later as Susan Spence's computer came alive.

He leaned forward and appeared to be searching through a million different files at once as he simultaneously uploaded the malware.

Grian stood behind, fascinated and in awe, as he watched. Jeffrey was definitely good with computers.

"Your granda's scent still stops dead in de middle of that room!" Shelli sighed, walking into the office. "I can't understand it…"

"Look!" Jeffrey interrupted her excitedly. "I've found the Tipping Point volunteer database. It may take a few seconds to decrypt but then we could get Solas's address – it'd make it much simpler to locate her then once we're properly in the city."

Grian tensed as his friend whizzed through various complicated-looking screens on his hTablet again before turning back to the main computer. Finally, he typed Solas's full name into the search bar of the computer and pressed enter. Within seconds a list appeared.

"It just says she's in 'Area Thirteen'." Jeffrey sounded a little disappointed. "All the names on the list above and below your sister's say the same thing – seems a bit vague."

"Area Thirteen?" Grian repeated. "But what does that mean? It doesn't seem like an address."

"Hey, look at this," Shelli said behind them.

She was standing in front of a huge flatscreen attached to the back wall of the office. On the screen was a 3D model of a city.

"It must be a map of the Tipping Point!" Grian gasped, walking over.

The layout of the Tipping Point had always been top secret. In all the advertisements, even in the exhibition stands outside, Grian had never seen exactly what Hansom's purpose-built smart city looked like. Hansom said they kept it secret for the volunteers' privacy and so that only those brave enough to sign up got to experience every detail of the place.

Studying the map, Grian could see the town was designed in a series of three concentric circles, like a shooting target. The exhibition centre, where they stood now, was located in the middle ring, called the *Parks and Recreation Zone*, the inner ring was labelled the *Central Business Zone*, and the larger, outer ring was the *Residential Zone*. The Hyperloop ran along the boundary between the two outer rings, the Residential and Parks zones.

As Grian zoomed into street level and navigated around the buildings – which looked more like works of art than places to live – something struck him as odd.

"All those people on the walls of the Hyperloop station," he whispered, "where do they live? The town doesn't look big enough for everyone. Doesn't Hansom need, like, millions of people to move here?"

"I'd say this will show us," Shelli said, tapping a red house icon labelled *Housing Estates* on the map key.

The view zoomed out so they could see the whole city again and the outer ring lit up with replica red house icons indicating the location of individual estates.

"None of those places are called Area Thirteen…" Grian mumbled, studying the names.

"What's this?" Shelli asked, pressing a green star icon on the map key labelled *Incidence Areas*.

Numerous green stars appeared round the *Recreation* and *Business* zones. Shelli clicked on one and a pop-up window sprang up on the interface, just as Grian was snapping a picture of the whole map with his Hansom.

The pop-up was filled with a list of times and seemed to be describing a road accident involving a child.

"What's that about?" Shelli asked.

"Maybe it's a police report." Grian shrugged.

"I've located the centralized door system and I'm about to unlock the main exit from the auditorium now! We'll have infiltrated the city and found Solas in no time!" Jeffrey interrupted the pair.

"Well, I'm impressed!" a strange voice boomed.

All three froze as the lights flickered on above them and a man stepped into the room.

CHAPTER 19

HOWARD HANSOM

Grian's eyes watered under the bright lights.

He could see the outline of a man standing at the office door. The man was tall, wearing plain jeans, a yellow hoody and a *PEOPLEPOWER* baseball cap, dark sunglasses resting on its peak.

Shocked, Grian reached out and grabbed the edge of a desk to steady himself. It couldn't be...surely it wasn't... Howard Hansom?

"Why are three children breaking into one of my offices?" His teeth were toothpaste white.

Howard Hansom walked closer and removed his sunglasses and cap. Jeffrey bent his knee and lowered his head as if he was meeting royalty. Grian was speechless –

his jaws felt glued together as he tried not to imagine all the trouble they were in. Shelli simply growled.

"Now I'll ask again – what are you three doing here?" Hansom scowled.

"Ahem, we're just… Perhaps we should… We were…" Jeffrey stuttered.

"We were looking for my sister," Grian answered, opting for the truth.

Hansom's light-blue eyes popped from his tanned face, and his lips turned up at the edges as he smiled. Grian thought it made him look like the Joker in a Batman comic, but he also knew it made girls weak – at least that's what Solas said.

"And why are you searching for your sister in my city in the middle of the night?" the man asked, looking straight at Grian.

His dad said lots of people never looked you in the eyes when they spoke, and it was a good sign of a person if they did. Hansom definitely did.

"We…we…ahem…we thought she might be here. We think she's volunteered."

"Well, that explains why you were sitting at one of my computers! You know I could have you arrested for this?" Hansom said, his face unreadable.

Grian and Jeffrey quivered. Shelli eyed the door behind them, as if preparing to bolt.

"But I admire your spirit. What's her name?" Hansom smiled.

"Solas…Solas Woods," Grian mumbled, waiting for the minute Howard Hansom would erupt like a normal adult and call their parents or even the police.

"Liv – can you search our database for a Solas Woods?" Hansom said to his Hansom.

The screen in the middle of the room filled with a list of names.

"I infiltrated the database already," Jeffrey said, finding his voice.

Grian and Shelli winced.

"Oh right." Hansom snorted a laugh. "Well, I should have known you did!"

Jeffrey nodded. "I thought you'd have something a little more sophisticated but you're still on hOS 15.1…"

"We're onto it, we'll be updating our operating system soon – we've just had a few other things to worry about lately. What did you say your name was?" Hansom smiled, bemused.

"Jeffrey – Jeffrey Slight."

"Solas Woods confirmed," Hansom's watch interrupted. "She is in Area Thirteen."

"Is that a street here?" Grian asked.

"Of sorts," Hansom replied. "Now why are you trying to track her down? All Tipping Point volunteers are free people; your sister can talk to whomever she wants. Surely, she'd tell you where she was if she wanted to? Maybe she doesn't want to be found right now. In the Tipping Point we value privacy."

"She ran away, she's only fourteen," Grian whispered, sheepishly. "She left a note, but—"

"Oh well, that's different. We don't condone runaways here, especially not underage ones," Hansom replied, for the first time looking annoyed. "It's bad for our campaign. We're trying to save the world and we don't need that kind of publicity. Your parents must be worried sick. Well, let's see how she is! Liv, show us Solas, please."

Grian gasped as his sister appeared on the large screen. She was in a dance class. He recognized the teacher from one of those reality dance programmes Solas loved to watch. His sister was jumping, twirling and laughing. She was happy, as if she had nothing to worry about, and Grian felt a little stung.

"Liv tells me it's Solas's dance class." Hansom smiled. "It seems your sister signed up for stage school."

A schedule popped up over the video of Solas. She was taking ballet on a Thursday and singing with Seline on a Friday.

"Not *the* Seline?" Jeffrey asked, raising his eyebrows.

"The very same." Hansom winked.

Hansom walked up to the screen and began to swipe,

until Solas's statistics popped up.

"Your sister's vitals look good!" He smiled. "She's in perfect health, her cortisol levels are low and serotonin is high; she's very relaxed."

"Well...ahem..." Grian stammered, confused. "Does that computer show if Grandad is here too? We think he came to find her."

Hansom flicked through the notes again, shaking his head. "There's nothing about your grandfather here I'm afraid. But at least we've found your sister. I bet it'll be a disappointment when Solas finds out her family know she's here and she has to leave."

Grian felt a little uneasy staring at the screen lost in thought. If Grandad wasn't here where was he?

"Yes?" Hansom quizzed furrowing his brow as he watched Grian closely. "Is there something wrong? Your parents do know you're here to get Solas, don't they? Please don't tell me your sister is not the only runaway!"

"My parents don't know I'm here." Jeffrey smiled. "But it honestly won't bother them."

Grian and Shelli looked away as Hansom's eyes fell on them. Why did Jeffrey always have to tell the truth? Grian's mam loved to say that if he and his sister told the truth they wouldn't get in trouble – but surely that didn't count this time?

"No, mine don't either." Grian was nervous and found

himself admitting everything. "Nobody knows I'm here. My parents are away. Grandad was looking after us, then Solas ran away. She left a note, so Grandad went to find her. He didn't come back, and then the Proctors turned up at my house and…"

"The Proctors?" Howard Hansom interrupted.

"They're a rogue gang who wear long capes with rather large hoods, making it impossible to recognize their features," Jeffrey informed him. "I think you're aware of the gang? I saw you interviewed about them once."

Hansom became agitated. He swiped at his watch, casting pictures of long, black caped, hooded figures onto the screen in front of them.

"You mean these people?" Hansom glared.

"Yes – exactly those." Jeffrey nodded.

The tall man stepped back and sighed, rubbing his hand through his hair before flopping down into an office chair and descending into silence.

Grian shifted nervously as he looked at his friends.

"The Proctors are a secret gang of hooded thugs trying to destroy everything I do," Hansom eventually said. "They accuse me of playing God. They believe if the planet is meant to fly off into oblivion and combust, then it should. I believe humans have the ingenuity to save ourselves – so why shouldn't we? Somebody needs to do something to save our planet and I am fortunate enough to have the motivation and means to be that person! I am pouring everything I have into the Tipping Point and the Proctors want to destroy it all.

"They have been kidnapping people who speak out *against* the Tipping Point, the Tilt deniers, and trying to pass the blame of the kidnappings on to me and my team – in order to say we are silencing debate, silencing our opponents. They want to dirty the name of the *PEOPLEPOWER* movement so it will lose popularity and ultimately fail."

"But if *PEOPLEPOWER* fails, the world will die!" Jeffrey stuttered.

"Exactly!" Hansom threw his hands into the air, exasperated, and collapsed against the back of the chair.

The room fell silent.

"Lots of de Wilde went missing a few years ago. De Proctors were spotted around de area at de same time," Shelli said softly. "Some said you had something to do with it…"

Grian looked at Shelli. She'd never mentioned before that people suspected Hansom was linked to the Proctors.

Hansom shook his head. "That's what the Proctors want people to think whenever they're spotted. It's so frustrating, but people often don't ask the obvious questions. The Wilde went missing before the Tilt – how would that have anything to do with me?

"But it doesn't matter, throw slander and it sticks. The Proctors' plans are working – destroy my name, destroy *PEOPLEPOWER*! But it's not just me they will destroy, is it?" Hansom looked at Shelli. "I trust you're one of the Wilde?"

Shelli nodded. "And my ma is one of de missing."

"I'm so sorry to hear that," Hansom said, getting up and reaching to hug her.

Shelli pulled away. The man stopped and bent down so he was eye to eye with her.

"I admire your people a lot," he soothed. "I've visited groups in southern forests. You're true caretakers of nature."

"Thanks," Shelli whispered, looking embarrassed.

"I get quite a lot of bad press," Hansom sighed. "When you're in a position of power, people write whatever they want about you, so I understand your surprise. But I love this planet just as much as you do. In fact, my own mother is originally Wilde, though she left the community a long time ago, when she met my father."

Grian was surprised again – he'd never heard that before either.

"The Techie – Edition 542 – I remember reading about your Wilde links," Jeffrey interjected. "It was a very informative article. The journalist had a rather nice style."

Howard was still staring at Shelli. "That's one of the

reasons why I'm so desperate to save our planet. The Tilt affected more than us humans. It's been disastrous for our animal population and for our ecosystems too. Did you know our insects are already dying out at rapid speed? And when they die, humanity is next."

"But Mother said that was happening before de Tilt, and—"

"Watch this!" Hansom interrupted, swiping his watch.

The screen in front of them played a video of a woman talking about animals in distress. She was wearing a *PEOPLEPOWER* T-shirt and feeding a baby bear.

"She works in our animal sanctuary here – it's just one of the things we're doing for our wildlife, but none of it is enough." Hansom shook his head in regret. "That little beauty she's feeding was found wandering lost and in a daze, with no sign of her mother."

"I've seen it too, in our forest," Shelli whispered. "Some animals look like they're missing their soul."

"An accurate description. It's because their natural rhythms have been disturbed," Hansom said. "Many animals have been rehabilitated here and released back into the wild, but others are still with us unfortunately. The Tilt has affected everything. All our calculations and modelling tell us the same thing – the Tipping Point will work. We can push the earth back to its original axis and this action won't just save ourselves, it will save all nature.

But we have to stop the Proctors first, before they undermine everything!"

The man was clearly upset and Grian wasn't sure what to say.

"Anyway, excuse me, I got distracted. Your sister…" Hansom said, swiping away the layers of Proctor images that had built up on the screen in front of them.

"Stop!" Grian gasped, moving closer to look at one of the pictures.

A tall man wearing a long black jacket glared out from a photo. His sleek dark hair was parted severely to one side and his crooked nose was prominent on his lined face. He was standing among a small group of people in the middle of a large stage behind Howard Hansom as a Proctor in a long black hooded cape floated menacingly to the side of the scene, just metres away.

"That's the man we saw in the tunnel earlier! Remember, Jeffrey?" Grian pointed.

"Are you sure?" Hansom quizzed, looking nervous.

"Yes, you're quite right, Grian," Jeffrey replied. "It is indeed him."

This time Howard Hansom disappeared into his thoughts for a long while before speaking again, slowly and seriously. "That man is the head of the Proctors. The most dangerous man in Babbage!"

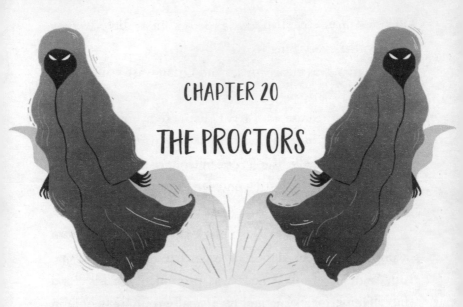

CHAPTER 20

THE PROCTORS

"But if that man is dangerous, why's he in a picture with you?" Shelli narrowed her brows.

"He worked for me once." Hansom sounded hurt. "The photo was taken at a product launch day which the Proctors turned up at and tried to destroy."

"He was acting rather odd in the postal tunnel!" Jeffrey stated, looking more closely at the photo on the screen.

"When was this? What postal tunnel?" Hansom asked, now animated again.

"The one from Tallystick to Turing. We found it when we were trying to escape the Proctors," Grian answered. "There are postal tunnels all over Babbage, they're just not used any more."

"You were escaping the Proctors... So they were chasing you?"

"Yes, they broke into my house," Grian replied. "I had to run to Jeffrey's—"

"I'm his neighbour, you see," Jeffrey explained.

"The first time they chased us we hid in the forest, where we met Shelli," Grian continued. "But the Proctors found us again in Tallystick and we escaped through the postal tunnel. We don't know why they were after us!"

"Your grandfather – you said he disappeared?" Hansom said.

"Well yes, we think so. He didn't come back after he went looking for Solas," Grian answered. "I thought he might be here in your city—"

"Here trying to get Solas to return home, that is," Jeffrey interrupted again. "Grian's grandfather certainly wouldn't sign up as a volunteer for the Tipping Point, as it'd be against his principles. He doesn't believe in the Tilt. He's a denier!"

Grian cringed and could feel himself blush.

"It's okay." Hansom smiled. "I've met non-believers, and do you know what? I envy them. I hope the Tilt deniers stay that way, because if they think that I'm misguided for the rest of their lives, and in years to come their adult grandchildren still think the Tilt was a hoax, it means the world didn't disappear into outer space.

It means we fixed the Tilt and beat the time bomb. I am happy to be a laughing stock if we can save humanity."

"Good point." Jeffrey nodded, giving Hansom a thumbs up.

"So your grandfather's a Tilt denier..." Hansom continued, "exactly the type the Proctors look for. Has he been vocal about it?"

Grian nodded, still a little red-faced.

He remembered hiding from his grandfather when he spotted him protesting at Hansom's rally in Tallystick just the other day. And he'd never forget the day his grandad decided to walk through Tallystick dressed as a papier mâché globe of the earth, holding a banner above his head with *THE TILT IS FAKE NEWS* scrawled in marker across it. Grian had tried to block the embarrassment from his mind loads of times, but the school bullies wouldn't let him.

"That might help explain what has happened to your grandfather then," continued Hansom. "I don't mean to cause alarm, but the Proctors kidnap people who've been vocal in their distrust of the Tilt and *PEOPLEPOWER*. They then point the finger of blame at me and say I'm trying to silence my opposition."

"So you think the Proctors do have Grandad, like Shelli thought?" Grian's voice shifted up an octave. "But my sister sent me a message—"

"That both myself and Shelli think may have come from your grandfather," Jeffrey interrupted.

"Look, of course, I don't know for sure," Hansom cautioned, "I wouldn't want to point the finger without evidence. But perhaps the Proctors were looking for your grandfather when they came to your house. And if he hasn't returned home since then…yes, I believe the Proctors may have found what they were looking for."

"The note!" Jeffrey said, looking at Grian. "We found a note in the tunnel. We think that man – the head Proctor, may have been looking for it. It might be evidence to support your theory, Howard."

"Do you have the note?" Hansom asked, his eyes almost popping from his head.

Grian took the crumpled paper from his pocket and handed it over.

V – Find out exactly what Adler knows about the White Rose. The postmen found a letter. Urgency needed. Y.

Hansom turned a little pale as he studied the note carefully before looking back up.

"Umm, strange." He coughed. "Do you know what any of it means?"

"No – Grandad isn't even into gardening! But I did

hear him on his radio a while ago talking about a 'white rose'. I didn't think anything of it until we found this note. The head Proctor left another note saying something about not getting any orders and heading back in," Grian said, passing that one over too. "Both notes had the same stamp on them but in different colours."

"Well, if nothing else, this proves that the Proctors are interested in your grandfather," Hansom said, "so we do need to find him. Their leader, the man in that picture, can be somewhat unpredictable – he's sent me death threats."

"Death threats?" Jeffrey gasped, horrified.

"Yes, but I'm not worried about that," Hansom dismissed. "I can take care of myself – it's humanity that concerns me. The head Proctor can be difficult to track down though. He's a shadow."

"A shadow?" Shelli asked.

"A person with almost no digital footprint," Jeffrey replied. "They're an anomaly!"

"We all know you're intelligent, Jeffrey," Grian sighed. "You don't need to use big words to prove it."

Jeffrey ignored his friend and spoke straight to Howard Hansom. "Shouldn't you get the police involved?"

"We are working with the police," Hansom replied, "and I have a team set on finding the Proctors. They are clever though – they wear hoods so they cannot be recognized on camera and from what we can tell they are all shadows, making them almost impossible to track.

"This postal tunnel you spoke about might just prove useful, though. It may be how they move around unseen and, judging by these notes, how they communicate. Could we question all three of you? See what you remember? It should help us get your grandfather back, Grian."

"Ahem, okay…" Grian answered, looking at the other two.

Both nodded, Shelli adding a shrug for good measure.

"Great," Hansom replied, "then I will contact your parents now and let them know you three adventurers are safe with me. I'll tell them about Solas too, if you don't mind?"

Grian nodded, a little relieved. If Hansom was looking for his grandad then surely everything was going to be alright. And his parents couldn't get too angry if Howard Hansom called them. His mam was just like Solas when it came to the tech entrepreneur – although she seemed to have gone off him a little lately. Grian remembered her silencing the TV with a huff when he was interviewed about the Tipping Point last week.

"I will speak to your sister tonight after her class and see if I can set up an hFaceCall with her and your parents. They can read Solas the riot act – I'll stay well out of that one if you don't mind," the man laughed. "I'll also tell your parents you're helping with our investigations and see if I can get them to agree to you having a short stay in the Tipping Point. You'll get VIP access…"

"Does that mean…we can…try the latest Hansom technologies?" Jeffrey interrupted, breathless with excitement.

"You can try absolutely everything!" Howard's smile erupted on his face. "The hHover, the hMate, all exclusive to the Tipping Point experience. You'll stay in a suite in the Peoplepower Plaza. It's a five-star hotel in the centre of town. Our volunteers stay there of course and we often give away trips to it so people can experience a night in the Tipping Point – most people who stay go home and sign up, and so do their friends! It really is unique – at least we like to think so!"

Hansom spoke to his watch: "Liv, contact Bonnie. Tell her I have some guests that I'd like her to take to our best available suite."

Grian's stomach felt woozy again but not in a horrible eggy way, it was more of a birthday feeling. Jeffrey looked like the definition of happy, while Shelli…well, she seemed a little scared.

"What's wrong?" Grian whispered. "This is probably the best thing that will ever happen in our whole lives!"

"If you like sleeping indoors. And what about Nach?"

she hissed. Grian looked at the fox, who was hiding under an office table.

"Just tell her to hide somewhere. You're able to talk to her, aren't you?"

Shelli nodded and closed her eyes.

"You could sleep on the balcony, Shelli. I'm sure there is one," Jeffrey stated. "All good suites have balconies these days."

Grian had never been in a suite – he'd never actually been in a hotel, except to use the toilet.

"Now…" Howard clapped his hands together. "Bonnie is on her way to collect you. She'll take you on the Hyperloop to the Plaza. I'll meet you three there in the morning with an update."

Grian couldn't believe their luck – he'd thought they'd be in serious trouble but instead they were being treated like VIPs.

A few minutes later a young woman appeared at the office door, displaying her bright white teeth as she smiled and wearing the usual *PEOPLEPOWER* uniform.

They said goodnight to Howard Hansom and the girl led them across the empty auditorium, under the huge globe, and down the mirrored hall to the Hyperloop station.

On the short journey Bonnie explained how the Hyperloop ran in a circle under the city, on the border between the Residential and the Parks zones. She told them the best way to get around during their stay was to take the Loop to the stop nearest their destination and then take a hoverboard from the docking points that were outside every Hyperloop station – just as they were about to do. Jeffrey looked like he might combust when the Hyperloop and hoverboards were mentioned in same sentence.

The Loop stopped and the doors slid open without a sound. Grian hesitated at the sight of what looked like a sea of water covering the platform.

"It's just a screen," Bonnie laughed. She jumped out and the floor beneath her rippled. "This is the Aquarium stop, the city aquarium is near here, so Hansom's team used the sea as inspiration for their station design. Isn't it cool? Now come on – let's get you each an hHover and make our way to the Peoplepower Plaza!"

Grian forgot to breathe as they followed Bonnie onto a tubular travelator designed to look like the inside of a whale, its giant ribs encasing them as they travelled upwards towards the night sky. In just moments they were stepping out of the mammal's mouth, into the heart of the Tipping Point.

CHAPTER 21

THE TIPPING POINT

Grian woke to warm sunlight on his face, gently pulling him from the most comfortable night's sleep he'd ever had. Somewhere he heard the sound of birds and rippling water. He was looking around for his favourite blanket when he spotted Shelli and remembered he wasn't in his own room.

"It's de circadian timer thing Bonnie told us about last night." Shelli pointed to a small white box almost invisible against the white ceiling. "De sun and bird sounds are pretty decent. I prefer de real thing, but de windows won't open."

Shelli was sitting shrouded by a thin lace curtain, making her look like a ghost. Her back pressed to a large expanse of glass that overlooked the streets below.

Grian yawned and stretched before sitting up. Jeffrey still snored soundly in the middle single bed of their triple room.

"These Hansom mattresses are cool," Grian slurred, still a little sleepy. "It knew exactly the position I wanted to sleep in and formed my shape, even changing whenever I turned. I have to get one!"

"Mine didn't work," Shelli yawned. "I don't have a Hansom. I think I might be an anonomanaly thingy!"

"A what?" he asked, rubbing his eyes.

"What Jeffrey said yesterday," she replied. "A shadow! All these things need information on ya to work, and they don't have any on me."

"No. I bet they'll work for you. Watch," Grian said, clapping twice like Bonnie had shown them. "Let's order breakfast!"

A ghostlike hologram of a man appeared in the room, wearing the same *PEOPLEPOWER* uniform they'd seen everywhere.

"Yes, Master Grian, how may I help you?" the hButler asked.

"Breakfast, please!" Grian smiled.

"Of course, sir. I see you're a fan of Cheerities cereal and milk. Also toast with melted real butter. You like orange juice too, freshly squeezed, so I will add a glass to the side. And we mustn't forget your vitamin shot! Anything else, sir?"

"No thank you, butler." Grian smiled, delighted, as the pillow plumped itself up behind his back. "I could really get used to this."

The hologram disappeared before addressing Shelli.

"Ya see." She smirked.

"But you didn't say anything," he replied, clapping his hands again.

"Yes, Master Grian," the hButler announced, appearing right by the edge of Grian's bed. "Is there something else?"

"You forgot Shelli." He pointed at his friend.

The hologram looked around, its expression confused.

"I'm afraid I'm puzzled, sir. Master Jeffrey is asleep, and I don't detect anyone else in the room. Can the guest reboot their Hansom – I should be able to pick up their details then."

"She doesn't have a Hansom," Grian replied.

"Then reboot whatever system your fellow guest is on. I can sync with all devices."

"She doesn't have any devices – she's Wilde," Grian added as explanation.

Shelli frowned.

"Then I recommend the Hansom desk downstairs; they will sort her out with the latest in hWear. Or she can

187

always fill in our guestbook manually and her details will be forwarded to our hButler system."

A long administration form appeared, hovering in mid-air beside the Butler.

"See," Shelli said, disgruntled. "Do ya believe me now? And I'm not filling out that form. Why would ya want a machine knowing more about ya than your own family – it can't be a good thing!"

"Okay – just two of my breakfasts then," Grian sighed, nodding at his virtual host.

"Perfect, sir. You're certainly a hungry traveller this morning." The hButler smiled before disappearing again.

"You just need to get a Hansom and stop complaining! You'll be able to do everything then." Grian exhaled, before flicking his hand at the TV to turn it on.

"I'm able to do way more *real* things than you and Jeffrey can. Anyways, don't ya ever get tired of all de screens – they're already hurting my head!"

"Well, I'd say that's just cause your brain's not big enough!" Grian joked as the room door slid open and the breakfast rattled in on a self-driving trolley.

The smell of fresh toast woke Jeffrey. His tummy rumbling, he shimmied up and ordered his own breakfast.

Grian hadn't realized how hungry he'd been. After filling his belly with as much cereal and toast as possible, he got dressed and raced out of the room down the blue carpeted hallway with the others. They stopped at a large glass elevator cut into the side of the hotel that overlooked the whole city.

As he stepped into the lift, Grian could see the circular layout of the Tipping Point, just like it appeared on the map in the exhibition centre office.

As they had hoverboarded, mesmerized, from the Aquarium station to the hotel the night before, Bonnie had explained to them the layout of the smart city.

The hotel, she said, was in the centre circle, which contained all the shops and businesses and a series of high-rise apartments where those working in the city lived. The centre circle was surrounded by a ring of beautiful parks and recreational spaces where the exhibition centre was situated – Grian had almost crashed his hHover when Bonnie pointed out its large glass dome poking up above the trees the night before. Beyond the Parks and Recreation zone, she said, was the outer ring of volunteers' housing, which was only connected to everything else by the underground Hyperloop.

Now, as the glass lift descended, Grian stared out in awe at the buildings that filled the Tipping Point centre. They were unlike anything he had ever seen before – their various shapes bent and twisted at impossible angles, the brainchildren of some of the world's top architects. He recognized the Hive from adverts. It was the city's main shopping centre and looked like the inside of a beehive, its hexagonal shapes covered in copper and gold metal like some sort of alien spaceship. Behind it, a little further in the distance, he could see the famous Dandelion, which appeared in almost all the Tipping Point press pictures. Its huge stemlike tower stretched right up into the sky to a central circular hub. Springing from the hub were numerous fine metal poles topped with seedhead-like platforms that acted as viewpoints.

Grian was stuck to the glass, still taking in the smart city, when the elevator doors pinged open. The interactive lobby floor greeted them with a multicoloured *Hello* displayed on the tiles, before directing the threesome using moving arrows to the hotel entrance. Their hButler had already told them Hansom was delayed and they were now scheduled to meet a town guide there.

The guide handed them each a pair of Hansom glasses and a Hansom hoverboard. The boards were just like the ones they'd taken with Bonnie the night before.

"These are the hMate," their guide said, popping the dark glasses onto Grian's face. "Compliments of Mr Hansom! Just turn on your hEarPods so you can hear the glasses, and you're all sorted. The hMate will sync with the hHover, so don't worry about directing your board, it'll stay in the traffic lanes – there are no cars in the recreation or business zones of this smart city, only hoverboards and scooters."

The rubber of the shades self-moulded around Grian's face, neatly cupping his cheekbones and brows so all daylight interference disappeared. Then the glass lit up like a screen in front of his eyes, and he could see everything around him again.

"Welcome to the Tipping Point, Grian," the glasses suddenly spoke into his hEarPods, pulling Grian's attention away from his friends. "I'll be your virtual guide for this morning. I've just connected with Bob and I see you're a huge fan of 'Beat the Barber' – want to see how it's made? Team Zion, the creators of the game, have a studio in our smart city. Would you like a tour of their company?"

Excited flutters filled his belly as Grian agreed. Then he lifted up his glasses to look at Jeffrey. His friend shivered with happiness.

"The hMate told me I'll be shadowing Auguste Screen as he directs part of his latest movie this morning. He'll be giving me all kinds of directorial advice!" Jeffrey beamed. "I dream of being many things when I grow up and a cinematographer has remained steady on my 'quite possible' list, so this will be a very valuable experience on the ladder to my future creative career."

Grian laughed. He was beginning to see Jeffrey's funny side – even if Jeffrey didn't see it himself.

"Uck! I'm not wearing these. They make me feel seasick and they're just asking me a million questions about what I like to do!" Shelli huffed as she pulled the hMate off her head and popped the shiny new hEarPods out. "But I've just had an amazing idea – I think I'm going to find my way round this place *ALL BY MYSELF*! And without one of those boards – I really didn't like going on one last night, I prefer using me legs."

"Well suit yourself! See you at lunch," Grian shouted, ignoring her sarcasm as his hMate announced their departure and he hovered off.

His board brought him straight to the door of Zion's studio, where he was greeted by a bubbly purple-haired woman. The woman had metal studs everywhere except for in her ears, and cool tattoos appeared to decorate her whole body.

Everyone inside wore baseball caps, T-shirts, hoodies, and trainers – nothing like the boring uniform Grian's dad went to work in. When he grew up, Grian was going to get a job somewhere like this, where work didn't seem like work at all. He spent the next few hours enraptured, as if in the most amazing dream. He met all the creative team and even watched the latest version of "Beat the Barber" come to life.

He was in the middle of beta-testing a new augmented reality version of the game, where he actually became the

Barber, when Bob vibrated and his glasses flashed an appointment notice across his field of vision.

Meeting: Howard Hansom, The Peoplepower Plaza Hotel, 25 minutes.

Something bumped Grian in the back and he turned around quickly to find his hHover floating at shin height. He climbed onboard and high-fived the Zion team before zooming down the stairs and straight outside, back towards the hotel.

Grian was in bliss daydreaming about his morning as the hHover navigated its way along the busy street, when he was pulled from his thoughts by a woman screaming hysterically. A small boy wearing a bright yellow jacket had just broken from her grasp on the pedestrian zone and run onto the road in front of a stream of oncoming scooters and hoverboards.

A group of people on the opposite side of the street cried out in alarm as they witnessed the scene.

Grian's hHover jolted to a stop – he flew forward, winding himself against the handlebar. Every other vehicle in the area did exactly the same thing, at exactly the same time – two electric scooters stopping just millimetres from the terrified child. The kid screamed for his mother, who raced onto the road and sobbed as she held him so tight Grian thought her son might burst.

"A parent worries about their child night and day – at the Tipping Point we aim to take that worry away," a holographic traffic warden announced as it appeared right at the scene. *"All our roads and electric vehicles have child sensors. You secure the safety of this world and we secure your world!"*

The crowd of horrified people now clapped and cheered on the opposite side of the street. From what Grian could see, they seemed to be on one of the Tipping Point Tours.

The virtual warden then restarted the traffic before disappearing.

Rattled by the event, Grian shivered as his hHover continued onwards. Something unnerved him about the whole thing – probably the fact that in any other city the boy would have been knocked down. Grian's mother would love it here, he thought – she had always been terrified of him around traffic and, to his embarrassment, still insisted on holding his hand whenever they crossed the road together.

A few minutes later his board glided to a halt at the Peoplepower Plaza, and he caught sight of Jeffrey darting inside.

The foyer was abuzz with activity.

"Isn't this beautiful, babe?" the influencer Grian

recognized from the day before gushed as she linked her partner's elbow. "I'm so happy we were gifted this stay. My followers are going to be soooo jealous! Let's move here. It's an adventure, isn't it? And, like, I won't be short of content to create – just look at this place! We'll be doing our bit for the planet, too, and that's so cool right now!"

Her partner, engrossed in his own Hansom, nodded absent-mindedly as Grian dashed past.

Shelli was sitting on a white padded chair that looked like an overgrown marshmallow. She was engulfed by it, as if the chair was eating her. Jeffrey was climbing onto a similar one across the table from her when Grian arrived. He'd just grabbed another chair when a hush fell over the lobby and everyone turned to stare at the hotel entrance before breaking into applause.

Howard Hansom had arrived. The man pulled his cap down over his head, waved a hand as if embarrassed with the greeting, before hurrying across the lobby to the three children.

"I had the most magnificent morning of my life, Mr Hansom," Jeffrey gushed as the man exhaled and sat down. "I had a beverage with Holly Wood, the most celebrated actress in the whole world, while she took a breather between takes. And Auguste gladly took my advice on a difficult camera angle, rightly praising me for it."

"Of course he did." Grian smirked.

"Holly's good like that!" Hansom smiled. "And, Shelli, how were the animals?"

"You know about that?" She narrowed her eyes.

"Oh don't worry, I wasn't following you! I know you didn't wear the hMate. The Wilde have always been suspicious of our technologies – though I did hear they've embraced them a little more lately, to keep up with world news. No, a friend of mine works at the centre and she was describing a girl with a unique closeness to the animals who visited there this morning – I presumed it was you!"

Shelli blushed a little.

"I can see why Solas wanted to volunteer," Grian admitted when Hansom turned towards him. "The Tipping Point is really pretty cool!"

"I actually wanted to talk about your sister," Hansom said. "Bonnie was speaking to Solas this morning and she will join us in the hotel at six this evening for dinner. She's signed up for some dance classes today that she doesn't want to miss."

"Oh," Grian replied, a little disappointed – he'd really wanted to ask her about the last message she'd sent him, "was Grandad with her?"

"No I'm afraid not Grian but don't worry we'll find him. Now I did manage to contact your parents. I just spoke to them actually. I must say they were worried. I told them you've been a great help here and they've agreed to allow you to stay a few days. Your dad said he'd send you a message."

Hansom was filling Jeffrey and Shelli in on word from their own families when Bob pinged.

You had us worried, Grian. Thankfully Mr Hansom told us everything. You shouldn't have gone off on your own but we understand you were worried about Solas and Grandad. Mam and I will be up to collect you soon and we can talk about it then. Enjoy the Tipping Point.

The message wasn't angry but it wasn't very friendly either – usually his dad would add a joke to his text messages. Maybe he was distracted with work and Grandad going missing and Solas running away. Or maybe saying they could talk about it later meant that Grian was in way more trouble than he could even imagine.

CHAPTER 22
THE ACCIDENT

"So," Hansom said after they'd eaten lunch, "I've been speaking to my team and we'd like to question each of you in relation to your recent encounters with the Proctors. Your memories might help solve some of the questions we have. We can pass what we learn on to the police and hopefully aid them in stopping this awful gang."

"What kind of questions?" Grian asked.

"It's nothing to worry about. I'll just be asking you to remember how you felt in those vital moments, such as when you first saw the Proctors or the man in the tunnel. I'll be using those feelings along with some of our latest technology to delve into those memories a little further."

"I don't like de sound of that." Shelli shuddered.

"It's harmless, honestly. You just place your Hansom in a slot and…"

"Amazing," Jeffrey interrupted, twitching with excitement. "Is it something from your R&D department? Possibly some of your latest policing technologies? I've read all about your projects under development. hDreamscaper sounds quite out of this world – being able to control my own dreams and do things I'd never imagined possible sounds…well, sounds like a dream!"

"You know all about us here, don't you, Jeffrey?" Hansom smiled. "Well yes, this is from our R&D department. It's still in beta, but I promise when it is finalized you won't have seen anything like it in your life. Now, are you ready to go?" He stood up. "Grian, if it's okay, we'll start with you."

Grian felt very important when people stopped them to shake Howard Hansom's hand as they crossed the lobby together. Once inside the lift Hansom swiped a plain marble panel on the elevator wall, which flipped over to reveal a hidden hand sensor on the back.

"Not many people have been privileged enough to see this." The man winked, placing his palm on the sensor. "We're going to the heart of my operations – the Howard Hansom Headquarters."

Instead of going up, the lift shot down underground.

Then the doors pinged open and the pair stepped out into a stark white corridor.

A hoverboard docking point, just like the ones outside the Loop stations, sat by the elevator and Hansom grabbed a board before handing another to Grian.

"Follow me," he called, flying off ahead.

Grian was in awe as they travelled along a series of intersecting white corridors, zipping around people in white coats or business suits, who disappeared behind doors labelled things like *The Tilt Research Centre* or *The Environmental-modelling Department*. Eventually Hansom stopped in front of a door with a large triple H on it. He placed his finger on a sensor and it slid open, revealing a huge black room beyond, a complete contrast to the white corridors they'd just passed through.

"Studies have found removing all colour adds a deeper level of concentration," Hansom said as Grian looked around, "and this is where my greatest minds reside."

They left their hHovers at another docking point and stepped inside.

"This, Grian, is where we're saving the world," the man said, walking across the black marble floor flecked with specks of white.

The silence was engulfing, their footsteps the only sound in the large space. They stopped at a row of shiny black orbs, which looked like huge cocoons sprouting from the dark floor.

"They're isolation stations – hPods for short. We had them specially made from laser-cut acrylic glass which we then had digitally woven. You can work away in there without disturbing anyone or anyone disturbing you," Hansom said, placing his hand on the side of one of the cocoons.

The glass cleared where Hansom touched it to reveal a woman inside. The woman was reclined on a chair sculpted into the wall of the cocoon-like orb. Every surface of the pod around her had become a screen filled with weird-looking equations and drawings of what looked like the dome of the exhibition centre, which she seemed to be interacting with.

"We've put these hPods in all our Tipping Point schools now and they're going down a treat."

Grian wouldn't mind having one in his school – he could probably sleep without his teacher ever noticing.

He really couldn't believe he was in Howard Hansom's headquarters! Grian smiled to himself – Solas would be so jealous when he told her.

They stopped at a huge reflective glass wall, which slid smoothly open. Grian followed Hansom inside and the wall closed behind them without making a sound.

The same marble floor continued in here and wrapped up onto the back wall behind an imposing black marble desk, which almost disappeared into its surroundings. There was a white leather chair behind it, and the back wall was lined with clear glass shelving that housed lots of gold trophies and framed photos of Hansom with his famous friends.

On the dark floor was a huge white fluffy rug that reminded Grian of a dog. Resting on the rug was a black leather reclining chair, which faced the large glass wall they'd just entered through.

"Sit down." Hansom smiled.

He clapped his hands so the glass wall turned into a giant interface.

"I need to ask you some questions, but first let me place this cap on your head."

Howard held what looked like a black beanie, though it appeared to be made of some sort of weird rubber material similar to the rim of the hMate glasses. He placed it on Grian's head and the rubber moulded to fit his skull, putting a little pressure on the soft skin of his temples.

"And place your wrist here so your watch fits into this slot," he said, pointing to a neat box set into the armrest of the seat.

Grian shuddered with a mix of excitement and nerves as Hansom walked back behind his desk to his white leather chair.

"This cap can pinpoint how you felt on particular occasions. Memories attach themselves to emotion, you see, and we have a little-known app on all Hansoms that turns on your camera and records the events whenever your watch is alerted to a surge in emotion. We developed it so you never forget the important times in your life – taking photos or video should be the last thing on your mind when you're living in the moment. During beta testing this system has also proved useful for solving crimes such as robberies and so forth – our Hansom cameras can pick up much more than any security camera footage and can really help the police in apprehending a criminal.

"Now let's find out what you've recorded on the Proctors. It won't take long, I promise. Just think back to the first time you saw them."

Grian concentrated on the night he saw them in his house. His heart beat a little faster.

"Great, that seems to be a strong memory – your cortisol levels are spiking," Hansom said, looking at a small screen on his desk, a larger version replicated on the wall in front of Grian. "That memory has a lot of fear attached to it so let's pull up some of the most recent footage that was captured when triggered by fear. Fear is an amazing motivator – one of our strongest emotions. We get great results from it, so we should spot the Proctors soon."

Suddenly images and videos and sound files populated the glass wall. There were lots of images of the Proctors on the patio of Grian's house, which looked to have been taken by his watch when he was hiding in his garden. There were pictures and video of the post office too, from when they were crawling across the floor. Plus some of the postal tunnel and of the head Proctor writing his note, and one of a small child in a bright yellow coat.

"I didn't take any of these," Grian whispered, surprised.

"No, but your Hansom did." Hansom smiled. "Isn't it cool? Your watch automatically captures all your greatest moments without you needing to do a thing.

"We had wondered if we'd be limited by the fact that the Hansom is worn on the wrist, but that hasn't proved a problem at all. People move their hands so much more than we ever realized and because such a vast amount of footage is captured so fast, we've taken luck out of the equation – your Hansom is always in the right place at the right time.

"Once triggered into life by an emotion, your watch takes millions of photos, videos and audio clips every nanosecond and stores them on the cloud. Then when you go to search your emotional memory bank, all events associated with a certain emotion can be accessed. The app filters out the bad angles and fuzzy shots, then stitches the best quality footage together, so you get perfect digital memories. You won't miss out on a thing in your life! We like to call it your emotional memory – or the hEmo for short."

Grian closed his eyes. He wasn't sure he liked the idea of Bob recording stuff without him asking it to. But then again, he did always forget to take pictures, so it was cool to know he had all his best memories there if he ever needed them.

"Great!" Hansom said looking back up from his screen. "Really great work, Grian! This should hugely help our case. I have a lot of good footage of the Proctors here and also of the man in the postal tunnel – he looks like our man alright. Now, can you think about the last time you saw your grandfather in his radio room for me – remember you overheard him talking about a White Rose... Try to access how you felt then!"

Grian cringed and tried to hide it as tears pricked the corners of his eyes. He hadn't been upset the last time he'd seen his grandad, but when he thought about him now worry took over. What if Grandad was hurt? What if the Proctors had done something awful to him? The screen filled rapidly with images, so fast Grian couldn't make out any of the pictures.

"Try not to allow yourself to be overwhelmed, Grian – it glitches the algorithm and all your emotions flood the system at once, meaning we can't access the data efficiently." Hansom's voice was gentle as he encouraged Grian. "Let's just try again, okay?"

Grian nodded, though his heart palpitated now as if it was about to burst. He concentrated hard but he didn't really know how he felt the last time he'd seen his grandad – it would have been different if he'd actually known it was the last time he'd see him for so long.

"Huh," Hansom huffed, sounding a little annoyed. "There's nothing coming. Think, Grian – how did you feel when you told your grandfather Solas was missing? When you heard him say the White Rose. Work with me – access those memories. It's for Adler."

Grian tried hard for what seemed like ages, at Hansom's insistence. He really wanted to help out, but the best he could do was to find the footage attached to the moment he realized Solas had run away – the trigger for those digital memories was anger.

Frustrated, Hansom tried to access Grian's hEmo's manually by time and date but he couldn't pinpoint anything.

"Never mind…" the man eventually said, though he seemed disappointed. "You did a great job, Grian. I'll question the other two and find out what they know next. By the end of the day, we'll have a better picture of things and can brief the police properly. I've arranged an assistant to take you back to the hotel. When you get there, please ask Jeffrey to come down with my assistant next."

Grian nodded and stood up, exhausted and dizzy. He took off the rubber cap, feeling like he'd let both Hansom and his grandad down. Stars blotted his vision and he was a little light-headed as he held tight onto the hHover and was guided through the maze of corridors back to the lift.

When he arrived at his room he told Jeffrey to go down next before collapsing onto the bed. His head felt fried, and he pushed his hands into both temples, trying to stop the constant throb.

"You okay?" Shelli asked.

Somehow her fox had gotten in and was curled round her feet at the end of the bed.

"I snuck Nach in a side door. No one noticed." She smiled as Grian eyed the creature. "So what happened anyway? Ya looked wrecked."

"Hansom wanted to look at my memories. My watch records them without me knowing whenever I get a strong emotion. It was kind of weird. I'm not sure I liked it and I wasn't much good at it anyway. I was able to find stuff on the Proctors but then he wanted me to remember Grandad in his radio room and I couldn't – I kept fogging up my memories. I think he was annoyed with me."

"Your watch records stuff without ya knowing?" Shelli shuddered. "I don't like de sound of that."

"It's not everything, it only records important things. And if it helps find Grandad..." Grian's head throbbed and he slipped into silence, closing his eyes.

The pillow moulded into perfect shape round his head and the throbbing eased a little. Annoyingly he kept seeing the boy in a yellow jacket in his mind's eye.

The incident unsettled him at the time and for some reason it was still unsettling.

Suddenly he bolted upright.

"Bob, open the picture I took of the map of the Tipping Point in the exhibition centre office last night, please."

Bob pulled up the image and Grian zoomed in on the pop-up window that was attached to the star icon Shelli had pressed. He scanned down through what he'd previously dismissed as a police report.

SCENE 5 – TIPPING POINT (PIXEL STREET)

11.43 – tour approaches the scene.

11.43 – child in yellow coat stands on path with mother.

11.43 – child runs out onto the road in front of scooter.

11.43 – mother screams.

11.44 – road security system reacts, everything stops.

11.44 – child screams.

11.44 – mother removes child from scene.

11.45 – traffic warden hologram appears –
Hansom message.

11.46 – hologram redirects traffic.

11.48 – normality resumes.

11.49 – tour moves on to Byte street.

"Grian, what is it? You're white," Shelli said as Nach tensed, the fox's hair standing on end.

"Eleven forty-three," Grian whispered, his voice rattling. "Bob, where was I at eleven forty-three this morning?"

His Hansom was silent for a minute.

"At eleven forty-three this morning you were stationary on Pixel Street, having just witnessed a near-accident."

Now fully rattled, Grian shoved Bob under Shelli's nose and pointed at its screen.

"This happened in real life this morning – exactly as it's written here. I was there, I saw it! But I took this picture last night before that boy ran right into the traffic – it's almost as if it was predicted," he rambled. "But… but what does that mean? Was the accident a set-up? And if it was, then why?"

CHAPTER 23

THE REAL THING

Grian stared at Bob's screen, reading the words over and over again.

"What do ya mean, it happened?" Shelli asked, shaking her head.

"Like it was a scene in a movie or something," Grian answered in disbelief. "The accident happened exactly like it's described here – I mean, the boy even wore a yellow jacket!"

"But I don't understand..." Shelli mumbled.

"Neither do I," Grian whispered.

The pair were discussing possibilities for why the accident might have been staged, when Jeffrey returned and Shelli reluctantly left for her own interview.

Jeffrey was so in awe of the hEmo and how it worked that he appeared to barely listen as Grian filled him in on the strange event he'd witnessed that morning, and how it seemed to have been predicted on the map they'd seen the night before.

"Maybe you were on a film set?" Jeffrey dismissed. "I was on a film set this morning after all."

"But there were no cameras or directors or anything, Jeffrey. A group of people on one of the Tipping Point Tours saw it happening – they definitely thought it was the real thing too!"

"Perhaps it was a set-up then, Grian. Perhaps it was staged to impress those people on the Tour. Look, it even mentions the Tour on that list. If I was a parent, I'm sure I'd be very impressed that my child was safe here. It would encourage me to make the move."

"But that's the same as lying, isn't it? That means Hansom lied to all those people," Grian stated, feeling a little uneasy.

Jeffrey stared at his friend, flabbergasted.

"Why would you think that? If I'd built this town and I needed people to move here, I'd make sure I brought out all the bells and whistles when they're here to witness it – wouldn't you? I don't see how that's a lie."

"Because those people thought the accident was real. You should have seen how scared they were and then how happy they were when the boy was fine! I think it's creepy to fake something like that…"

"You were quick!" Jeffrey said, distracted by Shelli slipping back into the room.

"I don't have a watch, so Hansom wasn't able to do anything much except ask me questions. I told him what I saw. I asked him if he knew anything about what happened to de Wilde who disappeared years ago, but he didn't." She sighed. "Anyway, have yous thought any more about de accident?"

"There were people on a Tipping Point Tour who witnessed the accident too. Jeffrey thinks it might have been staged to impress them. If that's true, it feels wrong, like a lie! Something's off here… I want to talk to Solas now. She hasn't contacted me and she knows I'm here. She hasn't posted anything on any of her social platforms either. It's weird."

"Think logically, Grian. Hansom told you Solas has her dance classes, so she's clearly busy and we will see her at dinner in a few hours anyway," Jeffrey stated.

"Grian's right," Shelli said, and Jeffrey's mouth dropped open. "Hansom's memory thing creeps me out – why would he want to take sneaky pictures of people's lives? And his office was creepy too! I think we should find Solas now – talk to her alone before we meet her with Hansom later. Maybe there's something going on, and if there is she definitely won't tell us in front of him!"

"Shelli's right! Let's go find her! We haven't much time." Grian jumped off the bed with an impulse and urgency that surprised even him.

"I'm really not convinced about this," Jeffrey muttered, following the others out into the hallway. "I mean, what do you possibly think could be going on? However, I'm not going to entertain myself all afternoon – I'll come."

Outside the hotel they found an interactive map. A large red arrow jumped up and down on the flat screen, indicating exactly where they were in the city.

"We would like to go to Area Thirteen," Grian instructed the map.

Shelli bent down to rub Nach, who was already starting to gather a bit of attention.

"There is no Area Thirteen in the Tipping Point," the sign replied, "do you mean any of these?"

A pop-up window appeared over the map, showing a list of suggested place names.

"Why wouldn't there be an Area Thirteen?" Grian said as Jeffrey peered over his shoulder.

"That's probably a code name of sorts for Hansom's own records. Can you give us a list of housing estates in the Tipping Point?" Jeffrey instructed the map.

"All Volunteer housing is located in the Residential

Zone, which is in the outer ring of the city. It can be accessed via the Hyperloop Residential Zone stop. Only volunteers or Tipping Point staff members have clearance to access this zone – it is strictly private for the safety and security of our volunteers. Is there anything else I can help you with?"

"No," Grian snapped.

"It can't be hard to find our own way to de outer ring," Shelli whispered. "We might be able to sneak in ourselves without going on de Loop. Nach can track Solas down once we're in there."

Grian looked around to make sure no one was listening, "Okay." He nodded. "Let's go!"

Jeffrey didn't move or say a thing as Grian stepped onto an hHover at the nearby docking point. Nach and Shelli sprinted off ahead.

"Are you coming?" Grian asked his friend.

Though still reluctant, Jeffrey climbed onto another board and hovered behind Grian through the busy city-centre streets. The beautiful buildings of the Tipping Point zipped by until they passed tall apartment blocks and the place opened up to a sea of green.

"Welcome to the second ring of the Tipping Point – enjoy all that our parks and recreational areas have to offer you," a holographic guide announced, appearing out of thin air as the pair hovered over the grass boundary.

Ahead were fields of green, zigzagged with cycle paths and dotted with woodland. Tennis courts, football pitches, swimming pools and playgrounds decorated the rest of the open space, alongside museums, art galleries and theatres.

Grian zipped past an outdoor gym class where a virtual trainer was busy shouting at red-faced people in bright Lycra, some of whom he recognized from the hotel. Then they passed a huge, heated pool made to look like a natural volcanic spring, and an elaborate art museum where holographic versions of long dead painters waited outside for visitors to guide through their life and art.

Finally the expanse of park came to an abrupt end and Grian was forced to stop his hHover in front of a huge curved screen that appeared to trace the edge of the whole parks and recreation area, separating the rest of the city from the Residential Zone.

Text floated across the enormous screen, saying things like *"Past this point is your future while you save ours"*, *"Join a community of dreamers and believers"* and *"Homes so comfortable you'll never want to leave"*. The text was interspersed with images and video of children playing in beautiful houses with large back gardens and smiling parents.

"Behind that must be de volunteers' houses," Shelli panted, catching up to them.

"But how do we get in?" Grian asked, dismayed. "The screen is huge, we'd never climb over it!"

"Look, there's a Loop station near de trees over there." Shelli pointed a little away. "De map at de hotel said de Residential Zone stop is de only way to get in there, so maybe we'll have to go that way…"

"The sign also said you need to be a volunteer yourself or a staff member to gain access!" Jeffrey interjected.

Shelli ignored him as she sprinted across the grass towards the station, Nach at her heels. Grian and Jeffrey hesitated a little before following her to a web of huge triangular glass that spanned like a sail over the grass. A sign outside read "Natural History Museum Station".

Under the sculptural glass roof were steps down to a bright white platform beside the Hyperloop track. The screen walls of this station were filled with mesmerizing moving clouds, the edges of which were silver and seemed to vibrate as if asking to be touched. Grian pressed on one cloud and his hEarPods filled with a song – *Every cloud is silver lined, even when it rains…*" – and a list of facts about clouds appeared on the wall.

Irritated by the too-cheery song, Grian switched it off and turned round to his friends. Other than them, the platform was quiet. Only one other person waited, listening to something on their hEarPods.

Shelli bent down eye to eye with Nach, then the fox

darted back up the steps to the outside.

"I've told her to hide for a bit. Now come on!" she whispered as a Hyperloop burst from the dark tunnel on their left and pulled silently to a stop in front of them.

The doors opened and Shelli jumped onboard.

"What are we going to do about access at the restricted station?" Grian whispered.

"I'm not sure, but usually when I follow my instincts something good happens – and my instincts are telling me to just get on de Loop!" Shelli answered, beckoning them onboard.

Grian was cautious as he stepped inside, Jeffrey tutting as he followed behind. Both took up blue seats opposite Shelli and waited as the multicoloured belts moved automatically down over their shoulders, strapping them in.

Grian's tummy did a spin as they took off. The Loop wasn't as busy as he'd imagined it should be for a city filled with people.

"They're all at work," Jeffrey dismissed when Grian voiced his observation.

After a minute a holographic guide appeared in the middle of the aisle.

"Next stop is the Aquarium station. Get off here for the city aquarium, or take the hHovers for the Peoplepower Plaza or the Hansom shopping mall."

"Excuse me," Grian said before the hologram could dissolve, "how do we get to the Residential Zone?"

"Only those with clearance can access the Residential Zone through the Residential platform, five stops from here."

The Loop pulled into the Aquarium station just as the hologram disappeared.

A large crowd was gathered on the shimmering platform. They all looked giddy and overly excited, like Grian's class on a school trip.

"Everyone onboard," a holographic guide said as she led the crowd onto the Hyperloop. "If you've forgotten anything from your stay in the Peoplepower Plaza Hotel we'll have it sent straight to your new home, so don't fret. Now take your seats and we'll be at the Residential Zone in moments."

"They must be new volunteers!" Grian hissed. "Everyone stays a night in the Plaza before they move to their homes – I read it on the website."

Shelli's eyes lit up, as Jeffrey shook his head. "I sincerely hope you're not thinking…"

"That we should sneak in with them?" Shelli nodded. "See? Didn't I tell ya something good would turn up!"

"We're kids – we'll easily slip in without being seen, it's a big crowd!" Grian said, trying to feel brave.

"Well, if you insist on breaking the law then I'd better

adjust the station cameras, the system is still compromised via the malware I installed last night – better safe than sorry. And we better turn off our watches before disembarking, Grian – just in case they set off the sensors. We can turn them back on of course once off the Loop," Jeffrey instructed as he fiddled with his Hansom.

Grian switched off Bob and tried to settle as his stomach did flips. His butterflies escalated along with the excitement of the volunteers, who counted down each stop until a huge cheer almost rocked the Hyperloop as it pulled into the Tipping Point Residential Zone platform. The elated crowd then pushed forwards towards the doors.

"Come on!" Shelli jumped up and disappeared into the middle of the large group.

She slipped past the holographic tour guide, who was checking everyone to make sure they swiped their Hansoms as they disembarked.

Grian and Jeffrey followed Shelli and, once on the platform, switched back on their watches. Then all three kept close to the wall, hiding behind the sea of adults as the Loop pulled away from the station.

"Everyone, pay attention! Step this way, step this way," the tour guide announced, directing the excited crowd towards a moving walkway.

The automatic walkway snaked through a long tunnel

and appeared to be the only way off the platform. Grian, Shelli and Jeffrey stepped on at the back of the group as they all moved off.

"Wow!" Jeffrey gasped when the curved tunnel walls turned into a simulation of the night sky.

Grian was speechless as constellations and shooting stars moved across the surfaces around them, making him feel as if he were floating in outer space.

"Life on earth began when the solar system settled into its current layout about 4.5 billion years ago," a voiceover said, as the floor slid slowly onwards.

Then the starry sky started to swirl and fill with all sorts of beautiful floating colours that lit up the dark, a bit like the aurora lights Grian had learned about in school. The group *Oohed* and *Ahhed*.

"Earth formed when gravity pulled swirling gas and dust in to become the third planet from the sun."

As the group passed through the tunnel, they were immersed in a mesmerizing history of planet earth up to the time of the Tilt. Then the floor stopped and five hidden doorways in the tunnel wall opened to their left. A holographic Tipping Point staff member waved as they stepped out of each one of the doors to greet them.

"Welcome to the adventure of your life," the guides announced in unison.

CHAPTER 24
ALL AN ACT

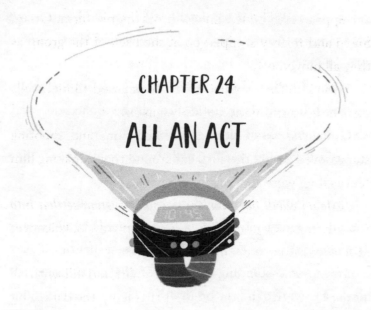

The large group was split into five smaller ones, each with a separate virtual guide. Grian, Jeffrey and Shelli's group guide wore a wide smile and held a *PEOPLEPOWER* branded hTablet.

"Our expert moving crew have assured us that all your belongings have been moved into each of your homes exactly as you requested, and there is a welcome pack waiting for every one of you on your kitchen tables. All you have to do when you get there is put your feet up and enjoy your first night in your new home!"

The group cheered – Jeffrey, Shelli and Grian joining in so as not to look suspicious.

"But before you move to the Residential Zone and

relax into the Tipping Point lifestyle, we'd like to make you famous. You deserve to let the world know you've played a huge part in saving this planet! So, follow us..."

Grian, Shelli and Jeffrey hid at the back of their group as they followed their guide through the arched doorway that opened behind him.

"What's going on?" Shelli whispered when they stopped.

Grian looked around nervously as the arched door closed, locking them inside a dark room. They were now in a queue that ended at some stark green sheeting ahead. Someone was standing in front of the green backdrop under the glare of a very bright light, facing a large camera. It looked like they were being interviewed by another hologram.

"I haven't the faintest idea," Jeffrey hissed, "but we'll just have to go along with it now and hope nobody is alerted to our presence. There appears to be no other way out." After a moment's pause he said, "You know, if I'm not mistaken that's a green screen ahead. They're used all the time in movies."

"Isn't it exciting!" a woman in the queue in front of them said, turning around. "I can't wait to see our new home. Rumours are they all have a swimming pool and an hButler – just like the one in the Plaza Hotel!"

"Shush." Their holographic guide pointed to a sign

above them where the words QUIET ON SET were lit up in red letters.

The woman giggled and placed her finger on her lips. Slowly the group each took their turn in front of the green screen until only Grian, Jeffrey and Shelli were left.

Grian shivered as he faced the camera. He was sick with nerves. What was the holographic interviewer going to ask him? Surely, it'd know he wasn't meant to be there?

"Watch that and pick your preferred background," the interviewer said, pointing to a large monitor in front of him.

Grian could see himself on the monitor outlined against the green background – then all of a sudden the backdrop disappeared, and it looked like he was standing in the middle of the water park in the Tipping Point, then he was standing on a viewing platform at the Dandelion, then in a classroom filled with the latest technology. As the next screen flashed up his stomach did a flip – he was standing in front of a huge roller coaster exactly like Solas had been on the billboard in Turing.

"Is that the one you want? Great choice," the holographic interviewer said, mistaking Grian's reaction. "First tell us your name and why you signed up. Then why you love living in the Tipping Point and visiting places like our Tipping Point Theme Park."

"I've never been to the Theme Park..." Grian answered, confused.

"Not yet," the interviewer replied, "but you're moving in just after this photoshoot so there's plenty of time to go there! It's Hansom policy not to disturb our volunteers once they've moved in – that's why we do all our filming now. Once you're living here we leave you alone to enjoy your new home in peace – so just pretend for now, but you know you'll love it!"

Afraid he'd be found out, Grian played along as the hologram encouraged him to say things about how much he loved the Tipping Point. He shuddered part way through as something occurred to him – had Solas been acting too?

The whole thing felt wrong, like the fake accident with the boy in the yellow jacket.

"I think I'd be good at acting!" Jeffrey smiled when all three of them had finally finished.

"Don't you think this is a bit weird?" Grian whispered, looking over his shoulder in case anyone heard him.

"Yeah, it's definitely creepy," Shelli replied, her face white. "I was raving about how great de water park is when I've never even been there."

"I don't understand why you two are so worried." Jeffrey tutted. "The interviewer explained the whole process to you, Grian. They simply record everyone now so as not to disturb people when they move into their homes. It's quite an efficient way of doing things. I'm sure it's cost effective too and makes perfect sense to me."

"Quick, this way!" Their holographic group guide ushered them into an adjacent room. "Take a seat and enjoy the next part of the journey to your new home!"

They now appeared to be in some sort of cinema. The lights were out, and hushed sounds of excitement wafted through the space from those already settled. Three vacant seats illuminated out of the darkness at the back.

Grian's palms were sticky with nerves as he sat down and gripped the armrests of the large cinema seat. It reclined automatically and moulded round the shape of his body, before massaging his back as it warmed up.

Their guide now stood on a stage at the top of the room, quietening the animated crowd.

"Listen up, everyone, there is someone I would like you to meet before we take you to your new homes!"

The *PEOPLEPOWER* theme tune began playing from surround sound speakers as a hologram of Howard Hansom appeared centre stage. The virtual pair began to interact like a comedy duo and the crowd laughed and cheered with gusto.

Still Grian couldn't shake off his unease.

"The holographic technology here is quite astounding really," Jeffrey whispered in awe as Hansom turned to address the crowd.

"Welcome, Fiona and Philip Phillips, Frederick and

Marina Fallow, Jonathon, Jonah, and June Jones..."

People in the room stood up and waved as the Hansom hologram listed off their names. Grian slipped down in the seat, hoping to hide the fact that they weren't meant to be there.

"I'm so proud of you all." The Hansom hologram smiled, its virtual teeth as sparkling as the actual man's real ones. "It takes courage and a whole heap of guts to give up your life and move here to help humanity. I assure you, though, you will not regret your decision."

Another huge cheer shot round the room.

"Now, we've prepared a short video to explain what to expect from your new life. After that you will be shown to your luxury homes in the exclusive Residential Zone. But first let's get a bit of housekeeping out of the way before you're whisked off to live here in the Tipping Point, the world's first purpose-built smart city," the Hansom hologram announced to another round of applause.

Virtual Howard Hansom disappeared as a film started showing what life in the Tipping Point was like. It began with an interview of a family in their new home, then a principal discussed what school was like and the ins and outs of a pupil's day. He was followed by a teenager who talked about all the shops and cool things kids could do, then a life coach, a sports coach, a wellness guru, a pop star and loads of others who raved about the benefits of the smart city, until finally a woman introduced herself as the Tipping Point chief physician. She explained how every volunteer, young and old, would be screened and how any health issues would be addressed for free in their new city by a team of the world's best healthcare providers. This seemed to really impress the adults.

"All you need to do is insert your Hansom into the space provided in the armrest of your chair and wait until it turns green, which shows we've uploaded all your vital statistics," the doctor smiled.

A slot similar to the one Grian had placed his watch in earlier in Hansom's office pulsed red beside him. He stared as a woman the row in front placed her device in her slot. After a few seconds the hollow turned green and she removed her watch.

"Don't put your Hansom in," Jeffrey hissed, "it may alert their systems to our presence."

After a few minutes of gentle bustle as everyone uploaded their watch's data, the Howard Hansom hologram reappeared.

"We're almost there," it announced. "You'll notice a friend of mine now sniffing round your seats."

A few people giggled up the front and Grian spotted a brightly lit, small, robotic dog running around near the stage at the top of the room.

"My little friend is called Fido and he loves nothing more than eating Hansoms. So, I'd ask you all now to please take off your watch and place it in Fido's mouth as he passes by. We're taking away your old device and replacing it with a new one! Don't worry, we are a sustainable brand and your watches will be reset and passed on to those less fortunate than yourselves. Your next generation Hansom watch will be waiting for you in your new home. Nobody else on the planet has these devices. It's just one of our ways to say thanks for all you are doing!"

Grian stiffened. Was that how Solas lost her Hansom?

The small robotic dog zipped by, and people laughed and giggled as they placed their device in its mouth and watched the robot swallow it whole before moving on. The dog even barked at a lady who teased it, pretending she wasn't going to hand hers over.

"We need to get out of here," Grian whispered, spotting the exit. "I'm not handing over Bob and if I don't that dog will definitely give us away!"

"I have an idea," Shelli muttered, closing her eyes.

Moments later a woman screamed as giant spiders appeared on the cinema screen. Suddenly people were jumping up on their seats and crying out as the invasion quickly grew in numbers.

"Go now!" Shelli hissed as the Hansom hologram tried to calm the panicked crowd.

"But there are huge arachnids everywhere," Jeffrey stuttered. "They are a crippling fear of mine!"

Shelli pointed to the back wall at what looked like an infestation of small bugs crawling over the projector lens.

"They're my friends and they're tiny!" she whispered, smiling. "Now come on – let's go!"

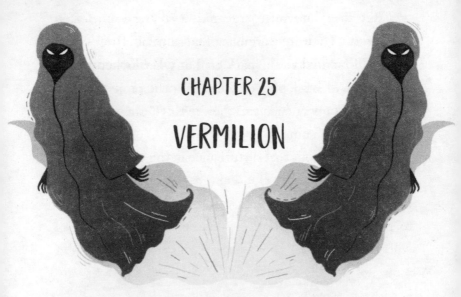

CHAPTER 25

VERMILION

As people stood screaming on their seats, the threesome snuck out through a door marked *Exit* into a long, narrow room. The walls of the room were just like the exhibition centre Hyperloop station – the tiny tile-like screens played videos of happy people and families waving wildly.

At both ends of the room were a set of sliding doors. One of them was plain white, while the other was decorated in *PEOPLEPOWER* branding with the words *Welcome to the Residential Zone!* splashed across the middle.

Grian, Shelli and Jeffrey tried to blend in as the volunteers piled out to fill the space, some of them still swiping invisible spiders from their clothes.

Once everyone was packed tight in the room, their holographic guide appeared, standing right in front of the branded double doors. The *PEOPLEPOWER* theme tune filled the air. Grian couldn't help but pick up on the buzz of excitement that seemed to bounce off everyone in the space.

"I'm sorry about that disturbance in the cinema room." The hologram smiled. "But don't let it put you off. Behind this door is your future! As you pass through remember to give the camera above a wave and videos of you all will play on the walls here as encouragement for the next group of volunteers, just as the previous group are encouragement for you!"

Then the theme tune ramped up, the doors slid open and the virtual guide was the first to walk through. People followed directly after, each stopping under the camera to wave hysterically at it.

"I wonder if it'll be easy to find Solas's house once we're in there," Grian whispered as the crowd inched forwards.

There was a small fuss ahead.

"Hey, what are you doing!" a woman in front of them snapped as she was shoved into her partner, who almost fell against the wall.

"Everyone keep coming," the hologram shouted from somewhere up ahead, "nothing to worry about. I think someone got a little lost, happens all the time with new volunteers!"

Jeffrey gasped. A tall figure pushed roughly past them, heading against the flow of people. The man wore a long black coat and a stern expression.

"That's the head of the Proctors!" Jeffrey stuttered, craning around as the man swiped his finger over a panel by the other set of sliding doors and disappeared through them.

"What's he doing here?" Shelli asked, startled.

"He came from the Residential Zone," Jeffrey continued. "We have to follow him. Hansom said that man's threatened to kill him! We need to raise the alarm. If anything happens to Howard Hansom, the whole world is in jeopardy!"

"But…but we need to find Solas…" Grian stammered, looking at the volunteers as they continued undeterred through the double doors.

"Solas is fine! In fact, I'm sure she's more than fine. But if that Proctor does anything to harm Howard or his plans then I'm afraid there's no hope for our planet – or any of us," Jeffrey said drastically. "The man looks angry and he's not even trying to disguise himself. That speaks of desperation to me. He could do anything!"

Grian looked at his friends as the last of the volunteers waved at the camera and passed through into the

Residential Zone, the sliding doors zipping closed behind them.

He really wanted to see Solas but what if Jeffrey was right? What if Howard Hansom was in terrible danger?

"Can't either of yous contact Hansom with them watches?" Shelli asked.

"No." Grian shook his head. "His details are private."

"Come on. There isn't time to waste – we must stop that Proctor!" Jeffrey said, sprinting to the opposite set of double doors that the tall man had just disappeared through.

Grian knew his friend was right. He raced over to Jeffrey, who was already fiddling with a tiny fingerprint sensor on the panel by the door frame.

"But how would the Proctor have access to Hansom's system?" Grian quizzed over his friend's shoulder.

"Their security system uses ultrasonic 3D imaging, which is relatively easy to hack if you know what you're doing," Jeffrey muttered as he spilled the contents of his backpack onto the floor and began riffling through the pencil case of oddities he'd packed earlier. "I just need something to dust the prints and some glue. Both of which I'm sure I have. Then I should be able to open that door."

"That could take ages," Grian said, anxious as he looked around. "There has to be another way in!"

The holographic guide might have been able to sound the alarm but it had disappeared with the volunteers behind the other set of sliding doors, which now appeared to be locked too. Grian desperately searched Bob for Tipping Point contact details so he could alert anyone to the Proctor's presence, but all he could find was the Tour ticket desk.

When he looked up from his watch, Shelli was standing silently with her back against the wall and her eyes closed. Grian braced himself for something weird when an annoying buzz filled his ears and he swiped at a fly hovering near his nose.

"Stop!" Shelli ordered, slicing him with a stare.

She began repeating something under her breath as she followed the fly around the long narrow room, Grian just behind. His recent experiences with Shelli convinced him she would probably lead them somewhere useful.

A smell of burning wafted through the air and he turned around in time to see Jeffrey brush something black onto the fingerprint sensor before struggling to open a roll of Sellotape.

"Grian, quick, there!" Shelli pointed to a well-camouflaged ventilation cover in the ceiling.

"Brilliant! If we can get into the vent, we should be able to crawl along it over the door. At least that's how it works in films," Grian said, racing to her side.

He slid to his knees and Shelli climbed onto his shoulders. She was feather light. Grian stood up, wobbling as she moved onto her feet. Shelli reached for the hatch and clicked it open, then grabbed the rim of the ceiling and swung like an acrobat up into the dark ventilation shaft above her.

Quickly she hung back down from her knees as though part of a circus act, grabbed Grian's wrists and, with a strength her small body belied, yanked him up beside her.

"Jeffrey, this way!" Grian called, poking his head back down.

"Don't disturb me...I'm almost there..." the other boy replied, deep in concentration.

"Come on," Shelli said, pushing him forward, "we don't have time to waste."

Cold air blew in their faces as they crawled on their hands and knees along the tight space. Grian was certain they had to be near the door when he heard it zip open somewhere beneath them.

"I'm in!" Jeffrey whispered below. "Oh my! I'm in Howard Hansom's Headquarters!"

Grian picked up speed, his body on fire – the Proctor must be in there too. They had to save Hansom. Muffled voices filtered along the vent from up ahead. The voices grew louder, as if an argument was brewing nearby.

Grian stopped a little short of another hatch, Shelli

just on his heels. Sweat dripped down his brow as he listened in the darkness.

"Where have you taken them all?" someone snapped below.

Grian could only hear snippets of the heated conversation.

"It's none of your business any more!" This voice sounded like Howard Hansom. "And it's too late – besides, I know what you've been up to!"

"Stop, Proctor – you will not hurt Howard Hansom!" they heard Jeffrey shout as something clattered below.

A scuffle erupted. There was a crack and a heavy thud. Glass smashed. Their friend cried out.

"Jeffrey!" Shelli roared as Grian surged forwards and slammed his feet into the hatch.

The vent flew open. Anger took him over as he dived down into the room, launching himself on the Proctor below. The man fell forward and Grian winced as he knocked his shoulder off Hansom's solid black marble desk before both of them hit the ground with a thump.

As Grian wrestled the Proctor, Howard Hansom shouted "Help!" into his watch. Suddenly two security guards rushed inside as shutters flew down all over the office.

"Grian, Shelli, Jeffrey," Hansom panted while the Proctor was dragged to his feet. "You saved me, you saved my life. You've saved the Tipping Point and *PEOPLEPOWER!*"

For a while, time passed in a blur. The security team asked Jeffrey, Grian and Shelli all sorts of questions and they had to go through their whole evening from start to finish over and over again.

"Thank you," Hansom whispered to Grian as the others were finishing their statements. "I don't know what would have happened if you three hadn't shown up. Even though you were sneaking around, I know it was for a good reason. Shelli said you'd spotted the Proctor and followed him down here, trying to save my life – I owe you a debt..."

"Umm, yeah – thanks," Grian responded blushing. He wasn't a good liar. "What will they do with him?"

"I don't really know," Howard replied. "He'll stay in the Tipping Point for a while until we get the information we need from him. We must ensure that the Proctors can never harm anyone again."

"Do you think the information he gives you will help find Grandad?" Grian asked, a thick lump in his throat.

"Yes, I suspect so. I'll make sure Adler is the first person he's questioned about. The Proctors have kidnapped a lot of people, especially the Wilde. I promise I will find out about Shelli's mother too – like I said, I owe you all my life."

Relief washed over Grian. The head of the Proctors was caught, his grandad would be okay and they might even find Shelli's mam.

Hansom's watch buzzed. His face changed as he read the message.

"I'm so sorry, Grian, in the middle of all of this I forgot we were to meet your sister! Bonnie waited with her but she says it got too late and Solas has gone back home to the Residential Zone. I'll arrange a meeting for tomorrow. I really am so sorry about this. I'm sure you're disappointed."

"Can't we go into the zone to meet her ourselves – we're practically beside it?" Grian asked. "I promise we won't cause any trouble!"

"Trouble seems to follow you about, Grian," Hansom joked. "Look, I know it's frustrating as I'm sure you'd love to see your sister, but only volunteers can access that zone. It's for their privacy, you see, and I've signed contracts with all the volunteers. If word got out that I let anyone in who wasn't meant to be there, then I could be sued – but worse still, I would lose the trust of all those people who put their lives on hold for humanity. I feel so bad not allowing you inside, but I hope you'll understand?"

"It's okay. I can wait until tomorrow to tell her she's in trouble!" Grian joked, masking his disappointment.

"Thanks," Hansom replied, "I'll call someone to escort you three back to the hotel now. You must be tired and hungry. I just need to speak to security for a moment first, see if they've found out anything more."

He said goodbye and walked out of his private office into the larger open-plan space of his headquarters.

As Grian watched Hansom speak to one of the security guards by the hPods, he noticed the handcuffed Proctor standing near the glass office wall, glaring in at him. Uncomfortable, he looked away. When he glanced back the man was still staring but was now mouthing something too.

"What are you looking at?" Shelli asked, joining him.

"He's saying something to me." Grian nodded in the Proctor's direction.

Shelli glared back at the man, then she stood up and walked closer to the glass.

"For million." She shrugged, sitting back down. "I think he saying 'for million' or 'for a million' or something like that – does it make any sense?"

Grian shook his head and looked away, avoiding the Proctor's threatening glare.

The three friends were escorted back on hHovers to the hotel lift via the underground white corridors they'd travelled through when Hansom had questioned them earlier that day. Once they arrived back at their room they ordered dinner, but Grian couldn't stomach much of it – he felt off.

He lay on the bed playing "Beat the Barber" before trying to fall sleep. Even though the mattress was moulded to his exact body shape and set at his preferred temperature, he just couldn't doze off for long.

Grian looked up at the virtual star-filled ceiling, throwing the words Shelli thought the Proctor had said over and over in his mind.

"For million, for a million…"

He couldn't make any sense of it.

"*Vermilion* is a colour originally made from the powdered mineral cinnabar," Bob stated out of the blue.

"Vermilion!" Grian gasped, bolting upright.

Grandad said Vermilion was the name of one of his radio friends. Surely that couldn't be what the Proctor was saying?

CHAPTER 26

A QUESTION OF TRUST

Grian's unease deepened and he shifted in the bed.

"Can't sleep either?" Shelli whispered from across the room. She wriggled up and sat with her back against the wall.

"No, you neither?" Grian asked.

"I can't get used to sleeping indoors…" she replied.

Shelli moved back the curtains and peered out. She seemed nervous.

"And I don't feel good – it's hard to explain. I feel like this sometimes when things aren't…right."

"I know what you mean," Grian answered. "You know that word the Proctor was saying – could it have been Vermilion?"

Shelli thought for a moment. "Yeah, that sounds more like it!"

"Grandad knew a Vermilion! I think he was talking to him on the radio just before he disappeared..." Grian's voice trembled as he spoke.

"So do you think de Proctor knows Vermilion? Does he know your grandad too, then – is that what he was trying to tell you? Or is de Proctor Vermilion – that note he left in de tunnel was signed with a V!"

Grian shrugged. "Maybe. I don't know...but we think that Proctor was looking for the first note we found in the postal tunnel, the one that talks about Grandad and the White Rose. And Grandad was talking to Vermilion and mentioned the White Rose the night I interrupted him on the radio. So they all have to be linked somehow – I just can't figure out how."

Shelli sighed, then stared off into space and closed her eyes. Grian hated it when she zoned out like that. He tensed, waiting for whatever weird animal she was calling to appear.

"De Wilde aren't happy..." she whispered, opening her eyes again.

"What?" Grian asked, confused.

"I can tune into Mother's energy," Shelli answered. "I feel she's nervous. Everyone is. There's something up – something big."

"What are you two talking about?" Jeffrey yawned, rubbing his eyes.

Grian and Shelli explained what the Proctor had said earlier that night and what Grian remembered about Vermilion.

"Maybe it's a trick." Jeffrey was now alert and sitting upright too. "Perhaps the Proctors saw the name Vermilion on your grandfather's map – they did break into your home after all. It is quite possible he's trying to trick you somehow, to lure you in by pretending he's a friend or something!"

"But why?" Shelli said suddenly. "I think we should speak to de Proctor. At least he can tell us himself why he said *Vermilion*."

"And fall straight into his trap?" Jeffrey shook his head. "Leave that to Howard Hansom and his security guards, I'm sure they have experts in the field of interrogation on their team!"

"No – I agree with Shelli. I think we should find the Proctor and ask him ourselves. Hansom won't know to ask him about Vermilion anyway," Grian replied.

"Well, he would if we told him!" Jeffrey stated.

"I don't..." Grian looked at Shelli, who shook her head.

"You both don't trust him?" Jeffrey gasped. "Howard Hansom is saving the world! Everybody trusts him – if he was doing something wrong surely there'd be protests everywhere."

"That accident Grian saw and de way de hologram asked all those volunteers to rave about living in de Tipping Point before they'd even moved in – that's all fake, and why would they need to fake anything if this place is so good? It's a little creepy if ya ask me," Shelli replied.

"And some people do protest…" Grian whispered, a shiver darting down his spine. "Grandad and his radio friends di—"

"All Tilt deniers," Jeffrey huffed.

"We're only talking about asking the Proctor questions, Jeffrey, that's all. You don't have to come but I think if we're going we should really go now. We don't have much time before morning."

"But you don't know where he is located! And I'm sure he's locked up. You won't be able to get near him," Jeffrey said, flopping back on the bed, folding his arms and closing his eyes. "This is a complete waste of energy!"

"You might be right but that doesn't stop us sniffing round!" Shelli smiled, climbing up from the floor.

Within seconds she was ready and waiting impatiently for Grian. The pair said goodbye to Jeffrey then tiptoed through the hotel and out an open side door on the ground floor, not wanting to pass through the lobby in case they were stopped.

Once outside they crouched behind a large flower bed that spelled out *The Plaza Hotel* in plants. Grian startled as Nach burst through the colourful blooms, landing on Shelli's lap.

"Where do we start looking?" Shelli whispered.

"Underground?" Grian replied. "It seems everything important happens down there. What about those corridors near Hansom's office, the ones we came back along this evening? There's loads of rooms there where the Proctor could be kept!"

"We'll be caught if we try to use de lift in de hotel," Shelli said. "De only other way we know to get down there is through de Residential Zone Hyperloop stop. Remember, de volunteers' waiting area leads to Hansom's headquarters, which leads to them corridors."

"But how will we get in? I'm sure all those rooms we went through with the volunteers earlier are kept locked."

"I imagine I can help with that," someone said behind them. "I still have the Proctor's thumb print – it was too time consuming to do in the tunnel earlier but I 3D printed a silicon copy of it on my trusted mini printer before bed. This version should be more reliable than the glue copy. There's a good chance Hansom haven't updated their security protocols yet after the Proctor's breach, so we should still be able to explore underground!"

"Oh Jeffrey," Shelli exclaimed, throwing her arms around the boy in unfamiliar affection.

"But I thought you trusted Hansom?" Grian quizzed.

"I do." Jeffrey shrugged. "I just don't trust you two! Without me, you'd likely fall into a drain and perish, never to be found again. I'd have no friends left. So, I've decided I'd like to keep you two around."

"Were you making a joke, Jeffrey!" Grian teased.

The three friends burst out laughing and Grian could feel his tension easing. It was the first time he'd laughed with friends in for ever and it had never felt so real.

As late night wrapped the quiet streets of Hansom's smart city, Grian, Jeffrey, Shelli and Nach snuck through the city centre and the park and recreation zone into the Aquarium Hyperloop station, where they nervously boarded an empty Loop heading for the Residential Zone stop.

CHAPTER 27

SOLAS

Grian shivered as he stepped off the Hyperloop onto the Residential Zone platform. Earlier he'd been mesmerized by the starry night and shooting stars that had filled the tunnel, but now this place felt eerie, as all the lights and installations were turned off for the night.

"For de only way into de volunteers' houses this stop is a bit quiet, isn't it?" Shelli whispered, lighting up her Glimmer. "Where are all de people who live in de Residential Zone?"

"In bed, I imagine," Jeffrey retorted.

Grian shivered as they hurried through the tunnelled walkway away from the platform, stopping at the door into the photographic studio where they'd been earlier.

Jeffrey fiddled with the Proctor's fingerprint on the sensor panel until the door slid open.

"We're in! As I suspected, Hansom mustn't have updated the security system yet – it's quite slack for such a large organization, especially after a dangerous breach." He tutted. "I'll have to tell Hansom to be a little more cautious."

"Maybe wait until we're finished sneaking around down here!" Grian teased, trying to lighten his own mood as they slipped past the large green screen into the cinema room and finally out into the volunteers' waiting area that led on one side to the Residential Zone and on the other to Howard Hansom Headquarters.

Suddenly Nach started to whimper.

"What is it, girl?" Shelli whispered, bending down to cup the animal's face.

The fox turned left towards the Residential Zone and clawed at the double doors.

"Open them, Jeffrey. She senses something," Shelli ordered.

"But how, she has no scent to follow?" Grian asked.

"She has a good memory. Maybe she's picked up a different scent, one she knows from before."

"It's probably Solas," Jeffrey replied. "She lives on the other side of those doors after all, and she must have passed down this way going home this evening! We're meant to be searching the corridors on the other side of Hansom's office for the Proctor. I suggest we don't get distracted."

"There's something up. I trust Nach. Open the doors, Jeffrey!"

Jeffrey looked a little disgruntled as he used the Proctor's print once more and the double doors slid open. Nach bounded across a small landing and straight onto a mesh metal stairwell that spiralled downwards.

Grian shivered as the sudden cold hit him.

Nothing on this side of the doors was branded in *PEOPLEPOWER* colours or inspirational Tipping Point quotes. The place felt eerie and unwelcoming.

Distant voices whispered on the air as he descended the steps behind Nach and Shelli. Further down the voices grew louder and he could just make out words. Some wept for their mothers while others raged at Howard Hansom.

Nach's whimpers intensified, along with Grian's anxiety. What was this place? It didn't feel like they were going into the Residential Zone, or at least not as Grian had imagined it.

His teeth chattered as a chill seeped into his bones.

He reached the bottom of the staircase and stepped out into what looked like a huge underground warehouse.

"Oh!" Shelli gasped, frightened.

Grian had never seen her afraid and he followed her horrified gaze across the concrete floor, lit up by crude fluorescent strip lights, to an enormous stack of large metal cages on the opposite side of the space. The cages were layered one on top of the other in long rows that spanned the width and height of the warehouse. A lot of the cages were empty…but others were packed with people.

Grian tried to rub some sense into his eyes, sure he wasn't seeing straight.

A worn and weary man in one of the bottom cages gripped the bars as he sang a haunting song. The sad sound echoed off the cold concrete walls. Others were packed motionless into the man's small cage, slumped against the bars or across the floor. Grian retched, afraid at first that the others were dead, but then he noticed movement and realized most were sleeping in whatever cramped position they could find.

"What is…is this place?" Shelli trembled. "We're meant to be in de Residential Zone!"

"It appears to be some form of prison facility," Jeffrey stated.

"Hey you, down there!" a woman cried hysterically.

Grian quickly spotted her, imprisoned on the third row of cages up. She was pointing at them. Deep shadows rimmed her frightened bulging eyes and her hair hung in thin dark threads by her dirty face.

"You three children...how did you get out? Break us out too! Now!!" she screamed, growing frantic.

Now others were standing at their cage bars too. They were shouting and pointing down at them. The voices were desperate and terrifying as they echoed in the cavernous space.

Nach began to howl.

Confused, and petrified they'd be caught, Grian told his friends to run for the cover of the stairwell, just as a piercing alarm cut through the cave. Everyone stopped shouting. People scrambled back from the bars of the cages, crawling over each other to get away.

"I'm not afraid! I don't care any more!" the woman who'd first spotted them roared.

She was holding her ground as others tried to drag her away from the bars, when a cloaked and hooded shape hovered into the warehouse, stopping ominously in front of the cages.

"Isn't that a Proctor?" Shelli gasped, holding tight to Nach's neck while the animal growled.

The Proctor pointed across the space and an enormous mechanical arm with a metal claw hand at one end craned out from the wall directly opposite the cages. People started to scream, the sound terrifying, as the bars of the woman's cage flew open, leaving her standing on the edge of a huge drop.

Grian choked as she stepped forward into thin air.

Wind whipped through her ragged hair as she fell for a moment before the metal hand opened and seized her like a rag doll. She laughed recklessly as the mechanical fist then dropped her down a silver funnel sticking up from the rock floor. Her laughter echoed round the cave for a few seconds after she'd vanished.

Silence cut the air as Grian, Jeffrey and Shelli huddled close together.

A low whimper fell from the lips of a terrified young child who now stood where the woman had been moments before. The bars of the cage moved back into place and the Proctor disappeared.

Grian was numb. He was about to speak when the sound of his name floated like a butterfly across the space. It was so faint he was sure he'd imagined it.

"Grian…Grian…Grian."

His heart ached and the hollowness left him. He knew that voice. Tears fell freely. He was on his feet and, before he could think, he ran to the base of the cages, searching for a face.

"Grian…Grian, up here… Up here." The voice was weak.

She was on the second level, too far away to reach. A plaque on the top corner of her cage read *Area 13*. He wanted to hold her, to squeeze her tight and take her away. She was frightened, the light robbed from her once-bright eyes.

"Solas!" he breathed.

CHAPTER 28
THE PRISON

"What...happened? What's...what...what is this place?" Grian couldn't make sense of anything as he stared up at his sister, who was meant to be happy living in the Tipping Point, saving the world and taking dance classes.

"I...I don't know." Solas's voice was faint. "I signed up for the Tipping Point. I'm so sorry, Grian, I didn't mean for any of this to happen."

Tears streamed down her face as she held the bars so tight her knuckles whitened.

"I should never have done it. I just...I thought the place looked so cool and I wanted to get out of Tallystick...I wanted to save the world...then Howard Hansom called me and I couldn't believe..."

"Howard Hansom called you?" Grian interrupted, surprised.

Solas nodded, her eyes left raw by tears.

"I couldn't believe he called me. He said that my name was picked at random after the rally in Tallystick and I'd won a prize to visit the Tipping Point. I knew Grandad wouldn't let me go, so I left a note and snuck away. I know I shouldn't have but Hansom said he'd call Mam and Dad and he'd make sure you all came too. He said we'd get special treatment. He was so nice, Grian... The first day I got dance classes and singing, it was..."

She started to cry again.

"The videos...he showed us a film of you dancing..." Grian stuttered.

"I had a film crew follow me – it felt like a dream come true..." Solas continued shaking now. "He even took me to his office. He put a cap on my head and read memories my watch had recorded. He asked loads of questions."

"Questions about what?"

"About Grandad. Most of his questions were about Grandad. He kept asking something about a letter that he was sure Grandad had. Something to do with a white rose."

"A white rose?" Grian gulped. "He asked me about that too. And the White Rose was written on a note we found that mentioned Grandad. Did Hansom say what this White Rose was or why he wanted to know about it?"

"No." Solas shook her head.

"Grandad's missing!" Grian blurted, even more scared now.

"Oh no! Does Hansom have him?" Solas asked petrified.

"I don't know... He said the Proctors had Grandad!"

"Who are the Proctors?" she asked, confused.

"Those dark-cloaked things. Like the one that was just here..."

"I didn't know they were called Proctors. We just call them the guards. But...but hold on – were you talking to Howard Hansom?"

"Yes." Grian nodded. "We came to the Tipping Point looking for you. I thought you knew something about where Grandad had gone because of the message you sent me."

"What message?" his sister asked.

"The one you sent after you left... You said Grandad was here."

"I...I didn't send you a message about Grandad. I didn't think anything was wrong. I was so stupid, Grian," Solas whimpered. "After he questioned me, Hansom told me I was going to our new home in the Residential Zone and you'd all be joining me. I got on the Hyperloop with all the other volunteers. I was so excited. Everyone was.

It all looked so cool. In the cinema this robot dog took my watch – we were promised new ones, but then we came here… I haven't had a watch since – nobody has one down here."

"But who sent the message then?" Grian questioned.

"I don't know," Solas replied, "but we don't have much time, you have to get us all out of here soon. They are emptying the whole prison! The Hyperloop just left with another load of volunteers, and I think I'll be next!"

"What…? To where?" Grian asked, dizzy with fear.

"I don't know." Solas shook her head and pointed to a track cut through the middle of the warehouse floor. "Some people say that Hansom has built an extension to the Hyperloop track, but nobody knows where it goes. I've heard that just after the track was finished a few weeks ago, the guards started filling the Loop every night and taking people away.

"Rumours say that all these cages were full with people once, but now lots of them are empty. More volunteers still arrive and fill some of the empty cages every day, but people are saying we'll all be gone soon. You know we're all volunteers here…everyone believed they were going to save the world," she wept.

Other prisoners now stood at the bars of their cells, staring down at Grian. Desperate whispers circled round him as they begged and pleaded for help or asked what was going on. Some who grew too loud or tearful were quietened by their cellmates.

"I'll get you out, Solas," Grian said, desperate to save her. "Is there a button or code or something to open these cages?"

His sister shook her head. "I don't know. We've tried loads of ways to escape but the locks are solid."

"I might know a person who can help," he replied, thinking quickly.

"You better stop fooling yourself, kid, and run before that arm grabs you too," a man yelled at Grian, the sound echoing off the concrete walls.

Everyone tensed as a door banged somewhere nearby.

"Grian, Grian, we need to hide!" Jeffrey and Shelli were calling across the space, their eyes wild with fright.

"Just go!" Solas urged. "The guards check on us sometimes. You'll be caught if you stay here!"

"I'll be back," he replied, holding her terrified stare. "I will get you out. I promise."

"I love you, Grian," his sister whispered through her tears before disappearing back into the shadows of the cage.

Solas had never told him she loved him before. She normally slammed doors in his face and screamed at him to get out of her life. Now Grian wished she would do that again – then it would mean all this was just a dream.

Quickly he took pictures of the locking system, then snuck back across to his friends, wiping the tears from his eyes as he slipped out of the warehouse and up the stairwell.

"That was Solas?" Jeffrey stuttered.

Grian nodded, speechless.

"But what was she doing there? Why isn't she in the Residential Zone? What is this place? Why are the Proctors here?" The other boy stammered.

Shelli held up her hand to stop Jeffrey's questions as Grian sat down on a step. Nach placed her head on his lap, her large brown eyes somehow soothing.

"Howard Hansom put my sister in there." His voice trembled as he told his friends everything his sister had just told him.

"But he's saving the world..." Jeffrey replied in disbelief. "So why? Why would Howard Hansom lock people up?"

"Solas said all the cages were full until lately, that there were lots and lots more volunteers, but the Proctors take them away at night..."

"So is everything Hansom told us about de Proctors a lie too?" Shelli growled. "Are they working for him? If they are, then who's that man we helped catch? Maybe Hansom has your granda too then, Grian – that must be why my animals tracked him to here!"

"I don't know," Grian replied, feeling sick, "but we have to get my sister out soon. She said the Hyperloop takes people away every night and she thinks it's her turn next."

"Takes them where?" Shelli asked.

"She doesn't know." Grian shivered as panic wobbled his voice. "But look at this place – it can't be anywhere good."

Then he swiped across Bob, sharing his recent photos to Jeffrey's Hansom.

"These are the cage locks. Can you open them?" he asked.

Jeffrey studied the images. "These look like hLocks, which are part of Hansom's new police tech. They must sit on an isolated network, Grian. The malware I installed earlier only has access to the open network. Anything down here underground appears to be a little more secret. I would imagine they're all controlled from a central computer, so we'd need to break into that..."

"Hansom's computer!" Grian jumped in. "The one in his office..."

"Yes, I imagine you're right." Jeffrey nodded. "I just – well, it's – I can't believe..."

"Come on!" Shelli growled, sprinting up the steps. "I don't like zoos – animal or human! We'll free Solas and all those people and stop whatever it is Howard Hansom's up to. I bet he's never come up against anything like us before!"

If it was any ordinary moment Grian would have laughed at Shelli's outburst, but instead he felt fierce as he charged after his friends. They had to save his sister!

CHAPTER 29

THE SUN

Grian raced up the metal stairwell two steps at a time and through the double doors, moving so fast even Shelli was left in his wake.

Jeffrey puffed and panted as he stopped at the doors into Hansom's headquarters. His hand trembled and he had to reposition the fingerprint a few times before pressing it onto the sensor. Grian tapped his foot off the floor as he willed the doors to open.

"Your intensity is a little off-putting," Jeffrey huffed when the sensor flashed red.

He fiddled with the fingerprint a little more before trying a second time. The panel flashed red again.

Anxiously Shelli turned towards the ventilation hatch

they'd used earlier, just as – on the fourth attempt – the panel flashed green, and the doors zipped open.

Wary, Grian was the first to step into the large black room beyond. The place was eerily quiet as the threesome slipped silently across the sleek marble floor, past the empty hPods and in through the door in the huge glass wall that separated Howard Hansom's private office from the rest of the space.

Once inside, Grian swiped at the glass wall just like he'd seen Hansom do to activate the screen.

"That won't work," Jeffrey whispered. "That glass screen must be connected to Hansom's personal computer, which has to be located somewhere in this room. If I'm right, that computer should give us access to the isolated network. Once I've infiltrated it I should be able to open the cages so we can free Solas and everyone else."

Grian and Shelli were searching the dark office, using Bob and the Glimmer for light, when Jeffrey snorted.

Grian turned to see his friend sitting on Hansom's large white leather chair, staring at a small, embedded computer that had just popped up from a hidden section in the expansive desk.

Jeffrey took out his hTablet and sClerk before turning on Howard Hansom's tiny computer. The large glass wall lit up.

A huge array of grainy rectangular black and white images filled the screen. It seemed they were looking at the security camera footage for what appeared to be the whole of the Tipping Point.

Grian recognized some of the places, like a few Hyperloop stations, the empty auditorium in the exhibition centre and the hotel lobby.

"Can't Hansom see us on these cameras?" he gulped.

"I've been diverting the city cameras with the malware I installed whenever we're up to no good – I told you this before." Jeffrey smiled proudly as he looked up from the screen. "Unfortunately, I don't have access to the cameras down here, but I will be able to wipe tonight's footage before we leave and upload the same malware to this computer, should we ever need it."

Grian was half listening to Jeffrey while he continued studying the grainy video footage, when his heart skipped.

Under the glare of one of the security cameras, two weary-looking men sat in an empty room. Grian gasped.

"What's wrong?" Shelli asked, now beside him.

"Grandad!" he exclaimed.

"What!" Jeffrey exclaimed, looking up from his work.

Grian pressed on the small security-camera view, which then enlarged to fill the full screen.

His grandad sat with his head in his hands as the second

264

man paced backwards and forwards across what looked to be a very small space.

"And that's the head of the Proctors," Grian stammered. "The one we helped arrest."

"Grian? Grian...is that you?" His grandad's voice filled the dark office as, on screen, the old man stood up and looked around.

"Who is it, Adler?" the Proctor said, looking around too.

"Grandad! It is me. Can you hear me?" Grian replied.

"Yes! Where are you?" his grandad exclaimed.

"Howard Hansom's Headquarters..."

"Get out of there – now!" his grandfather ordered urgently. "That man is dangerous!"

"No, they could help get us out, Adler. They could..."

"No, we can't leave, Grandad – not yet," Grian spoke over the Proctor. "We need to break into Hansom's system to free Solas! He has her in a cage with loads of other people!" Grian swallowed a lump in his throat as he tried to sound brave.

"Have you seen her? Is she okay?"

"Kind of – but she said the Hyperloop is coming to take her away. We need to get her out!"

"Oh, thank goodness," his grandad cried, shifting onto his knees. "When Hansom gave me her watch he said – he said she was gone for good. I thought..."

"Solas's watch?" Grian looked at Shelli. "You had it?"

"Yes," his grandad answered, "Hansom gave it to me. He told me he'd already hurt her – and if I didn't give him what he needed he'd do the same to you. I knew he didn't have you yet as otherwise he would have shown me, so I tried to send you a message in secret, but Hansom caught me. You know how bad I am with technology! Anyway, he called some robot dog that ate the watch in front of my eyes."

"It worked!" Grian replied. "I got a message from Solas – well, from you… That's why we're here! But what's going on, Grandad? Where are you?"

"That's enough talking," the other man snapped as he stepped forward towards the camera and glared down the lens. "You put me in here, you clueless child – now get me out! There's work to do!"

"Vermilion, stop!" Grandad commanded. "He must save my granddaughter first."

"Vermilion," Shelli said, surprised, "so *you* are Vermilion! Hansom told us you're a Proctor."

"Is that one of your friends, Grian? Vermilion told me there were others with you," his grandfather asked.

"Yes, it's Shelli, she's from the Wilde. And our neighbour Jeffrey Slight's here too."

"Vermilion is not a Proctor, Shelli," Adler corrected. "He's a radio friend of mine. The Proctors work for

Howard Hansom. They're the ones who captured me the night I was looking for Solas."

"Of course, I get it now – Hansom told you I was a Proctor!" Vermilion spat. "It's a double bluff. He's the world's best liar! He pretends the Proctors are after him and trying to destroy *PEOPLEPOWER* when all along they work for Hansom, silencing anyone like me who speaks out against the Tilt and the lies he's spinning!"

"But…but…if Hansom is lying, how does the whole world love and trust him?" Jeffrey asked.

"Everybody is told to love and trust him, young Slight!" Grandad replied. "Don't you see, those blasted watches everyone wears are programmed to make you believe Howard Hansom is a god – even our fridge sings his praises with a jingle. We're hardwired to fall for everything the Hansom Corporation tells us."

Jeffrey blushed. Grian looked at Bob. The watch was, up until recently, his best friend. Could it be true – could Hansom really be controlling what everyone thinks?

"But what exactly is he lying about?" Grian asked, confused.

"The Tilt, of course – it never happened," Vermilion snapped.

"But then why does he need all those volunteers in cages, if the Tilt is just a lie? Why would he kidnap Solas?"

Grandad shook his head. "We don't know the answer

to that, Grian. I wish we did. But I can guarantee it's not for the good of humanity. You have to get Solas out of there!"

"The Tilt can't be a lie! No…no…no," Jeffrey said, holding his head. "I'm not listening to that!"

"The science is fake – the Tilt never happened!" Vermilion snapped, his frustration spilling over. "The world hasn't shifted further on its axis. The earth's obliquity is still approximately 23.5 degrees, give or take a few thousand years. But why believe me? I'm just part of a group of some of the world's most brilliant minds, chaired by the planet's most eminent astronomer. But you go ahead and trust Hansom. See where that gets you!"

"Vermilion, they're just children!" Grandad reprimanded.

Grian's head was spinning. He'd heard his grandad say things like this before and hadn't been sure what to think. But now, faced with the other lies Hansom had told them, the Tilt not being real wasn't such a leap.

Yet he remembered sitting at his desk in school and the windows shattering on the day of the earthquake, the day they said the world tilted. He pictured the black mark on the sun, the slightly darker days. The constant news reels about the devastating effects of the earthquake, the Tipping Point exhibition stands showing how the planet's instability meant it would someday fly off into outer space and explode. All these things they said had happened or would happen because of the Tilt.

He'd learned about it in school, seen constant videos on his Hansom, on bus screens, on billboards – everywhere. All the experts agreed. So even though he felt in his gut that Vermilion was right – how could the Tilt not be true?

"But there's a black shadow on the sun – nobody can deny that!" Jeffrey replied. "Our daylight hours have changed. Even Shelli's insects are dying! Those are facts. Everybody agrees. I'm not listening to Tilt deniers – this is the stuff of lunacy!"

"I've heard Mother say things about de Tilt not being real..." Shelli whispered. "I just don't say it much. People already think de Wilde are crazy enough... De insects were dying out before de tilt happened, de animals were acting strange too – that's what my mam was protesting about when she went missing years ago. She said human greed was killing the planet – she called it climate change. Mother said after de Tilt nobody cared any more about fixing it, they all got distracted trying to tilt back de earth."

"The Wilde were always ahead of their time, Shelli." Grandad sighed, looking straight at the camera. "Grian – remember the map on the back wall of my office?"

Grian nodded.

"Vermilion and my radio friends helped me draw it by sharing their observations of the sun in their countries. We found that the shadow on the sun looks the same from every country in the world. If our earth had tilted over further, the shadow would be different depending on where on earth you live. Daylight hours would shift too, but contrary to what's reported – the sun still rises and sets at the same time as normal, in every country on the planet – the days are just slightly darker, which makes it feel like the hours have changed.

"The earth hasn't shifted. Vermilion has loads of scientific studies by world-famous scientists that contradict everything we're told. It's just they're being drowned out by all Hansom's noise – which is hardly surprising, since he owns so much of the world's media."

"But why is there a black mark on the sun then? Why are the days darker?" Jeffrey asked, still flabbergasted. "No matter what you say, that can't be fictitious!"

Adler shook his head and turned his back to the camera, whispering something to Vermilion. The pair appeared to be arguing.

"Grandad…tell us!" Grian pleaded.

"What's happening to our sun?" Shelli sounded scared. "Ya have to tell us!"

"We're not sure. Some say the sun's sick, as if it's been poisoned somehow," Vermilion replied sharply.

"Vermilion!" Grandad barked. "They are just children!"

"Children are simply smaller adults, Adler! They need to know the sun might be dying – after all, it's their future we're fighting for!"

"Dying?" Jeffrey, Grian and Shelli cried.

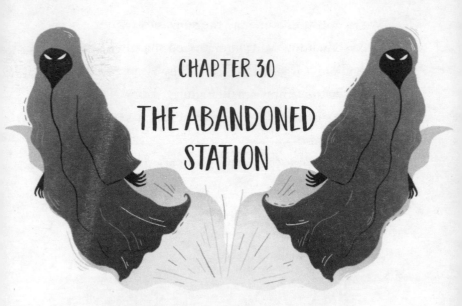

CHAPTER 30

THE ABANDONED STATION

"But – but the sun can't be dying. We learned in school that we need it…for…for everything. What will happen to us? What will happen to the world?" Grian murmured.

"We're working on it," Vermilion assured him.

"What do ya mean, *we*?" Shelli asked.

"The Council of Colour – we're searching for the truth so we can *really* save the world," Vermilion answered with passion.

"Who are the Council of Colour?" Grian asked, as Jeffrey resumed his hacking.

"They are scholars and scientists and free thinkers – normal people who are not afraid to ask questions or to think critically," Vermilion said, pointing to a small badge

Grian could just make out on the lapel of his coat. "This is our symbol – a colour wheel. Anyone wearing this is a friend."

The badge had exactly the same symbol on it as the stamp on the envelopes they'd found in the postal station.

"We...we found a note. It was marked with the same colour wheel – I thought it was a flower..." Grian stuttered. "It was in the old postal railway tunnel on an abandoned platform under Turing's post office. We saw you there, Vermilion – I...ahem...I think you might have been looking for it."

"What? How stupid of you to take something that's not yours!" Vermilion snapped. "What did it say? Tell me – now!"

"Vermilion!" Adler barked. "I've told you, they are just children. Stop it!"

"It...ahem...it said something about the White Rose and about postmen finding a letter."

Grian didn't mention the note said anything about his grandfather. He wasn't warming to Vermilion, even if he was meant to be on their side.

Vermilion's eyes popped. "They found a letter? Hansom will panic if he finds out!"

"Ahem...he already knows – we told him. And he saw it too and he saw you when he looked at my digital memories," Grian winced as he replied.

"Huh...so that explains how my cover was blown! I was working for Hansom as a data scientist in order to spy on him. I hadn't been in the warehouse in a while so on my break earlier I checked in on the volunteers. I knew at some point Hansom would need to move people to free up space but I got nervous when I saw all the empty cages. I went to his office to ask him about it. But he'd obviously already suspected me as a spy when he saw your memories, so he told you I was a Proctor. When you three played the heroes, you gave him the perfect opportunity and he had me arrested..."

"No, he told us you were a Proctor before that, I think," Shelli interrupted. "Grian recognized you when Hansom was showing us pictures of de Proctors."

"However it happened, I'll have to get word to the Council of Colour to stop all communications and movement via the underground postal railway lines. If one of our members is caught sneaking into the Tipping Point through the exhibition centre station it'll be on your heads!" Vermilion snorted. "Hansom must be moving everyone because he's growing more nervous of the White Rose and those rumoured letters."

"But who is the White Rose and what are the letters?" Grian asked. "Hansom thinks you know something about the White Rose, Grandad – he asked me and Solas about it. Is that why he wants you?"

"I told him – I don't know anything," his grandfather snapped.

"The security parameters on this computer are too tight. I can't access the cages to free Solas!" Jeffrey interrupted as files opened and closed at breakneck speed on one half of the large glass screen in Hansom's office. "I'm afraid if I persist I'll alert Hansom to a breach."

"Then the only way to get into his system is to find me first," Vermilion replied quickly. "I developed a secret access card. It's secure and I can ghost Hansom's personal network without being caught. I've been copying files, looking for evidence of his lies. With my access card we can unlock the cages and release the remaining volunteers..."

"But we have to know where yous are if we're going to get ya out." Shelli stepped forward.

"We don't know." Grandad shook his head. "I don't remember and neither does Vermilion. I was held somewhere else first. I think Hansom must have drugged us before he brought us here because I don't remember being moved. This place is distinctive though – it's not an ordinary room, if that makes sense?"

"What do ya mean?" Shelli quizzed. "Describe it."

"We're in a square clear box encased in some sort of white styrofoam," Vermilion said as he paced the room, rapping his knuckles off the walls. "Earlier I thought I could hear voices, as though a lot of people were nearby, but they've gone now…"

"Maybe they're in the warehouse where Solas is?" Jeffrey guessed. "There are a lot of people there."

"Is there anything else? Anything at all that might help us? Even tiny details?" Shelli encouraged.

"There is something," Grandad answered. "It's odd, though, and sometimes I wonder if I am imagining it. But every hour or so I think the room moves a little. So at times it feels as if the floor is slanted away from my feet and other times it's straight under me. When it happens, I can hear a tiny clink, as if there are some hidden mechanics making us move. It's not easy on the stomach."

Jeffrey took notes on Betty as Grandad spoke.

"Also, Grian," he said a little quieter, "you might think me mad for even mentioning it, but something about this place reminds me of the puzzle boxes we used to solve when you were little. It might be the tiny clink or the odd movement, I really don't know, but it all feels familiar somehow."

Grian remembered hours of frustration mixed with moments of pure excitement when he had opened the latest of his grandad's puzzle boxes. Most were made of wood and square or circular in design. He and Solas had to figure out how to open each box piece by piece, like a 3D jigsaw in reverse, to find whatever secret compartment lay inside. Grian used to imagine himself as the world's best puzzle master and even once made a red cape for "Puzzle Boy", his superhero self, which he hid under his bed in case Solas ever found it.

"We need to get out of here." Jeffrey sounded anxious. "In all Hansom's autobiographies he reports being an early riser and arriving at his office before six a.m.! It's precisely five forty a.m. now."

"He's right. You'd better go, Grian – but be careful, please!" His grandad's voice broke a little.

"We'll find you, I promise," Grian whispered, before Jeffrey switched off the computer.

Grian knew saving Grandad and Vermilion and getting that access card was the only way they'd be able to break into Hansom's system and save his sister. But time was a problem – Solas was certain she didn't have much time left and, for all Grian knew, neither did his grandfather.

He was eaten up by worry as the three friends snuck out across the dark office. They debated whether to take the hovers to the lift that Hansom had brought them on the first time they'd seen his headquarters or use the Hyperloop to get back to the hotel. Eventually they decided the lift could be too risky.

It was still dark as they boarded the deserted Loop and rode it back, slipping in the rear door of the hotel. They crept unseen up the stairwell back to their room.

Grian shivered as he climbed onto his bed.

For distraction he turned and looked out the window to watch the rising sun. The shadow on its bright face never bothered him much before, as catastrophe seemed so far away. But now, well – now things were different.

"We'll find Vermilion and your granda," Shelli tried to reassure him.

"But it could take ages to find them, and that's time Solas doesn't have!" he argued. "Hansom wants Grandad because he thinks he knows something about this White Rose. So I don't think Hansom would hurt him, at least not yet. Maybe Grandad has time that Solas doesn't have. My sister said they're emptying out the prison every night. If she disappears, we won't know where she's gone or how to save her...

"Solas said that a new Hyperloop track had just been finished and that's when they started taking people away on it. What if we could find out where that track goes? Or what if we could somehow stop the Proctors when they've already opened the cages and people are boarding the Hyperloop?" Grian's ideas were growing as he spoke. "I just think we need to look into another way to save Solas in case we can't find Vermilion quickly!"

"But there are too many variables in your plan, Grian. Opening the locks is fail safe, we just need to find Vermilion and his access card," Jeffrey stated.

"What if we did both?" Shelli interrupted. "Me and Nach can search for Vermilion and Adler, and I'll get Fred back on de scent too, while yous work on a second plan to save Solas. Then if we don't find Vermilion in time, we can change to plan B?"

"Okay, split the odds…diversify… Yes, that makes sense." Jeffrey nodded. "If we're to find a way to save Solas then we should probably go back to the warehouse where she's—"

"Solas is in a sort of warehouse, Jeffrey, isn't she? That mechanical arm could have been used for moving post," Grian interrupted as a thought struck him. "Vermilion said something about the Council using the postal line to communicate and about members sneaking into the Tipping Point through the exhibition centre Loop stop. Maybe… Bob, find the picture I took of the map of the Turing District postal railway!"

His watch found the image and Grian cast it onto the TV screen in their hotel room.

Jeffrey and Shelli walked up to the map, inspecting it closely as Grian stood back and surveyed the whole thing. A numbered line ran from Turing to the last stop, which was labelled *Babbage Central Sorting Warehouse*.

"Look at stop nine." Grian pointed excitedly. "The letters T.P. are scratched into the metal beside it – surely that has to mean the Tipping Point? Maybe there's a way into the postal railway line from the exhibition centre Loop platform? And, see the last stop – it's called the Babbage Central Sorting Warehouse. Where Solas is kept is like a giant warehouse – maybe it's the same place! What if it's possible to sneak in there through the postal line? And if it is, then it should be possible to sneak people back out that way too!"

CHAPTER 31

THE hSWARM

After a short fitful sleep and some breakfast, Grian, Shelli and Jeffrey set off to try and solidify their plans.

"You three are up early!" Howard Hansom smiled as the lift opened and they stepped out into the hotel lobby.

"Oh, ahem…" Grian spluttered, in surprise.

"Howard, how lovely to see you!" Jeffrey replied, not missing a beat. "We wanted to explore more of the City. We haven't been to the Dandelion yet and by all accounts it's jaw dropping."

"It'll be quiet there now too." Hansom nodded. "A good time to visit before the crowds. Anyway, I was on my way to your room to tell you I've been in touch with Solas and you'll be pleased to know you'll see her this evening. She's in on a little secret, you see, and is helping me plan a very special surprise for you three tonight…as my way of saying thanks.

"Stopping that Proctor saved my life, and ultimately the world, and I want everyone to know. That's all I can tell you for now, but I can promise you'll have the evening of your young lives – in fact, it will be life-changing!"

Grian tried to appear relaxed – it'd be strange if he didn't at least smile – but he was finding it hard to force his lips apart. Shelli barely held in a growl.

"Well, that's marvellous news, isn't it?" Jeffrey exclaimed.

"Yes, great! Thank you!" Grian imagined he was probably grimacing, though he tried hard not to. "And… ahem…has the Proctor told you anything about Grandad?"

"Not yet, but we're working on it, Grian. My team started questioning him again early this morning. I promise we'll have an answer soon. I understand you must be so worried!" Hansom lowered his voice as he fiddled with a small toy replica of the world, throwing it up and down like a nervous tick. The toy looked like one of the souvenirs Grian had seen in the gift shop at the exhibition centre.

Hansom looked at his watch. "So…I'll meet you in your room at six. Now if you'll forgive me, I still have the world to save – thanks to you three!"

He threw the tiny toy globe into the air once more before depositing the small object back into his pocket and walking away.

"Do you think he suspects anything?" Grian asked, a little shaken, as they headed off in the direction of the Dandelion so as not to raise suspicion.

"I don't know," Shelli replied. "But we can't worry about that now. We need to stick to our plans. Yous go to de exhibition centre stop and see if ya can find a way into de postal tunnel, and I'll see if Nach and Fred can track down your granda or Vermilion. Give me that note Vermilion wrote, Grian."

Grian took out the crumpled note that they'd found in the postal tunnel and handed it to Shelli.

"It'll have a bit of his smell on it at least," she said. "Right, we'll meet back at de hotel at four."

The three split up. Grian and Jeffrey made their way to the Aquarium Hyperloop station and caught the next shuttle to the exhibition centre. Grian shivered as he got off at the platform. The faces of all the volunteers on the tiled screens around him were now chilling instead of inspiring.

The pair hung around, trying not to look suspicious as they searched the platform for some sort of a doorway. Grian was investigating behind a bin when Jeffrey called him over. A small wax stamp was stuck on a fire hydrant that was hanging on the wall hidden discreetly in the shadow of a platform pillar. The stamp looked exactly like the symbol of the colour wheel that Vermilion had shown them.

"That's the Council of Colour sign," Grian whispered, looking over his shoulder to make sure no one was watching. "The entrance must be somewhere near here."

They waited until the next Loop, which brought a gaggle of day trippers, left and the platform had emptied again before Grian pulled on the fire hydrant, trying to remove it from the wall. But surprisingly it clicked and turned easily in his grasp. He rotated the small red tank sideways until he heard another click, then he leaned back with all his weight and a round door opened into a hidden tunnel.

The pair jumped in excitement, then took a cautious look around before scrambling through the opening and shutting the door behind them.

The same cobwebbed industrial strip lights they'd seen in the tunnel in Tallystick ran along the centre of this one too. Those not broken flickered enough light that Grian could just make out the arched concrete beams tracing the rounded ceiling. A railway line ran along in front of them, disappearing into the distance to their left and right. An old postal train sat abandoned on the tracks nearby. The train consisted of three rusted metal wagons, similar to the one the boys had crashed before.

"If we could somehow get Solas and the others into this tunnel," Grian said, "they could escape along it to the Turing Post Office stop – where we saw Vermilion. Come on, though, first we need to see if this track leads to the warehouse, like the map seems to show."

Using Bob's GPS to figure out which direction to head in, the pair raced along the postal line.

As they travelled, Bob's torch highlighted the cobwebs that hung like unwashed veils from the ceiling. Grian had to pull some of the sticky threads from his face. It seemed nobody had been along this part of the track in a very long time.

They'd been moving for about twenty minutes when they reached a dead end where a large dusty metal barrier spanned the width of the tracks in front of a rough clay wall.

Grian tried not to panic as he searched for a way through. This couldn't be a dead end – the tunnel had to lead them to Solas!

"Over here," Jeffrey whispered.

Grian spun around.

Jeffrey, almost blinded by Bob's torch, stood by a large metal map screwed to a strip of concrete embedded in the clay wall. The map looked just like the one they'd seen in the post office before, except this one showed three postal lines connected at a central spot, like the spokes of a bicycle wheel. A raised plaque in the top right-hand corner of the map read *Babbage Postal Routes – All Districts*.

"We're at the end of the Turing line, so we must be here." Grian pointed to the large dot that all three lines ran into – a small label above it read *Babbage Central Sorting Warehouse*. "Look, the Turing, Quantum and Hopper district lines all meet here. I've heard Dad talk about a huge sorting office before. They closed it when I was younger because nobody was using the post that much any more."

"I imagine an underground warehouse like that would be large enough to hold lots of people. Especially if they were in cages," Jeffrey replied. "If the Tilt isn't true, then Hansom didn't build the Tipping Point here for a geographical reason, like he said – but perhaps the storage facilities played a part in his decision!"

Grian shuddered as he walked towards an old iron lever that jutted out from the wall near the map.

"I wonder what this does," he said as he forced the lever into movement.

With each rotation a long metal chute, resembling a battered playground slide, clunked as it lowered down from the curved ceiling. It chugged to a stop just low enough for Grian to reach up and touch from his tippy toes.

"Look." He pointed to a hatch in the ceiling that the chute had come out from.

"I imagine they used to drop post down this chute to the trains waiting below – quite a quick and efficient method really," Jeffrey said, eyeing the contraption.

Grian scrambled onto his hands and knees, forming a bridge.

"If you stand on my back, Jeffrey, you should be able to reach the slide and climb up through the hatch."

He groaned, his arms buckling under the weight, as Jeffrey climbed awkwardly on to his back and struggled up onto the chute. The metal creaked as his friend inched up the slope until he reached the hatch and shimmied through.

Then Grian grabbed a large chunk of rock nearby and dragged it into place under the chute. The rock gave him just enough height to catch hold of the metal slide and wriggle up onto it. Once he was within reach, Jeffrey leaned down from the hatch above and grabbed his jumper, dragging Grian up through the opening until he was lying on his tummy on the floor of a tiny room.

Only when Grian flipped over onto his back did he notice thin blue lines criss-crossing the air above him.

"Don't move! Not a muscle," Jeffrey whispered urgently.

"What are they?" Grian hissed.

"Sophisticated lasers. They must be attached to a security system."

Grian's view was limited from his spot on the floor. But just past his feet was a metal door. It had to be the way out.

The room was lined with steel shelving. On the lower shelves were black rubber fingerless gloves with large cuffs, on the upper shelves were black rubber boots with thick block soles. Clear face visors hung from the ceiling and by the door was a tall shelving rack packed with what looked like thousands of small shiny black coins.

"It must be some sort of a storeroom," Grian mumbled to a strangely quiet Jeffrey.

"Perhaps the most advanced and technologically exciting storeroom I have ever laid witness to!" the other boy gasped. "Those gloves and boots are Hansom's latest policing technologies – 'for a powerful, peaceful force', according to *Cyber Monthly*'s most recent publication. Before that announcement there were really only rumours and whispers about this stuff, from other hackers.

"From what I know, when the wearer puts them on, the boots hover and the gloves can knock anything down using sound waves. The visors have facial and voice recognition and can tell if you are lying using sonic heartbeat sensors. The magazine said Hansom was only working on prototypes; however these appear to be much more advanced than that... But those," Jeffrey said, pointing out the small black coins on the rack, "they truly prove that Hansom is a genius. They're called hSwarms."

Grian held his breath as Jeffrey shimmied across the floor, almost hitting a low-lying laser beam in his eagerness to slip an hSwarm off its shelf.

"Watch this!" He smiled, placing the thing on his flat palm and rubbing it.

Suddenly the black coin morphed upwards into a tight ball before elongating until it looked exactly like a slug, then it changed to a beetle, a bee, an ant and he was pretty sure a maggot until it finally settled on a fly.

"What...what is it?" Grian shivered.

"It's an hSwarm," Jeffrey repeated as if his friend hadn't heard the first time. "They're made to replace insects and certain invertebrates."

"Why would Hansom make something like that?" Grian asked unsure he wanted to hear the answer. "Shelli won't be happy – she says we need insects!"

"Shelli is of course correct. Insects do a multitude of good work needed for our basic survival, but according to the world's most accomplished scientists, insects are dying all around us," Jeffrey said, sounding like a virtual encyclopaedia. "So, Hansom has invented these. They're much more efficient than the real thing – they won't bite, they are hypoallergenic, the bee mode even pollinates plants. And their very best feature means we won't be required to leave this room to see what's going on outside of it."

Grian stared, bewildered, as Jeffrey turned the tiny machine over and pressed his finger to a sensor on its black underbelly. Then he swiped his watch.

"Pairing," Betty, his Hansom, stated.

"I downloaded a beta testing application for the hSwarms a few months ago. It was released by Mushka, a supreme hacker. Watch this, I can make it move!"

Jeffrey placed the coin on the floor and it morphed into a beetle. Then he flicked his wrist and the hSwarm scuttled across to the door. With another subtle wrist movement, it changed into a worm and slithered out under the gap.

"Yes," Jeffrey gasped, looking at his Hansom, "we're in!"

Jeffrey shared his screen and Grian watched Bob in amazement as the cave wall, then the large metal arm, and finally the cages came into view.

"The hSwarm's flying and it's got a camera!" Grian whispered, astonished, as the hollow faces of those standing behind the cage bars whizzed past.

"That's only a tiny proportion of this object's capabilities." Jeffrey almost sounded boastful, as if he'd invented the thing himself. "They're more of a spy tool than a pollinator, if you ask me!"

The cage bars were coming up fast and one filled Bob's screen as the image suddenly jarred and blurred for a moment before returning to normal.

"Oops! Accidents are of course to be expected. It's the first time I've steered an hSwarm and trying to manoeuvre in between those cage bars is tricky," Jeffrey said. "Aha, there we go!"

Grian watched as the bug landed on someone's shoulder. He could see the side of a pale neck, then the lobe of an ear, and then he was staring down what he thought might be the translucent red tunnel of an ear canal.

Someone grunted and the camera shook, blurring the image again.

"Stop, stop," Jeffrey whispered. "Don't speak. Just think. We can hear what you think."

"What?" a computerized voice slipped quietly from Jeffrey's watch into the tiny room. "Who is this?"

"It is I, Jeffrey Slight, and your brother Grian."

"Is this a dream? Am I dreaming?" the computerized voice spoke again. "I was sure I was awake…"

"Is that Solas…? That thing can really hear what she's thinking?" Grian whispered in disbelief.

"Grian! I can hear you! Where are you? What's going on? Oh, maybe I'm totally flipping out now. I'm hearing voices in my head. Oh, please someone help. Someone get me out of this place—"

"We're aiming to do precisely that," Jeffrey interrupted.

"I must be dreaming...but why am I dreaming of Jeffrey Slight..."

"Solas, please stop! Control your thoughts or it's hard to make sense of what we're hearing. You're not going mad," Grian pleaded. "There's a small insect machine thing in your ear. Reach up and feel it."

The image wobbled a little as if something had touched the hSwarm.

"We're talking to you through that. It's listening to your thoughts."

"And converting their wave frequencies back into words," Jeffrey added.

The camera angle shifted, shaking a little again. Grian could see his sister's palm, the lines like crevasses up this close. Then the hairy black holes of her nostrils came into view, before finally the image steadied on two large brown irises flecked with hints of gold.

"Solas!" he whispered.

CHAPTER 32

THE HYPERLOOP

Solas stared in disbelief at the tiny creature in her hand before putting it back in her ear.

"How? What? I'm hungry! I'm scared! Is Grian really here?" Her jumbled thoughts fell over each other.

It seemed that listening to someone think wasn't as easy as listening to someone speak.

"We're going to get you out," Grian insisted.

"Get me out? Now? But how? The cages. The arm, the guards, they'll catch us..."

"Solas, pretend you're speaking out loud and your thoughts will be much more coherent," Jeffrey instructed.

"Ahem...out loud, but, like, in my head. What? I don't know, this is wei—"

"Stop thinking, Solas!" Grian ordered. "Just listen. We have a few questions."

Jeffrey jumped in. "We need to know exactly when the Hyperloop will take you away – if you have that information?"

"Okay – I think I have the hang of this... At night. A man in my cage has one of those old watches with hands. He says the Loop has left every night at twelve the last few days. They're slowly emptying out the whole prison down here. There are just enough of us left to probably fill one Hyperloop now, even with new volunteers arriving. It's my turn tonight, Grian – I'm sure of it..."

"We can't open the cages," Grian said quickly. "Is there another way to get you out?"

"Overpower the guards once they've opened the cages," Solas's thoughts interrupted him. "But how? No... it'd be too dangerous. Grian could get hurt!"

"How many Proctors, I mean guards, are there?" Grian asked, jumping on her thought.

"Not many," Solas answered. "Two, three maybe. People are scared of them because the guards have weird powers – so they don't need many of them to get us on the Loop."

As Grian looked at the shelves of equipment surrounding them, then back at Bob, an idea started taking shape.

"Can we take some of these boots and cuffs without

setting off alarms?" he asked Jeffrey.

Jeffrey looked uncertain.

"Take what?" Solas thought.

"I'm not talking to you, Solas," he whispered. "Look, we have to go now, but I promise we'll save you. Expect us tonight before the Hyperloop comes! Be ready to run."

"Solas, I'm going to leave the bug with you," Jeffrey added. "It'll enable us to fill you in on our plans. Use it if for any reason you need to contact us – I'll check in on the app during the day. But keep it hidden, please. Your position will be a lot more precarious if you're caught with an hSwarm!"

"Okay, thanks, Jeffrey," she responded. "And Grian… I love you."

Jeffrey switched off the hSwarm app and looked at his friend. Grian tried to hide his glassy eyes.

"A good cry is often necessary in testing times." Jeffrey sighed. "In fact, some psychologists even suggest we may be doing ourselves a disservice by not crying regularly."

"I'm not crying," Grian insisted. "You didn't answer me. Can we take some of these boots and cuffs without setting off the alarms? Can't you access the security network or something?"

"I'm afraid not," Jeffrey replied. "These are Hansom's latest and probably deadliest invention – nobody even knows the final products are in production and exist outside of a research lab. To be frank it's a little scary that they do, given what we're beginning to understand about Howard Hansom. Their security is bound to be controlled through Hansom's isolated network."

There was a clatter of metal in the tunnel below. Grian froze. Had somebody followed them?

"Hey, what are yous doing up there?" a voice hissed.

"Shelli?" Jeffrey whispered from his spot on the floor. "Aren't you meant to be locating Adler and Vermilion?"

Metal clanged below them again before Shelli's fiery red hair popped up through the opened hatch.

"Don't break the lasers!" Grian barked.

"Oh, right, sorry," she said, a frizzy curl stopping short of a thin blue line. "I tried to find your granda's and Vermilion's scent again but de same thing happened – both Nach and Fred led me back to de same spot in de exhibition centre and then wouldn't move. Maybe they didn't have a strong enough reading off Vermilion's letter, but that doesn't explain why your granda's smell always brings them to that spot. Anyway, Fred was sniffing de air and squeaking – it's normally a sign he's found something but there was nothing there again. Then an annoying girl spotted Fred and screamed, and we had to run. It's so weird how people don't like rats!"

"Have your animals ever stopped like that before?" Grian asked.

"No." Shelli shook her head in frustration. "I tried to direct their search then, make them go somewhere else but Nach and Fred weren't having any of it. I checked around de exhibition stands just in case, but I couldn't see anywhere your granda and Vermilion could be hidden. So, I tracked yous down instead. Is plan B is going any better?"

The two boys explained everything that had happened since leaving her that morning.

"And I think I have an idea – that is, if we can just get hold of some of those boots and gloves without setting off the alarms, but Jeffrey thinks it's impossible," Grian finished.

"Nothing is impossible, Grian. I meant it's merely improbable!"

Without warning Shelli disappeared back down into the tunnel below. Grian and Jeffrey were still arguing about whether or not they could take some of Hansom's equipment, when something grey and furry scurried into the room.

Grian stiffened as the large rat sniffed round the waist band of his trousers.

"Fred'll handle it," Shelli called up from below. "Just take what ya need, though not enough that anyone will notice, and let Fred take de blame for de alarm! People love to blame rats for everything. They can barely think of anything else once they've seen one! I promise they'll be so panicked they won't even question how he got in there – it's hilarious! And Fred can get out of any sticky situation so don't worry about him!"

Grian wasn't exactly worried about Fred and he didn't need to be told twice.

The alarms pierced the air as he jumped up, breaking the blue lasers, and grabbed a set of gloves and boots. Jeffrey grabbed a set too and had already gone out through the hatch when Grian spotted shrouds of black material hanging by the side of one of the shelves.

His heart skipped as he realized these must be the cloaks the Proctors wore. He unhooked two of them and followed his friend down the chute. Sharp pain coursed up his legs when he landed with a thud on the tunnel floor.

Shelli grunted, as she levered the metal chute back up, locking Fred inside the room.

"Run!" she hissed, and the three of them took off at lightning pace back along the derelict track.

CHAPTER 33

ℏTHOUGHTTECH

"Quite an ingenious idea, if a little unnerving, Shelli! I just hope Fred will be okay," Jeffrey rasped, bent over at the waist, when they eventually stopped running, at the hidden entrance to the exhibition centre Loop stop.

Grian had stopped a little way behind them and now he tried to hold in a snigger as he burst from the darkness, lunging towards his unsuspecting friends.

"Boo!" he cried.

"Argh," Shelli screamed, stumbling backwards. "A Proctor, a proctor!"

Grian burst out laughing as he threw back the large hood of the black cape he'd just put on.

"Your faces," he snorted. "My Proctor costume is

convincing, then – so my plan might work!"

"Oh my!" Jeffrey gasped. "Where did you find that?"

"In the storeroom." Grian smiled, pleased with himself.

"Oh – of course – now it all makes sense! The Proctors wear Hansom's boots, the cape hides the boots, and the Proctors appear as if they're floating on air," Jeffrey exclaimed. "Look at this!"

He searched his Hansom and then shared a video to Bob. Shelli peered over Grian's shoulder as they both watched the small screen.

Howard Hansom stood at the side of a glistening lake. It was a sunny day. He was wearing khaki shorts and a smart shirt – the black rubber gloves and boots covering his wrists and lower calves looked out of place.

"Man has always dreamed about walking on water," Hansom said as people snapped pictures wildly around him.

Then he flicked his wrist, kicked his ankles, and stepped out onto the lake. Grian and Shelli gasped in time with the small group as Howard Hansom walked across the water, leaving not even a ripple on the blue surface below him, before returning to dry land.

"But we can't all walk on water." The man winked at the camera. "Some of us have to walk through it."

Then Hansom flung his arms wide like a bird about to

take flight. To sounds of disbelief, the waters split apart, creating a passage through the middle of the lake. The camera kept rolling as the small group, full of nervous excitement, followed Hansom out onto the sandy lake bed, while towering walls of water gushed either side of them.

"But how and...why?" Shelli asked, confused, as the video stopped. "What could anyone want with something so powerful? Mother says only bad things come with too much power!"

"Hansom has tapped into the energy waves around us. These technologies enhance the human experience, they push boundaries. It's progress," Jeffrey answered. "If used in the right way, of course."

"In tracking, sometimes you make de best progress when you stop and turn round!" Shelli replied.

Grian ignored his friends' squabble as he continued to flesh out his idea.

"What if we were waiting in the warehouse when the Hyperloop arrives and we attack the Proctors after they've opened the cages but before everyone gets onboard? Then we take Solas and the rest of the volunteers down into the post tunnel and away from here..."

"Attack de Proctors?" Shelli raised her brows. "You're sounding braver than me now!"

"But if we practise with these gloves and boots, we'll be just as powerful as them, Shelli. They must be normal people under these hoods. I'm sure we could overpower them."

Still wearing his oversized cape, Grian shoved on a pair of gloves, tightening the straps so the large cuffs felt secure. Then he pulled on the boots and kicked his ankles just as Hansom had demonstrated in the video.

Nothing happened.

"You need the neuro link," Jeffrey stated, walking forward and pressing a small button in the side of his friend's boots.

The button fell out onto Jeffrey's palm and he reached up and pushed the tiny round object onto Grian's temple where it stuck as if glued to his skin.

"Weird." Grian shivered as he reached up and felt the button like a mole popping out from his forehead.

"And you'll need the app," Jeffrey smiled proudly pulling out his hTablet. "You can only download it if you remove permissions for a few security settings on your Hansom, which invariably takes quite a while. Then you must have Mushka's hacker clearance. Supreme hackers like Mushka don't impart their secrets to everyone!"

"But they do to you, I suppose?" Grian sighed.

"Exactly!" Jeffrey beamed, strapping his own watch to his friend's wrist. "Of course, I can arrange it all on Bob, but for the present moment use Betty. Now concentrate on what you want to happen!"

Grian concentrated on his feet, willing the boots to move...and suddenly he wobbled upwards. He grabbed the wall beside him, afraid he'd fall over, and tightened all his muscles in an effort to balance. Then, using his free hand, Grian pulled the hood over his head, let go of the wall and weaved a crooked path through the air towards his friends.

"What do I look like?" he asked.

"A Proctor who's taken a rather serious knock to the head," Jeffrey answered.

"Another joke, Jeffrey?" Grian teased, pushing off the hood. "But with a little practice I think we could pass for the real thing."

"Well, he can move, but how does he fight off de Proctors?" Shelli asked Jeffrey.

"With force. Just concentrate on moving that train, Grian, then push the air." Jeffrey nodded at the postal carriage resting on the tracks near them.

Grian eyed the three rusted wagons and thought about moving them. Then he flung his arms forward. The line of metal buckets rattled a little on the tracks.

He jumped in excitement as Nach dived behind Shelli's back, growling.

Grian concentrated harder, imagining he was forcing the air around him forward to create a great big gust. The train moved further down the tracks.

"Genius!" Jeffrey beamed. "The policing gloves and boots are part of Hansom's new range of hThoughtTech -- just like the hSwarm. This technology can read your brainwaves and harness the energy around you to do exactly what you want – as Grian has demonstrated. Theoretically we should be able to move anything – our only limits are our imaginations!"

Shelli shuddered.

"What if we put the volunteers on this train and use the gloves to shove them down the tracks as fast and far away as possible, once they're in the tunnel? We could try to get them to Turing Post Office so they can escape up to the outside from there," Grian said, growing excited.

"Good thinking. We'll need to get them out as fast as we can once Hansom is aware of the escape. But how will we access the warehouse in the first place?" Jeffrey asked. "If we go through the storeroom, we'll alert security by breaking the lasers and most probably have a lot more than three Proctors to ward off…"

"So technology has found its limit…" Shelli smiled. "Well, what if nature hasn't? Me and my friends could cause a stir bigger than anything yous can imagine. It'll be so big Hansom won't even notice there's a problem in his storeroom!"

Grian and Jeffrey nodded, impressed, as Shelli filled them in on her idea.

"So we're agreed? Once we get everyone down the chute and in the postal tunnel, we take them to Turing Post Office. But where will they go after that?" Grian asked. "Hansom will be looking for us, so we need somewhere safe…"

"What about de Wilde forest? Mother won't mind, and everyone will be safe there until we figure out what to do next," Shelli answered.

"Perfect." Grian smiled.

While Grian and Shelli went over the plans again, looking for any holes, Jeffrey downloaded the hThoughtTech app and programmed Bob so Grian could use it to control the gloves and boots. He wore a proud, wide smile when he told Grian he'd also hidden the app within a dummy one, so no one else could see or access it.

It was agreed that, at eleven that night, Jeffrey and Grian would sneak into the postal railway line and put on the gloves, boots and cloaks that they'd leave hidden there. Then, disguised as Proctors, they'd wait under the storeroom until 11.50 p.m., when Shelli and her friends would cause a fuss in the Tipping Point.

Grian and Jeffrey would then break into the warehouse via the storeroom, wait until the Proctors had opened the cages, and then attack, before herding everyone into the postal tunnel where Shelli would meet them. There they'd pack as many volunteers as they could onto the old train and push them down the line as far as possible, before pulling the train back and sending more people out. They would all then escape via Turing Post Office to the Wilde forest.

After they'd worked everything out, they filled Solas in on their plans, via the hSwarm, then Grian and Jeffrey practised with the gloves and boots until they were able to push and pull the train up and down the track.

Finally, exhausted, they moved the rusted train into place, as close as they could to the chute.

"So I think we have a plan!" Jeffrey smiled, high-fiving his friends as they set off for the hotel.

"But what about your granda and Vermilion?" Shelli asked Grian.

"We'll save Solas and the others first, then worry about that. Hansom needs Grandad – I don't think he will hurt him."

Grian's niggling feelings had eased a bit. He convinced himself they had a good plan – they would save his sister.

All he had to do then was save his grandad. He didn't tell the others he intended to do that alone, once he was sure his sister and his friends were safe.

CHAPTER 34

WISE WORDS

Grian checked in with Bob as they entered their large suite in the hotel – it was twenty past five already. They only had forty minutes until whatever "celebration" Hansom had planned for them. He started to feel a little anxious about it.

"Hello." The holographic hButler appeared on their arrival. "A virtual closet has been set up for you, Jeffrey and Grian. Please look in the mirror and choose your outfit for tonight's celebrations!"

A little confused, Jeffrey stepped in front of the mirrored wardrobe as instructed. All of a sudden his reflection was wearing a smart suit with a cool blue blazer, which then changed to white trousers and a pink shirt.

They all laughed when his mirror image donned a bright yellow pinstriped trouser suit. Jeffrey chose the smart suit and then stepped aside for Grian, who didn't think long before choosing a shirt and jeans – he wasn't fussy.

"Those outfits will be delivered to you shortly. Enjoy what promises to be a magnificent evening." The hButler smiled before disappearing.

"I take it I don't get a choice because I'm a shadow." Shelli grimaced at the sparkling black dress laid out on the bed behind them. "I've never worn a dress in my life!"

She pinched the material up in two fingers, before dropping it back down in disgust.

"Mother always dressed me up in numerous smart outfits when I was a young boy and posted loads of pictures online." Jeffrey smiled, smoothing down his jacket, which had just arrived. "But then she grew bored of me."

"That's not true," Shelli said, throwing the dress over her head. "Your mam's just busy, Jeffrey. People in towns are always busy."

"Oh no, it is true, Father told me so. Mother grows bored easily. But I don't mind," Jeffrey insisted, admiring himself in the mirror. "Children must grow up at some point and be independent – at least that's what Father says."

"Oh." Grian felt guilty as he pulled on his jeans. "Well

maybe you can come to my house and hang out when we get home...so you're not alone as much."

"Why, thank you, Grian – that's remarkably kind." Jeffrey beamed. "I'd quite like that."

Shelli walked out of the bathroom, her sparkling dress tucked in so it gathered in a ball at the waist of her trousers.

"I don't think that's how you wear a dress!" Grian joked.

"Well, I don't care how they're meant to be worn, I'll wear it my way! Anyway, I didn't like de cold on my legs, so I put my trousers back on," she huffed.

"Trousers are a practical solution to that problem, I imagine," Jeffrey said, just as there was a knock on their door and Howard Hansom walked inside.

Grian shivered, but not with the cold.

Hansom was dressed in a smart jacket and trousers that stopped short of his ankles. He wasn't wearing any socks with his slip-on shoes.

"Well don't you all look lovely." He smiled, his eyes stopping for a second on Shelli's improvised outfit before moving on. "The world will toast you tonight!"

"The world? What do you mean?" Grian asked, trying not to sound concerned.

"Well, you've saved the Tipping Point and *PEOPLEPOWER* – so you've really saved the world, and my PR team have let everyone know about it. Tonight we will celebrate! Solas is a little delayed getting ready, because she helped with the whole surprise." He smiled. "But she'll be joining us later."

Grian fumed as he thought of his sister locked in a cage underneath the smart city while this man lied to his face. He tried to act natural as Hansom led them down the hall to the lift. Other guests on the same floor stood at their opened doors and clapped as they passed by. What was going on?

Grian blushed and looked at the floor, avoiding eye contact. Shelli was awkward too, while Jeffrey smiled and nodded at everyone, even shaking a few hands.

When the lift doors pinged open in the foyer of the hotel, the place erupted in applause. The atmosphere was frantic, and lights flashed from all angles, blinding Grian as people behind large cameras called his name. He tried to smile while answering questions about the Proctor attack and what it felt like to stop the "deadliest man in Babbage".

Shelli and Jeffrey were nearby but it was hard to see them as they too were surrounded by hordes of people.

After a few minutes of answering press questions, Hansom swept the three children towards the hotel's five star restaurant. Grian glanced up at the large TV hanging over the reception desk as he passed and gasped as he saw images of himself, Jeffrey and Shelli on the Babbage main evening news.

Bob immediately started to ping with messages of congratulations. Hansom was right, it seemed everyone was toasting them right now, at a time when all Grian wanted to do was disappear and get on with saving his sister.

The chef and waiting staff stood in a line to welcome their guests and Grian ate more than he imagined he had in his whole lifetime before they were led back through the foyer and outside.

Howard Hansom smiled and hugged each of them in front of more cameras before they climbed into a huge black convertible hovering smart car – it was unlike anything Grian had ever seen. Jeffrey was mesmerized as the driver told them to sit on the back seats. Hansom climbed between them, shouting things into the crowd like "These guys are real superheroes!"

Then the car paraded at snail's pace through the streets of the Tipping Point as people lined the roads three and four deep, screaming and waving *PEOPLEPOWER* flags while chanting their names.

Grian was overwhelmed and grabbed Shelli and Jeffrey's hands, squeezing them tight.

"We sent a press release far and wide stating real-life superheroes saved the Tipping Point and the story went viral. Everyone was desperate to see the heroes revealed tonight. We've even opened the city to the general public for one night only so we could have a huge crowd here to celebrate with us. It's going to be spectacular! Listen to them shouting. All of Babbage loves you!" Hansom exclaimed.

Grian shivered as the man smiled straight at him. Did Hansom know something was up?

Every few minutes the car stopped for autographs until, after what felt like hours and Grian's wrist was sore – he thought his hand might fall off from overuse – they pulled up to the exhibition centre and climbed out onto a plush red carpet. Cameras flashed like lightning round them as people screamed their names. Howard Hansom led the way up the steps, stopping to pose for every lens that turned in his direction.

Grian's heart pounded. They needed to rescue Solas, but how were they ever going to sneak away with the whole world watching?

His composure wobbled and he stopped for a minute as he reached the top of the steps. More crowds lined both sides of the red carpet that wound on through the large open double doors into the auditorium. Grian took a deep breath and avoided all eye contact as he walked forward into the huge space and up onto a newly constructed stage which rested just beneath the massive

PEOPLEPOWER globe suspended from the ceiling. For the first time he noticed a pattern of small hairline cracks tracing the surface of the enormous sphere. A memory bubbled up then washed away diluted in the chaos around him.

Beside him on the stage Hansom was fiddling with the same small toy globe he'd had in the hotel lobby earlier that morning. He caught Grian looking at it.

"Puzzles are a tuning fork for the mind!" The tall man smiled before stepping forward to the microphone.

Grian startled. He'd heard that saying before, from his grandfather. Every time he solved a puzzle box, Grandad would smile and say, "Puzzles are a tuning fork for the mind, Grian." He'd asked him once what the saying meant, but all his grandad told him was that it was something an old friend used to say.

"Thank you – thank you one and all for coming, and a very special thank you to these three heroes, without whom I literally wouldn't be here." Hansom smiled, turning towards Grian, Shelli and Jeffrey.

Grian felt hot and sticky as he swallowed a large lump in his desert-dry throat. He zoned in and out of Hansom's speech, trying to concentrate on their plans as he constantly checked Bob. Time was ticking.

"...but you three have selflessly saved our people and our planet," Hansom said, turning to look each of them square in the eyes. "Children really are our future!"

Then the man beckoned the three friends forward to the front of the stage and stood right behind them like a proud father as the room erupted.

Excited cries filled the space as people jumped around as though celebrating the World Cup or something. Grian felt removed from it all, as if somehow he was watching a film and not standing right there. All these people believed in Hansom's lies, while under their feet his sister and other innocent volunteers, who had all believed in the man too, were imprisoned in cages.

Grian shuffled from foot to foot, his nerves moving him to an invisible beat, when a small blue ball rolled against the side of his polished shoe. It looked exactly like the globe of the world Hansom had just been playing with – had he dropped it?

Curious, Grian bent down and picked up the sphere.

Puzzles are a tuning fork for the mind. The saying rattled round his head.

He shivered as goosebumps pimpled his skin. Was Hansom trying to tell him something?

CHAPTER 35

IN LUCK

After his speech, Howard Hansom mingled with the adoring crowd as the room filled with waiting staff, expertly carrying large plates of tiny food.

Grian avoided questions from the strangers who crowded round him as he hounded Hansom with his eyes.

"Stop!" Shelli whispered over her shoulder. "You're staring at him!"

"It's just…something feels off…" He shook his head.

"What?" she asked.

"I don't know – it's probably nothing. Just a feeling."

"Mother says gut feelings are everything, Grian. Listen to them," his friend whispered.

"Me and Jeffrey have to go. It's after eleven," he said, checking Bob. "Remember, you've to cause a stir. But make sure it's after the Proctors open the cages. We'll be waiting. Meet you in the railway tunnel after!"

"I've Fred on the case, he'll tell me when de cages are open. Just trust me," Shelli assured.

"I do," he said, before leaving to grab Jeffrey, who was stalking a stacked snack tray.

"We need to go now," Grian whispered. "Come on." The two boys tried to cut discreetly through the crowds, towards the Hyperloop station entrance.

In his urgency, Grian collided with a waiter, who stumbled into an elderly couple. The small woman squealed in fright and was about to cause a scene when a cheer erupted in the middle of the huge room. The crowd stood mesmerized while a flock of birds danced in sync through the auditorium, just as they had done the day the three friends arrived in the Tipping Point.

Shelli caught his eye and winked as he darted unnoticed into the mirrored hallway that led down to the Loop station, followed by Jeffrey.

The platform was empty and silent, only the gentle whistle of a breeze whispered round them. Grian tried to ignore the thousands of volunteers' faces smiling enthusiastically from their wall tiles.

He looked at Bob – it was almost half eleven. The

Hyperloop could already be in the warehouse, waiting to take his sister away.

Grian raced to the fire hydrant and unlocked the secret door, before climbing into the derelict postal line. Jeffrey clambered in after him, closing the door behind them. They both got dressed into their long black capes, and fastened tight their gloves and boots, then hovered as fast as possible up the track to the end of the line, where they were to wait for Shelli's signal.

Grian paced back and forth across the space, while Jeffrey lowered down the old postal chute. When he glanced up it, Grian could see the blue laser lines cut through the air in the room above.

He looked at Bob as the bottom of his cape swished round his feet. It was almost time.

Then he jumped as a tiny squeal broke the silence. It was followed by squeaks and rustles, until the tunnel was filled with strange sounds.

Something tugged at Grian's cloak, and he flashed Bob's light downwards. The dark pinhead eyes of a small rat stared up at him. Startled, Grian jumped back and, unused to his hover boots, collided painfully with the wall, where another creature was just burrowing out of the dirt.

Holes now appeared like pockmarks all over the walls, as creatures great and small dug their way into the old railway tunnel. A sea of insects also streamed from the floor, walls and ceiling, shimmering like snakeskin under the glare of Bob's torchlight.

"Shelli and her creature friends certainly know how to invade a city in style. If it's like this down here, imagine what the rest of the Tipping Point is experiencing right now. Hansom's security team won't know where to look!" Jeffrey smiled.

Grian was watching the blue lasers through the hatch above when suddenly alarm bells screeched around him. He covered his ears as the penetrating sound clattered off the walls.

"You're right. Shelli definitely knows how to cause a distraction," he shouted above the noise. "Let's go!"

Quickly he hovered up the metal chute, brushing all kinds of creatures out of his way as he struggled into the storeroom above. Barely able to hear himself think, he closed his eyes and concentrated on the steel door in front of him. His wrists tingled, then the feeling slipped into his palms until his fingers were on fire. He could feel the energy gathering round his hands as he forced them forward through the air, crying out with an anger he didn't know he owned.

Grian blinked in shock as the heavy metal door flew from its hinges, right across the warehouse, as though featherlight. It crashed into the far cement wall.

He steadied his shallow breathing and stepped out into the huge warehouse, a black-cloaked Jeffrey at his side.

The Hyperloop was sitting in the middle of the track between the cages, under the glare of the fluorescent lighting. Its doors were opening and closing to an erratic rhythm, as all sorts of animals rushed in and out of the stark white interior.

All around them the walls appeared to move in glistening waves of insects, while rats, rabbits, hares, badgers, foxes and moles pulled on the cloaks of two Proctors, who were herding terrified volunteers towards the Loop.

Sweat raced down Grian's brow and he wiped it away before it stung his eyes. He was finding it hard to breathe under the weight of the huge black cloak.

He moved past the cages – all now empty.

The Proctors had their backs to him, but he could see the petrified faces of some volunteers who tried to resist, only to be pushed forward by a powerful, invisible force.

Grian looked at Jeffrey and nodded, before concentrating on his gloves once more. His wrists tingled again, and the power grew faster this time. A roar burst from somewhere deep inside him, a surge of energy blasting from his gloves and crashing against the nearest Proctor.

The man screamed as he was propelled forwards,

landing with a sharp crack against the Hyperloop before collapsing to the floor.

"That was spectacular, Grian!" Jeffrey exclaimed, his hood sliding off in his excitement.

Grian was about to respond when a huge weight rammed into his chest. His breath was stolen as he was hurled backwards, hitting the warehouse wall with a thump.

"Grian!" Solas shrieked, breaking away from the group of volunteers.

He struggled onto his knees, gasping for air, as in a haze he watched his sister pound and pull at the remaining Proctor like a wild animal. Jeffrey was beside Solas now, his arms outstretched as he pinned the Proctor to the floor with his invisible power. But the Proctor was fighting back.

Grian had to do something. He winced as he pulled himself up, barely able to stand.

The Proctor was upright now, Jeffrey almost overpowered.

Grian concentrated on his boots and willed them to fly him across the space. He knocked into the Proctor, who faltered, their hood slipping off. A small, blonde woman glared at him, her blue eyes brutal in her vicious face.

The split-second allowed Jeffrey to regain control, then Grian joined his friend and together they shoved the woman backwards and into one of the cages.

"Take off her boots and gloves," Grian cried, holding her in a corner.

Some of the prisoners raced inside and removed the woman's equipment, flinging it out through the bars.

Solas and a few others ran to the second Proctor and stripped him of his gloves and boots too, before carrying him into the cage. Then they closed the hLocks, imprisoning both Proctors.

"Follow me," Jeffrey ordered, without wasting a moment.

As alarms continued to blare all around them, Jeffrey led the way into the storeroom and slid down the chute into the tunnel below. Grian and Solas stayed in the room above, guiding the weary volunteers to the metal slide as fast as possible.

There were fewer volunteers than he'd imagined.

"Where is everyone?" Grian asked his sister as they followed the last people down into the tunnel.

"They sent an earlier Hyperloop – I thought I'd be gone before you came but they left some of us behind." His sister trembled. "I couldn't contact you because one of the Proctors somehow found the insect thing you gave me! I was so scared – I thought I'd never see you again! But I got lucky…"

A shiver slithered up his spine and goosepimples mottled his skin once more. They'd found the hSwarm and Solas didn't get in trouble? This time Grian was sure his sinking feeling was real. His sister hadn't got lucky. Hansom knew.

CHAPTER 36

THE ZEUS BOX

"I believe this is yours," Jeffrey said as Solas and Grian landed down in the tunnel beside him. In his opened palm was Solas's pink Hansom watch. Grian's sister shook her head and pushed his hand back.

"I can't," she whispered. "I don't ever want anything to do with Howard Hansom again."

"Understandable of course." Jeffrey nodded as he put the watch back in his pocket before calling the volunteers to gather round the rusted postal train so he could explain the rest of the plan.

"We will load this train with as many of you as possible and I'll propel it forward as fast as I can down the tracks until we get to the Turing district maintenance line, it's just off the main track. You'll wait on the platform there while I come back and fill the train again. When we're all on the platform, we'll venture above ground. Then Shelli, our friend, will guide us to the Wilde forest, where we'll be safe."

Grian checked his watch again. Where was Shelli?

"I'm not following anyone into a Wilde forest, those people can't be trusted!" a woman said, holding tight to her young son.

"You are free because of Shelli. She's Wilde and has been helping you already!" Grian snapped.

He shook with anger as the words tumbled out.

The woman blushed and fell silent. It never bothered him before when people were mean about the Wilde, but now – well, now he knew Shelli.

As the volunteers crammed into the postal train, Grian fidgeted with the globe he'd found onstage in the auditorium and watched the tunnel anxiously for signs of Shelli.

"That's the Zeus puzzle!" Solas interrupted his thoughts, grabbing the globe from him. "It's Grandad's favourite. Where did you get it?"

"What did you say?" He stared at his sister.

"The Zeus puzzle box. Remember, the king of all puzzles? Grandad used to play it with us all the time! He locked sweets inside the secret chamber, and we had to get them out!"

All the loose ends and niggling feelings suddenly fit together. Nach and Fred had stopped under the huge globe in the exhibition centre. Shelli had said it was as if his grandad's scent had disappeared into thin air. His grandad said the room he was in somehow reminded him of the puzzles they played. Could he and Vermilion really be there, right above their heads – trapped in the most public place in the Tipping Point?

Now he was sure Hansom *had* given him a clue – but why?

"I have to go!" Grian said, grabbing his sister's hand. "I have to find Shelli – she's meant to be here, and I think...I think I know where Grandad is! Don't wait for me when you get to Turing. If Shelli doesn't turn up, go straight to the forest. Jeffrey will remember the way. He's the smartest person I know!"

"But...but...I'm coming with you," his sister stammered.

"No," Grian shook his head, "someone needs to stay here with the rest of the volunteers."

Before his sister could say anything else, Grian hovered back up the chute and into the storeroom above. He raced to the rack of shelving where the hSwarms were kept and grabbed a few before sliding back down.

"Here," he panted, handing one of the black coins to Solas and pocketing the rest. "If there's any trouble, let Jeffrey know via the hSwarm."

"Did someone mention my name…" Jeffrey said, interrupting the pair.

Grian explained why he needed to go. How he was worried about Shelli and thought he knew where Grandad might be.

"You can trust us to handle everything this end, Grian – just find Shelli and Adler," Jeffrey said as he paired the hSwarm with his watch.

"Okay." Solas nodded agreement before Jeffrey headed back to stand behind the crammed postal train, the volunteers waiting anxiously onboard.

Grian was almost unable to watch as his friend bowed his head in concentration.

"Brace yourselves," Jeffrey called.

The train rattled and some of the volunteers squealed. Then it shook again as if in anticipation before he flung his hands forward and the rusted wagon catapulted down the tunnel, to a soundtrack of screams.

Then Jeffrey turned and looked at Grian.

"You can do this, my friend – think of everything we've accomplished so far." He smiled before zipping into the distant darkness after the train.

Grian turned and looked at his sister. Solas's lip quivered as she threw her arms around her brother before stepping back and wiping her tears.

He half smiled, trying to hide his own nerves. Then Grian nodded and without a word disappeared through the secret door into the exhibition centre stop.

The noise on the platform was overwhelming. Piercing alarms mixed with the screams and roars of people in smart suits and sparkling dresses who were only moments before celebrating in the Exhibition Centre. Hordes of animals and insects clung to their clothes or played with their hair as they waited for the Hyperloop to take them home.

Grian sped up the stairs, ignoring the mayhem, the small plastic globe firm in his grasp.

The exhibition pavilion was dark and almost empty of people. Shelli's animals had taken over. Flocks of birds soared under the glass ceiling, armies of insects crawled the walls and a mass of different furry creatures scratched and pulled at the neon-blue *PEOPLEPOWER* carpet.

Grian stopped under the enormous suspended globe and hovered up to study the series of thin lines that criss-crossed its surface.

Could it really be a puzzle too?

He looked at the smaller globe in his hand and pushed on the piece he'd worked out might be the first one. It shifted a little, breaking the sphere, though not coming fully loose. He fiddled with it again until the small piece fell out into his hand.

Grian gasped at a sound of shifting from the larger globe above him. He zipped backwards just in time to avoid a large section of the suspended globe hitting him as it fell to the floor, landing with a soft thud on the carpet below.

The globe in his hand was somehow linked to the one above the auditorium! If he solved the smaller one, he'd solve the bigger. He couldn't deny Hansom was a technical genius, though a pretty twisted one.

Bob's torchlight reflected off the corner of a clear glass box that the missing piece had just revealed. Grian's stomach did a flip – he could make out his grandad and Vermilion inside.

Grandad was shouting something, but he couldn't hear him. The clear box seemed to be soundproof. Grian concentrated on his boots and hovered over to the corner. His grandad's face loomed forward out of the darkness as he pressed his nose to the glass.

Grian held the puzzle close enough for his grandfather to see it and pointed individually to all remaining pieces until the old man nodded at one.

Grian tried to move it, but the piece wouldn't release. It wasn't the right one. His grandad shook his head while Grian stared down at the puzzle. He took a deep breath. He could do this on his own. After all, he had once called himself Puzzle Boy.

Grian turned the sphere over and over, handling the object until he felt something give.

He cajoled the moving piece until it fell out into his grasp, the larger piece tumbling to the auditorium floor directly after its twin. His confidence grew and it wasn't long before the whole sphere had fallen away, leaving Grian with a small plastic box in his hand.

He'd been concentrating so hard on the puzzle that he hadn't looked up. Now as he did, Grian couldn't help but smile at the sheer pride on his grandfather's face as he stood, thumbs up, inside a glass box suspended high in the Tipping Point exhibition centre.

Grian hovered at lightning speed over to a door in the side of the large glass box and tried the handle. It was locked. A sensor rested just off the door frame – he needed to find a key.

His grandad was now pointing frantically at the smaller box in Grian's hand. He shook it and something rattled inside. There was no obvious way to open it – it appeared to be another puzzle.

Grian ran his fingers across the six faces of the box, even blowing on a few in case a pattern emerged from his foggy breath, as had happened with a puzzle that had taken him ages to solve before. Then he held the object to his ear, pushing very gently on each side until he heard a click – it was a trick Grandad had taught him. One of the sides locked in place, leaving a slight dip in the cube. Holding his breath he fiddled until another side moved downwards into the space left behind by its neighbour, before falling into Grian's hand.

The box was open!

He turned it upside down and a tiny rectangular chip fell out onto his palm. Grian's heart thumped as he waved the chip over the sensor. There was a faint click before the door slid open.

CHAPTER 37

SHELLI

"Oh, Grian," his grandfather cried, wrapping him in a huge hug as he pulled him inside the suspended box. "I knew you'd find us. I'm so proud of you for solving that puzzle! It's not easy under this pressure. Hansom is completely out of control. Hanging us from the ceiling like this is almost theatrical!"

Vermilion stood in the far corner, scowling as he watched the pair embrace.

"We saved Solas and some of the others," Grian said, filling his grandad in as the room spun below them. "They are on their way to Turing with Jeffrey. We're meeting them in the Wilde forest."

"They?" Vermilion asked. "How many are free?"

"Not many," Grian sighed. "Another Hyperloop came earlier than Solas expected. Most volunteers were taken on that. Solas thought she'd be taken too, but they left her and some others behind. I think that—"

"We have to get into Hansom's computer!" Vermilion interrupted. "We need to get whatever we can from his system before we leave – we might never have another chance like this! Now bring me down!" He grabbed Grian around the waist and shoved him out the door.

Grian cried out as the pair spiralled in free fall, before the Hansom hover boots adjusted to the extra weight and he was able to manoeuvre them both safely to the ground.

"Hurry! Get your grandfather," Vermilion ordered, before cutting across the auditorium.

Grian rescued his grandad and the pair raced after Vermilion, through the souvenir shop into the back office where they'd first met Howard Hansom. Vermilion dashed into an elevator hidden in the back wall, Grandad and Grian barely slipping inside after him before the lift doors pinged shut.

Vermilion placed a small square chip on the wall sensor and the lift shot downwards.

"How did you do that?" Grian questioned.

"It's the access key I told you about!" Vermilion growled.

The lift doors opened. Vermilion grabbed a hoverboard

from the docking station and sped off through a series of white corridors. Grian helped Grandad to work his board and the pair wobbled behind the other man the whole way to Howard Hansom Headquarters.

The place was dark and deserted as they crept across the black marble floor, past the cocoon-like hPods and behind the glass wall into Hansom's private office.

Grian was nervous. Something felt off.

Vermilion hurried round the large desk and opened Hansom's computer. He seemed very familiar with the place. The glass wall lit up.

Welcome, Howard the screen read.

Vermilion began to swipe through files.

"I think Hansom is on to us! We need to go now..." Grian whispered, desperate to leave.

Grandad gripped his grandson's shoulders and was about to reply, when the large glass screen wall in front of them changed to grainy security camera footage.

"What's going on?" Vermilion spat.

The footage looked to be from a camera high in the ceiling of the underground warehouse where Solas and the others had been held prisoner. Grian could see the two Proctors still in the cage and the Hyperloop waiting empty on the tracks. He could hear a weird shrill cry too, almost like a baby.

"Nach!" he gasped.

On screen, Shelli's fox raced in frantic circles, arching her head back and howling skywards.

Directly above the fox was the large metal arm that Grian had seen pick up and drop the woman volunteer earlier. The thing was stretched far across the middle of the huge space, and there was a figure slumped and unmoving in its mechanical grip.

"Shelli!" Grian cried.

"It's okay…it's okay," his grandad whispered, holding him tight as he turned him away from the screen.

Vermilion banged the computer with rage. "He's on to us! You children have ruined everything! We have to get out of here now, Adler."

"What? No!" Grandad replied. "Not without that girl. We have to save her, Vermilion!"

"Think of the bigger picture, Adler," the man snapped, racing over and grabbing Grian's grandad. "Do you want to save that girl or save our sun, which all life depends on? Hansom needs you – he thinks you have a connection to the White Rose and we have to figure out what that is. You're too valuable now!"

"What are you doing?" Grandad cried, struggling against Vermilion as he dragged him out the office door.

Grian tried to activate his gloves, when a huge crash shook the room. The floor beneath him moved, just as it had on the day of the earthquake, and he was knocked sideways.

Hansom's awards clanged and clattered, hitting the floor all around him as the glass wall split and shattered. He scrambled up just before the white leather chair collided with his head, as it flew across the room like a toy. Through the broken glass screen, he could see Vermilion shoving his grandad across the black marble floor.

"Leave Grandad alone!" Grian roared, racing out after them.

He closed his eyes and concentrated. First his wrists tingled, then the skin on the back of his hands came alive until he could feel the power rubbing his palms. He threw his hands out. This time he could almost see the huge surge of air engulf Vermilion, knocking him over like wild sea waves. The man crumpled to the ground, stunned as he hit his head off the cold black floor.

Grian sprinted forwards, grabbing the access key, which had fallen from Vermilion's hand, as he passed.

"Grandad, we need to save Shelli," he panted as he raced to the door that led out towards the warehouse. "I know the way!"

He stopped before placing the access key on the door sensor.

"I think it's a trap though," he wheezed.

"A trap how?" his grandfather asked.

"I'm not sure exactly – but I think Hansom is setting us up – I think he has been all along!"

"If that's true then there's something I have to give you now." His grandad reached inside his jacket and ripped away some of the lining to pull out a small cream drawstring bag. "I'm trusting you with this, Grian – you must hide it well and promise to tell no one. And I have a plan – this is what we must do…"

CHAPTER 38

DEAR ADLER

Grian shook his head as his grandfather finished speaking. He couldn't let him do what he was planning to, could he?

"Grandad, there has to be another way. Just leave here, please – I can save Shelli myself," Grian begged, as they stopped at the top of the stairwell that wound down to the warehouse. "Hansom could have hurt me any time in these past few days, and he didn't, so I'm sure he won't now."

"I'm not leaving you alone. What kind of a grandfather would I be? We're a team, you and me – remember all those puzzles we solved together over the years. We'll solve this one too – now hand it over."

As dust fell like snow around them and tiny bits of ceiling ricocheted off the metal steps, Grian took the small black coin from his pocket and placed it in his grandad's wizened palm.

"I shouldn't have told you about these," he trembled.

He had tears in his eyes. Grandad grabbed him squarely on the shoulders with a force that startled Grian.

"No matter what happens down here, you stick with our plan! Get your friend and get out. Find Yarrow, the head of the Council of Colour, and tell her everything. It's the only way." His grandfather's voice broke.

Grian nodded, unable to speak.

"You're the bravest boy I've ever known – you've even made friends again, good friends, and that was fearless. I am so proud of you, Grian!"

Then his grandad headed down the steps and walked straight out into the warehouse. Grian took a deep breath before following behind.

Everything was shaking. The Hyperloop rattled on the track in front of them. Grian shivered as cracks raced through the tall cement walls and huge chunks fell from the ceiling above them. Some of the debris whacked off the Hyperloop, while more deflected off the thick steel arm above, barely missing Shelli, who was still unconscious in its mechanical grasp.

"What took you so long?" a voice boomed.

Grian squinted through the dust and falling dirt as a figure stepped out of the empty Loop.

"I wasn't sure you'd come for one of the Wilde, Adler!" Howard Hansom laughed. He too was wearing hThoughtTech black rubber boots and gloves.

"What is this madness, Hansom?" Grian's grandad replied. "Just let the girl go home. What do you want her for now? Can't you see your city is collapsing? Whatever you're planning is turning to ruins!"

"Home?" Hansom laughed again as the ceiling rained down around him. "Soon she won't have a home to go to – none of you will! And all this destruction, Adler, it's all part of the plan. The Tipping Point was only the beginning of the end, and what a glorious beginning it was! You and those interfering children and that ridiculous Council of Colour, you'll all be blamed for this, you realize? They'll blame you for destroying me and the Tipping Point – the only hope our poor world had of survival. You've played right into my plans."

"What are you talking about, Howard? This is insanity!" Grandad replied, a slight quiver in his voice.

"Soon you, your grandson and his friends will be the most wanted people in Babbage. And when the media link you all back to the Council of Colour – and I guarantee you, they will – that organization will finally be destroyed! Everyone will be too distracted with finding you all to

339

even notice they're sleepwalking to their own destruction. Smoke and mirrors, Adler, smoke and mirrors."

"People are waking up to your lies, Howard – you'll be caught. Just give up now and stop this deadly game," Grandad fumed.

"Nonsense! People really are stupid, Adler – haven't you realized that by now? Especially children. You don't need to look further than your grandson and his friends. Grian, you fell hook, line and sinker for everything I fed you. Didn't you think your freedom here was a little strange? Did you really believe that idiot Jeffrey could outsmart my systems? I led you here and allowed you to uncover the darkest parts of this smart city. Bob is a good friend of mine, incognito mode or not – it likes to share everything you do with me!

"And I had such fun playing the game, especially that PEOPLEPOWER puzzle. Anyone else would have just locked you and Vermilion in a boring room, Adler, but where's the mastery in that?" The man laughed. "I had thought you'd be a little quicker to figure that one out though, Grian – in the end I had to literally drop you a clue. I mean those silly animals sniffed it straight away – and they're dumb beasts! They even found your sister's watch, which wasn't actually part of the plan. We sell all the Hansoms to the second-hand trade – never waste a penny! Gave me the perfect opportunity to display that ad of your sister in the Tipping Point, though, which started off our whole adventure together."

Grian realized he had known, deep inside. Everything these past few days had been a little too easy – from the miracle day-trip tickets, to his dad's message agreeing to him staying, to getting into the Residential Zone, to the puzzle.

His anger built, like a kettle about to boil.

"Of course, the world doesn't have to know how you've destroyed the Tipping Point, Grian... I mean, I don't have to share all the footage I have... We could just pretend there was another earthquake, like the last one. People will fall for anything I feed them – I mean, look how they devoured the Tilt. But I will only clear your name if your grandfather gives me what I want!"

"So, Grandad is right – the Tilt never happened? There was no earthquake, and the world is still spinning normally? So, what is going on with the sun then? Shelli said nature is dying and we will be next. What have you done?" Grian roared, shaking now.

Hansom laughed again as the warehouse rained down around him.

"Of course the Tilt never happened. The things you can get people to believe if you spread a little fear! Nature has been dying out for a long time though, Grian – long before my plans – and nobody cared.

"Let's just say I've come up with a solution. And I'm

not destroying ALL of humanity – humanity has done a good enough job of that itself this last century. I prefer to think of myself as saviour to a select few. Not everyone could get on the ark. Now if your grandfather tells me what he knows about the White Rose, maybe I'll give you and your family a golden ticket to a certain future… otherwise you'll perish with the rest! Do you think he'll do that for me, Grian? Time is ticking…"

"Don't you think I would have told you whatever it is you believe I know by now, Howard? This is evil!" Grandad cried, blue veins popping from the side of his forehead.

As his grandfather argued with Howard Hansom, Grian tore himself away from the argument to inspect the metal arm that gripped his friend. He had to follow the plan – he had to save Shelli.

If Grandad could keep Hansom talking, Grian could hover up undetected and get her out of the robotic claw before the whole warehouse came tumbling down.

He was about to move when he felt a sudden pull on his body. Like waves luring him into the sea, Grian gasped as he was dragged forward. He tried to flick his ankles to turn on his boots, but the invisible force tugging him was too strong. Grandad grabbed him but failed to hold on as Grian levitated involuntarily across the cave.

Hansom's arms were outstretched, welcoming him in,

as the man used his hThoughtTech to force Grian to his side.

"Let him go!" Grandad cried, fear in his tone.

Grian began to cough and splutter as the invisible force wrapped like a snake round his neck, blocking his airway.

"I'll tell you everything about the White Rose. Just let my grandson go!" His grandfather sounded frantic as Grian started to choke.

Suddenly the pressure on his windpipe eased and Grian gasped, thirsty for air. He was flooded with relief, though his feet still dangled a few centimetres above the floor and his whole body was powerless and stiff.

"Now that's the offer I was waiting for. I don't want to hurt you, Adler. When people come willingly it makes everything that much easier! Once you're on the Hyperloop I will let Grian go." Hansom smiled as a carriage door slid open.

"Where will you take me?" his grandad asked. "What are you planning, Howard?"

"All in good time!" Hansom shook his head and pointed to the Loop behind him.

Adler walked towards Grian, never lifting his eyes from his grandson's.

"Remember – you're the bravest boy I know!" he whispered, before entering the Hyperloop.

"Enjoy your new found fame, Grian – I couldn't have

asked you to play your part any better. You'll be the boy everybody loves to hate. You destroyed the Tipping Point and any future the planet has. I can't imagine what they'll do to you, but I promise I'll enjoy watching!" Hansom laughed one final time before boarding.

As the Loop shot down the track out of the warehouse and away from the Tipping Point, Grian crashed to the floor.

His body shivered out of control as tears streamed down his face. But he couldn't give up, he had to concentrate. He'd promised Grandad.

Shelli! She was still stuck in the claws of the metal arm above. He had to get her out.

Quickly he clicked his ankles and zoomed upwards, zipping in between large cement chunks as they rebounded off the walls around him, one whizzing just passed his head. Shelli's eyes were closed but she was still breathing when he reached her. He tried to shake her awake, but she didn't respond.

Nach grew more frantic below. Grian closed his eyes and concentrated on opening the mechanical grip.

The steel hand loosened a little and Shelli slipped out, free-falling for a second before Grian dashed down and caught her, cradling the Wilde girl in his arms. Rocks rained like bullets around them as he darted for the storeroom and down into the postal tunnel, Nach just behind.

CHAPTER 39

THE LETTER

Grian zoomed with his unconscious friend along the old postal railway track. By the time they reached the battered elevator up into Turing Post Office, Shelli was coming to. He checked the time; it was nearly three a.m.!

It was dark as they stepped out into Turing, Shelli's arm now draped over Grian's shoulder for balance. Neither spoke as they walked the streets to the nearest bus stop and boarded a late-night bus to Tallystick.

A man in the front seat gave them a strange look. Grian wondered why until he caught a glimpse of his reflection in a window. His once-smart clothes were now covered in a layer of white dust, as was his hair, which stuck out at all sorts of angles. Teamed with his black boots and gloves, he looked like he was in fancy dress costume. Shelli looked even worse in her mismatched outfit.

"Lucky you sent Nach home on foot or we'd definitely be the centre of attention," Grian whispered, trying to break the tension.

Shelli half smiled though she didn't reply. She looked paler than usual and fell asleep just after the bus took off.

As his friend dozed next to him, Grian turned off Bob and placed it in his pocket, before finally opening the small cream drawstring bag that had been calling to him ever since his grandad had entrusted him with it.

His hand trembled as he emptied an unusual piece of cut rock crystal onto his palm. The crystal was gold coloured and shimmered under the stark bus light with hints of purple and pink.

There was something stiff inside the bag too. Grian prised out a piece of paper folded in quarters. His heart thumped, drowning out all other sounds of the bus, as he opened the paper.

Dear Adler,
I have made many mistakes in my life – the biggest was leaving you. But I can't hide behind my cowardice any longer. After a lifetime I finally have the courage to suffer for the truth – I have to.
This is the first of four letters that I have sent out

on your beloved postal network. Each of the others will be addressed "Dear Postman" and in a red envelope. I chose the post as it is the only means of communication that cannot be hacked these days and because it's a proud profession built on discretion.

I hope you will understand, but for protection, I can't trust any one person with all of the information I have to disclose so I have split it up. Each letter will lead to a separate piece of a larger puzzle.

This crystal is the first of those pieces. When all the pieces are put together, they have the power to reverse the destruction I've unwittingly set in motion.

I have written the other letters as puzzles, just like the games we used to entertain ourselves with. This is not a game, though, Adler. I have written them this way in case they fall into the wrong hands. There are people who will kill if they get wind this information is out.

I know I am putting you right into the heart of this global deceit and in mortal danger, and for that I am sorry. But, if you are still the man I once knew, then you are still a truth-seeker and there is no other place you'd rather be.

If you need proof that what I write is real, then watch the skies. The black mark on our sun is just *the beginning of this thievery – it will extinguish in phases until only the embers are left.*

Once this phasing begins, time is running out. I beg you – find the letters, find the pieces, then come find me.

I have made it so I will not be able to go to you. I pray you know who I am, but I also insist it is vital you tell no one. If I am found and killed the final part of the puzzle dies with me and our world as we know it is no more.

My resistance is based on the power of love and now you have all of mine – please keep it safe.

You are my glimmer of hope.

The White Rose.

Shelli groaned and moved in the seat beside him, pulling Grian from his shock.

He panicked as he shoved the letter and crystal back in their pouch and quickly into his pocket, afraid anyone would see. Hansom, he knew now, had eyes everywhere.

He'd never wanted to save the world before, even when everyone was queuing up to do it. But now...well, now things were different.

CHAPTER 40

REAL PEOPLE POWER

Grian ran over snippets of the letter in his head, feeling sicker and sicker.

This is the first of four letters... There are people who will kill if they get wind this information is out... The black mark on our sun is just the beginning of this thievery, it will extinguish in phases until only the embers are left... If I am found and killed the final part of the puzzle dies with me and our world as we know it is no more.

What did any of it mean? Could he really help? He was just a kid and this...this was huge.

Grian was trying to calm down when a sudden newsflash flew across the screen inset into the headrest in front of him.

He gasped and sat forward, turning up his hEarPods.

Images and video footage of himself, Shelli, Jeffrey, Vermilion and Grandad played behind a bright red scrolling banner which ran in a series of headlines like *"From heroes to horrors"*, *"Explosion in the Tipping Point"*, *"Many feared dead"* and *"Howard Hansom presumed lost while saving lives"*.

He shimmied down in the chair and gripped the armrests to steady his shaking as he watched the newsreel.

First there was video from the party Hansom had thrown them. Then the report cut to security footage of Grian, Shelli and Jeffrey trying to sneak into the Tipping Point a few nights previously, then more video of them sneaking round the white underground corridors and breaking into Hansom's headquarters. Finally, the newsflash showed devastation on the streets of the Tipping Point and people screaming and crying.

Grian's heart pounded, and he slipped further down in his chair while an emotional newsreader dabbed her red-rimmed eyes as she explained how he, Shelli, Jeffrey, Grandad and Vermilion were part of a group called the Proctors, who it was widely known were out to destroy Hansom. She said they'd infiltrated Hansom's inner circle and gained his trust by pretending to save him from a Proctor attack, then set a bomb which exploded, taking out the smart city, and with it any hope of saving the world.

"But it's all lies! He set us up!" Grian fumed through gritted teeth.

Hansom had said Grian would be the most hated boy in Babbage – and now he was! If everyone knew his face, how would he ever be able to help his grandad and the White Rose? Hansom was right, everybody would be so distracted looking for Grian and the others that nobody would be trying to find out the truth.

He shuddered as he thought about the White Rose's letter – *The black mark on our sun is just the beginning of this thievery, it will extinguish in phases until only the embers are left*. What did it all mean? And the word thievery seemed strange. Then he felt sick as he remembered Hansom's words about how the world would sleepwalk to its own destruction.

He shook Shelli awake and convinced her to get off at the next stop. Once they were on the pavement, he explained what he'd seen on the news. He ditched his dusty jacket and Shelli her dress, so she was just in a dirty vest and trousers, then the pair crept along the streets, watching, on edge, in case anyone was about.

As they passed through the city, heading on foot for Tallystick and the Wilde forest, their faces were on every virtual bus stop and billboard in sight. A man across the street stopped, stunned, watching the breaking news unfold.

Exhausted and scared, the two children kept to back

streets wherever possible until they reached the Wilde forest on the outskirts of Tallystick. Both stuck in thought, neither had spoken much since leaving the bus. As they trudged through the densely packed trees, Grian barely noticed the branches that clawed at his clothes and scratched at his skin.

Having been forewarned by lookouts high in the trees, people were already gathered waiting on the rope bridges and platforms above them as the pair entered the Wilde camp.

Nach whined, sprinting through the undergrowth, the first to greet them. Shelli buried her face in the fox's deep-red coat, rare tears sliding silently down her cheeks.

As they continued on, the crowd began to clap until the clapping grew to shouts and cheers of joy. When Grian and Shelli reached the centre of the Wilde camp they were engulfed by a huge group of waiting well-wishers.

"Thank goodness you made it out alive!" Jeffrey cried, breaking through the crowd. "I must admit I was perturbed when Nach arrived back alone, but then I saw the news and knew you'd likely survived. Do you realize Hansom has the entire world blaming us for blowing up the Tipping Point? The audacity!

"Anyway, let's not focus on the negatives now – let's celebrate. I'm ravenous and we couldn't commence eating without you. Apparently we're heroes, you know!"

"Heroes?" Grian rattled with rage. "You said you've seen the news? Everyone thinks we've destroyed the Tipping Point, Jeffrey! They think we've stopped Howard Hansom from saving the world – that makes us the opposite of heroes! And it means nobody apart from the people here will believe anything we say!"

"But you and I know that's not the truth." Mother's gentle voice floated down on the air from somewhere above. "And the truth will out! Now come up – we'll talk, then we'll celebrate. Jeffrey is right, you are heroes; you've saved all these people. People with families who will tell their families the truth of what happened in the Tipping Point – whispers, just like streams, turn to rivers that turn to oceans. The battle has begun and it's important we celebrate the little victories!"

The old woman welcomed them from the platform of the meeting hut above, her warm dimpled smile comforting. The sun was just rising as Grian climbed up to her, Shelli and Jeffrey behind him. Each movement was an effort as exhaustion took hold.

The meeting hut was stuffy and crammed full of people as they all squeezed inside.

"Grian!" a familiar voice called from across the room.

His vision blurred with tears as the crowd parted.

"I was so worried!" his mam said, wrapping him up in her arms.

He hugged her tighter than he ever had in his life, never wanting to let her go again. Then Solas was there too, sobbing into his shoulder and holding him as though her life depended on it.

"Where is Grandad?" his sister asked.

Grian shook his head, unable to speak.

"It's okay," his mother soothed, gripping his hand.

His mam didn't let go until eventually he felt strong enough to clear his throat and slowly recount his story. The words caught as he described the last moments with his grandfather and how Grandad had given himself up for Grian.

He never mentioned the crystal or the White Rose's letter. Those were his secrets. Secrets his grandad had trusted him to keep and only tell to Yarrow, the head of the Council of Colour. They were also secrets he was already finding a burden to carry.

"Hansom thought Grandad knew something about the White Rose. He seemed desperate, but Grandad said…he said he didn't know anything," Grian lied.

"Then we must find out ourselves," Mother announced. "All we know about Hansom for sure, thanks to these children, is that he has been spinning lies for the last three years and making the whole world believe them. We know he must need people – lots of innocent people – to fulfil whatever plans he has, and we know the sun is somehow sick. That's it! Our only lead is the White Rose – Hansom is desperate to find this person, so we must be now too!"

"The White Rose is real," Saoirse, Grian's mam, said, stepping forward to speak.

Grian watched in disbelief. How did his mam know anything about the White Rose?

"My father, Adler Rothe, asked my husband to look out for letters a while ago now. We were sceptical at first, but we both knew Dad wouldn't make something like this up, so word was put out discreetly on the Postal Network and we formed a secret group…"

"Well that explains the need for a Faraday cage in the post office," Jeffrey whispered behind them.

"Then a postman in the Turing district found a letter. It was in a red envelope and addressed 'Dear Postman', just like Dad had said it would be. Dad also said…" Saoirse stopped for a minute, composing herself. "He said if anything happened to him we were to personally take the letters to The Council of Colour. So that's what my husband is doing as we speak. And we have postmen and women looking for the other letters – Dad said there'd be three in total."

Four, Grian thought, if you included the one Grandad had given him. His mam looked down at him and his sister, and grabbed both their hands again.

"The letters and the White Rose mean hope, and hope is what we need right now. Their existence has already brought us great things – they have brought us all together. The Wilde, the Council of Colour and the Postal Network. That's a strong alliance – that's real People Power."

Just as a cheer raced round the small, stuffy room, a little girl burst inside.

"It's gone darker, it's gone darker!" she screeched, jumping up into the arms of a man nearby.

Some people already on the platform started to cry and scream, pointing skywards, as those in the meeting hut streamed outside.

Grian stood between Jeffrey and Shelli. His knuckles whitened as he gripped the wooden rail in front of him.

"Oh my!" Jeffrey exclaimed as Shelli grabbed both their hands.

The morning light had dimmed significantly, as if a heavy rainstorm had just blown in a cover of dark cloud. But there was no cloud. The sun had blackened further and now darkness filled a quarter of its face.

Grian closed his eyes and tried to steady his racing heart as he felt in his pocket for the small bag that held the crystal and the letter.

If you need proof that what I write is real then watch the skies. The black mark on our sun is just the beginning of this thievery – it will extinguish in phases until only the embers are left.

Grian had his proof – what the White Rose wrote was real. His mind was a mess as he thought about the word *thievery* again. Was the White Rose saying someone was stealing the sun? But surely that was impossible! And it would mean none of this was an accident, or a natural disaster – the sun wasn't just dying. Someone was stealing it on purpose!

He shook with rage and fear as he remembered another sentence in the letter he half wished he'd never read.

Once this phasing begins, time is running out.

CHAPTER 41

SUPERHEROES

Grian shifted in the bed, unable to sleep, his head full of worry. Shelli, Jeffrey and Solas snored to varying degrees around him, exhausted from their adventures. His mam still hadn't come back from the meeting hut.

The adults had been going over things all day and would probably be up all night talking about the letters, the White Rose and why the black spot on the sun had suddenly grown much bigger. His mam had tried to pretend she wasn't worried, but Grian could tell she really was.

Everyone was.

The last few days played on a continuous loop over and over in his mind. He took out the letter and reread it again, trying to make sense of it all and wondering how he could ever keep this secret.

Then, like a twitch, he switched Bob back on for the millionth time. Each time was for just a few seconds, as he knew he couldn't trust the watch. But he also reassured himself that Hansom probably wasn't tracking him any more now that the whole world was after Grian and his friends.

Grandad had said the only way to find out the truth was to keep close to Hansom, so before they'd left the stairwell Grian had handed his grandfather an hSwarm.

Grian had just clicked the app again when an electronic voice filtered into the room. He startled and dropped the watch.

"Grian, Grian. I hope he can hear me thinking – oh this tech stuff better work. I'm in a city, there's a strange sky – it's familiar somehow – I don't know but I think, I think I'm in..." Static filled the air and the electronic voice dropped out.

Grian trembled as he picked up his watch. Grandad was alive – their plan had worked. But where was he? And was he still with Hansom?

Jeffrey spluttered an enormous snore.

Grandad had told him to trust no one, but he'd also told him making friends was one of the bravest things he'd ever done. Grian had always thought he was better off alone, but these last few days had taught him he was wrong. Shelli had told him to follow his gut feelings, and his gut told him he could trust his friends – they would help him carry the secret.

He needed Shelli, Jeffrey and even Nach now, if they were going to save his grandad and the world.

THE END. FOR NOW...

NOW WHO DO YOU TRUST TO SAVE THE WORLD...

A BOY AND HIS FRIENDS OR A BILLIONAIRE?

Is the sun really dying? What has happened
to all the people who thought they were saving the
planet when they moved to the Tipping Point?
Where is Howard Hansom and
what is he planning?

Look out for the second gripping adventure in
THE LIGHT THIEVES series as Grian, Shelli and
Jeffrey try to find some answers and save the world!

HERE'S A SMALL TASTER OF
WHAT'S TO COME

"It doesn't sound promising," Jeffrey stuttered, "what the White Rose writes about has to be true because the letter says if we need proof to look at the sun. It IS extinguishing in phases – that's precisely what happened today! It's a quarter black now. How long before the sun is extinguished completely? And what then…? I don't think life is even possible on the planet without the sun. I mean I'm not an avid geography or biology buff or whatever category this sort of issue falls under but I'm quite sure we're in enormous trouble and by we I mean every…"

"Stop Jeffrey!" Shelli growled. "We can't panic. This letter proves that de White Rose is real now. And whoever they are, they know we can fix what's happening to the sun and they've given us a way to do it. We just need to find de pieces and solve de puzzle – just like de letter says. And we have de first piece – that crystal. And Grian's dad has another letter – remember his mam said de Postman's Network found one and he's already bringing it to de Council of Colour. That letter has to have another clue, that's more good news. Let's just look at de positives and forget…"

"That the sun is somehow literally dying," Jeffrey exclaimed.

Shelli was right – Grian had forgotten his dad had another letter. A postman had found it. "We just need to find the Council of Colour, like Grandad said."

A small light lit up on Jeffrey's wrist as he turned on his Hansom.

"What are you doing!?" Grian gasped frightened.

"I'm doing what you said. Just a quick hNet search – there might be something on the Council of Colour. Don't worry I've all the security parameters on my watch switched…"

"No," Grian said grabbing Jeffrey's wrist to plunge the off button. "We can't use our Hansoms. They'll be tracked, everyone is looking for us now…"

"But I saw you check Bob!" Shelli eyed him suspiciously.

Grian hesitated for a minute before continuing. He'd already told his friends about the letter – now he'd need to tell them everything.

ACKNOWLEDGEMENTS

Firstly, I have to thank my friend, Howard Triggs, for lending me his name. He once mentioned a little downheartedly that he'd never come across a character called Howard in a book before – so I promised I'd make one up. As it turned out the name was a perfect fit and Howard Hansom my smart villain was born. Fortunately for Howard Triggs, the two men share very little in common apart from their genius. So, Howard thank you for being my guide for much of the science in this story though I take full responsibility for all of its loose use.

To everyone at Usborne especially Katie and Kath for their beautiful cover, to Jacob and Fritha for their masterful marketing and PR, to Christian for his sales savvy and to my editor Anne Finnis for her patience and eagle-like editorial eye – Anne you never fail to ask the right questions and to make me dig that little bit deeper.

To Rocky for his brilliant tech advice. I'll never hack a computer in your presence. "Not that you'd be able to" I hear you whisper in return.

To Jordan for his guidance and dogged determination – I genuinely feel so lucky to be on your team.

To my extended and ever-growing family – especially Willie for his open heart, Monica for her deep roots and Carmel for her third eye. They say you don't choose your tribe but I reckon I'd a hand in picking you.

To Mam for her courage and gentle acceptance of life. Thank you for letting me dream.

To Robbie for everything, even the odd growl. If I didn't have you by my side this story would be missing its soul.

And finally, to Jo and Bobbie – for choosing me.

I know deep in my gut, a place where my thinking can't reach, that you two will grow up in a new earth, where we have learned to live in harmony with the rhythms of nature, not against them.

I have promised myself I will do my part to make this dream your reality.

I believe that this world of ours has its own consciousness, and to think we understand its workings is naive. Shelli, my Wilde friend, told me if I seed the energy of this dream – my imagined new earth – it will connect with the dreams of so many others and grow.

And so I wrote it down.

This series *The Light Thieves* is my seeded dream. I'm growing it for you my girls.

To find out more about
HELENA DUGGAN and **THE LIGHT THIEVES**
go to **USBORNE.COM/FICTION**

🐦 **@USBORNE**
📷 **@USBORNE_BOOKS**
🐦 **@HELDIDEAS**
#THELIGHTTHIEVES